MATRYOSHKA

MATRYOSHKA

JOHN ANDES

iUniverse, Inc.
Bloomington

Matryoshka

iUniverse books may be ordered through booksellers or by contacting:

iUniverse
1663 Liberty Drive
Bloomington, IN 47403
www.iuniverse.com
1-800-Authors (1-800-288-4677)

ISBN: 978-1-4759-4202-6 (sc)
ISBN: 978-1-4759-4203-3 (ebk)

Printed in the United States of America

iUniverse rev. date: 07/27/2012

Dedicated to William David Andes and Dorothy Rose Hess Andes

With special thanks to Judy Wessells whose editing acumen made the mess readable and Helene who made the cover come alive.

Preface

Just when you think you know, you don't.

Snarl

The command of the dispatcher's voice is breaking up with building-caused interference.

"Sector Car 4-2. Proceed to 2-4-6-7 Amsterdam Avenue. Corner of 1-2-8 Street and Amsterdam Avenue. Disturbance. Possible robbery in progress. What is your ETA? Kay."

"Base, this is Sector Car 4-2. We are proceeding to 2-4-6-7 Amsterdam.

Corner of Amsterdam and 1-2-8 Street. ETA three minutes. Kay."

"Sector Car 4-1 will back up 4-2 at location. 4-1 Kay"

"Base, this is 4-1. We are proceeding to 2-4-6-7 Amsterdam. Corner of Amsterdam and 1-2-8 Street. ETA five minutes. Kay."

Patrolman Sean O'Malley in Sector car 4-2 switches on the lights and Siren. The *woop-woop* is so familiar to the neighborhood no one acknowledges the squad car as it turns the corner and races toward Amsterdam Avenue. Nor do they react to the screeching of the brakes as the car fishtails to a halt. *Amato's Produce & Provisions* truck is double-parked on the street and is blocking eastbound traffic. The westbound flow of cars and delivery vans is typically heavy this is Friday morning. Drivers and passengers wave and talk to the people on the sidewalk and stoops. An outdoor chat room. Promises for Friday night are made as young men and women flirt aggressively. The squad car is trapped. This stall could last ten to twenty minutes. Frustration gives way to cop logic and urgency. The only way out is a U-turn. Go west two blocks, then north two, then east three, then south two blocks to the location of the disturbance. O'Malley decides that the shortest distance between two points is a U-turn and three left-hand turns.

"Bobby, get out and direct traffic."

Bobby Joseph halts the westbound lane. O'Malley leans on the horn and the siren as he starts the process. Two forwards and two reverses, a couple of bumps and scrapes, four hard wheel turns, and he has extricated the cruiser from the vehicular quagmire. His partner re-enters. They are off on their circuitous route.

"Base. This is sector car 4-2. Revised ETA. Now eight minutes. Damned traffic. Kay."

Sector car 4-1 has run afoul of the set-up for the weekend's gala. Cars have been cleared from the curbs. But, they have been replaced by structures that will become booths and concession stands for the *Feast of San Paulo*. The congregating and dancing will cover three blocks all weekend starting at sundown tonight. Patrolwoman, Angela Rivera, has driven five car lengths into the first block when she realizes her dilemma. There is no exit. But, her u-turn is easy. The workers and the wannabes, hoot derisively at the squad car occupants.

Sector car 4-1's U-turn and new routes will delay arrival as back up.

The doorway at 2467 Amsterdam is foot printed in blood leading out to the street. The silver SUV roars north on Amsterdam Avenue, slides in and out of traffic, blends, then disappears within six blocks. Everybody noticed, but no one could recall. The license plate is not conspicuous by its absence. Lots of other cars in this neighborhood have no license plates.

On the other side of the storefront doorway are the remains of an office and four earless bodies.

R.E.A.C.H

The Plaza Hotel is festooned with four flags: Old Glory, New York State, New York City, and that of the Aksum Mission . . . a brilliant white field holds a pair of black hands cradling a gold cross. The letters **R.E.A.C.H**. are in blood red. The letters stand for **R**ehabilitated **E**ducated **A**dults in **C**hrist's **H**ands and clearly communicate the Mission of the Ethiopian Christian Church. Every April 30th, the Mission holds a very showy and very profitable fundraiser. Everything is donated. The food is donated by local purveyors, then brought to the hotel and prepared by members of the Mission. The kitchen union members take the evening off. It's their contribution. All regular hotel dining is closed for the evening. The hotel donates the facilities. Tables and chairs, table settings, and linen are free for the night. The servers are members of the Mission. The sole purpose of the entire evening is to raise money. This is done under the guise of a status report, which follows the meal. The meal follows the fellowship hour. No alcohol is served, so gentle conversation is held over tea or spring water. Many of the non-Mission attendees are sure to have a few drinks before arrival. Alcohol can grease the proceedings.

At the entrance to the main ballroom are the sign-in tables and name tags. This way the Mission can be sure who didn't show up and report that fact back to whoever cares. This threat of ratting ensures attendance. If you can't show, you are expected to regret with the full donation. Your seat is then offered to the next in line, who makes an equal donation and attends out of gratitude for the opportunity to be seen with the city's power base. The room is filled with 150 tables. Each sits 10. Each ticket donation is $500. With about 25% regrets, duplicate seat offerings, and no expenses, this evening makes big money. Net, net one million. Lieutenant Anthony William Sattill Jr. will be seated at table 72. Last year he sat at table 78. Forward motion is based on rank and attendance history. At this rate he will be at one of the ten front tables by the time he retires. It's always a pleasant surprise to meet his upwardly mobile tablemates.

The center of attraction is a spot lighted architect's model of the Mission with the addition of the new building. Huge renderings of the Mission's various buildings and the surrounding area decorate the vast room. The Mission started with one abandoned warehouse ten years ago and now covers three city blocks in Harlem. Tunnels and bridges connect all the buildings. On the roofs of two former warehouses are small vegetable gardens and greenhouses. The Mission buys the old and abandoned buildings by paying the back taxes. The city is glad to get the slums off the tax rolls and have a reputable buyer for what had been shooting galleries and flop houses. The neighbors are glad to rid the neighborhood of the junkies and hookers; glad to have the trash of humanity replaced by good, clean families. Former trash, just cleaned up. The city keeps the new Xenon streetlights fully functional to maintain this bright spot in the blight. Around the perimeter of the Mission compound there are gardens with plants and bushes of all manner. No fences can be seen anywhere, although the entrance gates are secured by armed guards 24/7 and the widows, regardless of floor are barred . . . decoratively.

When the Mission began to grow, some city residents feared a para-military complex. But, the Catholic and Episcopalian dioceses argued in favor of a safe haven for the down trodden. They argued that this would be an island of rehabilitation supported by the private sector. Their argument didn't obfuscate the fact that the Mission would keep society's lowest from overcrowding the diocesan Missions on the East Side and downtown. These two religious forces are incredibly powerful. The wasps and the Italo-Irish leaders became champions of the Mission are always at the city council meetings. A dozen or so of the two clergies are visible each year at the fund raiser. They sit up front. To see and be seen.

"Tony, my favorite Ivy League police Detective. How is the crime business, old sport?"

"Lucky, nice to see you again. Business is getting better. We're getting smarter and they're getting dumber. I hope all is well at the bank."

"Couldn't be better. Big announcement late next week. Blow the roof off the personal banking business."

"Can you give me a hint?"

"You're the Detective, you figure it out."

"I'll just hold my breath and read the papers."

"Read the financial section before the sports and local news."

"Rarely do I read the financial section. Tried to once, but the money just got in the way of the truth. For you and this one week, I'll read it first."

Latchazar Razdarovich, V. Pompous drunken lineage of the Manhattan Private Trust's founders. Tony went to Brown with Lucky. He was just one of the many snot-nosed suits who made sure Tony felt inferior . . . either because he was Italian or because he didn't go to one of the elite prep schools, known collectively as *St Grotlsex*. They knew about wine, fast cars and the right place to summer. Tony read about these places and recognized their names. The snobs were successful in stepping on his ego, because the feeling of inferiority remains etched on his soul to this day when he is around them or their type. Tony did not see or hear much of this cadre after college, except when he read in the newspaper about some merger or sailing accident. The bank, founded after the revolution, was, is, and will be where the very old rich keep money. It operates like a Swiss bank: very private, very secure, and very personal. A thousand families use the bank as their own piggy, and they pay a premium for that luxury. The bank has all the right legal and political connections. And, as president and majority stockholder, Lucky is not above using this muscle to extort favors or bend the rules for the bank or its clientele. Lucky shows up each day to make sure the wheels haven't fallen off during the night. He berates his Senior Vice Presidents during their morning briefings. Then he leaves for a long lunch and squash with one of the clients. He drinks heavily, but no one cares as long as no risk is taken with the fortunes. No risk that can't be corrected. He is just one member of the money crowd here tonight.

"Where's your better half?"

"Over there with daddy. See you later, old sport."

The banalities don't suit Tony, but they suit Lucky's toady audience. Melissa was Lucky's one grasp at humanity. She is the daughter of the Manhattan Borough President, Jerome D. Aylir. Jerome rose through the ranks of the wards to acquire the most powerful political job that has no term limits. Not shabby for a black man with a Community College degree. The fact that Melissa and her family are black has been a source of perverted admiration for Lucky, his family, and his peers. None of the other liberal elitists would marry a black, but they are oh-so happy to say one of their best friends is black. They never fail to mention that she went to Yale and her father is the borough president. It's their way of touting social equality. Lucky makes sure that Melissa is seen at all the right charitable and political events. Always gets her picture in the paper. She is statuesque and well tended. She spends more on clothing than Tony grosses in a year.

"Melissa. Mr. Aylir. Mrs. Aylir. It's nice to see you again."

"Tony, you look dashing in your tuxedo. I'm glad you didn't wear your dress uniform this year. It makes you look so military . . . so imposing."

"Thank you, Melissa. This year I was increased in stature and was moved toward the front of the room. So, better table, better clothes."

"Lieutenant, may I have a word with you in private. Would you excuse us, dear"?

"Yes, daddy."

Her attempted pouting was endearing. Both men smiled.

"Yes, sir. How can I help you?"

"How do you know I need help?"

"Candidly, sir, no one ever wants to talk to a cop or a priest unless they need help or are confessing. And, I doubt this is a confession."

The dour expression on the older man cracks into a slight grin.

"It's not about me, Lieutenant. It's about my daughter."

"If I can help either of you, you know I will. What is the problem?"

"In a word; Lucky."

"Her husband?"

"Over the last two years, I have begun to suspect he is abusing Melissa. Physically, I mean. I have no idea about any other way."

"Please elaborate."

"About eighteen months ago, Melissa had to be taken to the ER. She fell and broke her arm. No big deal. Clumsy, but not newsworthy. About a year ago she had Sunday dinner with her mother and me, and we noticed a swelling on her cheek and bruises on both arms. We said nothing. In fact, her mother and I have not discussed Melissa's condition at all. Nine months ago, she slipped in her kitchen. The fall nearly dislocated the hip. Very serious sprain. She claimed she had spilled some water on the floor and had had too much to drink. The ER attending physician told me the injury was consistent with the blow of a stick or baseball bat. Last Christmas she chipped two teeth and cut her lip when she fell ice skating at Wolman's Rink. The teeth were capped

9

and the cut stitched. Lieutenant, my daughter is not accident-prone. She is not clumsy. She is graceful and has all of her faculties. And, she never has more than two glasses of wine. On the other side of the aisle, Lucky is a bully and a drunk. On more than one occasion, he has raised his voice to Melissa in my presence. I am worried about her. The next so-called accident may cause her irreparable damage."

"Sir, if what you say is true, and I have no reason to doubt you, this is a matter better handled by marriage counselors, lawyers, or at worse, precinct patrolmen. How can I help you help her?"

"I would appreciate it if you would somehow watch over her. I know she's fond of you and I know you were a classmate of her husband. You could make an effort to be closer to them socially. Observe them as much as possible, but professionally. Get Melissa to open up and tell you what's really happening."

Out of the corner of his right eye, Tony spots Melissa homing in on him. No time to negotiate or get more information. He must say yes. To say no would be political suicide.

"Time's up, daddy. You can't hog the best looking penguin any longer. I want to show him the model of the new building. Now, if you'll excuse us."

"I am beholden to you, Lieutenant."

"Look at what the money raised tonight will pay for. An abandoned warehouse that will be converted into a three-story home for nearly 30 families. One, two, and three bedroom units. Each with a living room. The larger units will have a den also. Communal cafeteria-style eating. Designated tables. A pre-school facility for the children of working mothers. A vest pocket park with a waterfall.

High tech fire alarm and prevention system. All of this is the means to the end. A better life for those who want it and are willing to work for it. This building will get over 100 people off the streets and out of life's gutters. It will help dozens and dozens of junkies get clean and sober. It will help dozens of unfortunate hookers start a new life."

People had begun to gather around her. They hung on every word from her soapbox. When she became aware of the admiring crowd, she became embarrassed and quiet.

"Melissa, stop the sales pitch. I know the good the Mission does. I read the quarterly crime statistics. You're preaching to the choir . . . the professional choir."

"Ooops."

The sheepish grin was that of a teen. The lights flickered. Everyone headed to their respective tables.

"Please join me in a prayer of thanksgiving. Oh, gracious king, we thank you for the gift of your son, the love of family and friends, and the bounty bestowed upon us. We thank you for the strength of life, which enables us to put the gifts to your use. May we strive to keep your kingdom foremost in our hearts and minds. May we have the humility of your son, who showed us how to serve others. May we have the strength of purpose to bring more lost sheep into your flock. May we endeavor to spread the word of your kingdom throughout this earthly realm. We ask for all things, and receive all things through Jesus Christ our only lord and mediator. Amen."

Makeda spoke with the gentleness of a devout Christian and the strength of a warrior. As the head of the Aksum Mission, she is responsible for its inception and almost unbelievable growth during the past decade.

She is a tribal leader, a princess, in a metropolitan area. Her clan has grown from three families in a dilapidated brownstone to nearly five hundred families, three kitchens, an educational facility, and an emergency health clinic all in a refurbished five-building compound. She has been transformed from a street-corner proselytizer to a leader, who has the ear of every major power base in the city. She has evolved into someone who dines with the secular kings and queens.

On the dais are the representatives of the city's other tribes . . . business, financial, political, religious, police, fire, and the fourth estate. Each is there to pay homage to the great deeds done by the Mission and to be seen paying homage by the television and newspaper reporters who flit from table to table in search of something newsworthy or an innuendo. Lieutenants of the tribal leaders are sprinkled at every table in the first three rows. They are there to learn how to pay homage.

"Hello, my name is Brenda Linder. My husband is Robert Linder, Sr. Vice President of Manhattan Private Trust. What brings you here tonight?"

"Duty and honor Mrs. Linder."

"What do you do young man?"

"I'm a Lieutenant in the Police Department."

"That sounds fascinatingly dangerous."

With that dismissal, the short, slightly overweight and very over-dressed woman exits stage left.

"Lieutenant Sattill, right?"

"Right."

"Carlita Brown. We met in Captain Flaherty's office about six months ago. There was a meeting to discuss how the Gang Task Force could be better integrated with the other special units of the department."

"Yes, thanks for jogging my memory. It's nice to see you again."

"I think what the Mission does is nothing shy of miraculous. I know my job is easier because of the Mission."

It is bad form to talk cop-shop in at public gathering and particularly taboo to do so here among so many unaware. Not a big mistake just bad form. The meal is served and consumed with a din of idle pleasantries of children, the weather, the Mets chances, and the New York Football Giants, pride of the city. Lamb, curry-flavored rice, a mixture of arcane vegetables, and a chopped salad create a dissonance of flavors and textures that is strangely pleasant. The dessert consists of fruit and cheese, while a smoky sweet tea cleanses the palate.

"Ladies and gentlemen, brothers and sisters, I thank you for being here tonight at the Aksum Mission's annual dinner. I also thank those who prepared and served the meal. Please join me in showing appreciation."

Fifteen hundred people spring from the discomfort of small chairs and applaud. The loud politeness lasts three minutes.

"We at the Mission want you to know that your donations of time, goods, services, and money are deeply appreciated. We want you to understand just how much your contributions mean. In the past year, our flock has increased by 68 lost souls . . . men, women and children. In the past year, 36 souls of our flock have received Graduate Equivalent Degrees. That's 36 people who once had difficulty reading, doing math, and writing, who are now ready to tackle to day-to-day issues of work and managing a family. They have a brighter future. In the past year, we welcomed sixteen babies into the household of Christ. Up to delivery, each of the mothers-to-be received health and nutritional assistance from the on-site nurse, who runs our health clinic. Each year we seem to do more, because you do more. This year we will be able to continue the progress. If you have not seen the model in the center of the room, allow me to tell you about it. Through your generosity and with the understanding of the city, we will be expanding our work in Christ's name. Six months ago we began renovation of the newest addition to our Mission. This three-story former manufacturing facility is being converted into living quarters for families. On the first floor will be a new dining room. Plus, we will be moving the expanded the health clinic to this building and adding an exercise room for all the Mission's residents. All we can say is . . . ."

'Thank you', was yelled by the Mission members throughout the room and was followed by their applause. The appreciative thunder lasted four minutes.

"We are honored that you chose to support Christ's Mission. We hope you enjoyed your meal, and that you return home safely. Please, join us in a closing prayer. Dear and gracious giver of all things, thank you for those who help us in your Mission. Guard, keep and protect them through the coming year. May the peace of the Lord be upon us all. Amen."

The tingling of flatware on china and shuffling of the chairs is muffled by the diners' voices.

"Lieutenant, care for a round of fellowship in the Oak Room."

"Thanks for the kind offer Lieutenant Brown, but the crush of bureaucracy this week forces me to work tonight. I have to scurry home and plug in my laptop. May I have a rain check"?

"Yes you may, but next time you can't say no."

"That's fair."

Rather than wait thirty minutes at the hotel entrance, Tony walks four blocks east to find a cab. On the ride uptown, he contemplates Carlita's offer. He had heard rumors about her. How she had risen to the top by being on her knees. How she had stuck the knife into other officers, who were competing for her position of power and visibility. It's safer for his career to stay out of that spider's web. At home, he sheds his black and white costume, inserts an Enigma CD, pours three ounces of Balvenie Double Wood over a single ice cube and settles into his chair. What does the Borough President really want? The libation and hypnotic harmonies ignite Tony's imagination. When they are gone, Tony goes to bed.

Night Visitor

The rasp of the buzzer grinds Tony awake. Not once or twice, the buzzer screams repeatedly like a child craving attention in K-Mart. He ambles to the intercom and presses the button. The irritation stops. No need to ask who would be so bold as to interrupt his sleep. He knew before he fell asleep that the night visitor would appear. He just didn't know when. He pads to the front door and waits. The elevator in the four-story brownstone never hurries, regardless of the desires of the riders. The elevator car door opens and the intruder exits. As she approaches his door, he swings it open. She enters and wraps him in a lover's embrace.

"God, I can't stand being near you and not touching you. Please pour me a drink. Will you join me?"

"That's my intention."

"I mean in a drink, silly."

Two three-ounce Balvenie's, each over a single ice cube. She has tossed her wrap over his chair forcing him to sit with her on the couch. To his rudely awaken senses, she is magnificent.

"What did daddy want?"

"Your father asked me to do him a favor."

"I deduced that. What kind of favor?"

"Some off-the-record digging."

"About what?"

"Just some matter that deals with his office."

"Good God, must I go over there and pull all out your fingernails one-by-one before you tell me."

"Your father is concerned there might be some shenanigans with recent housing contracts."

"If he wanted to investigate that, he should call in the appropriate rats from another borough. Why you? Why some techno-cop?"

"Well, thanks for the ego boost."

"I didn't mean it derogatorily. I just meant there are squads of able bodies out there who would love to hang dirty laundry."

"That's the whole point. Your father wants me to dig informally and report back to him. Then and only then will he decide to initiate a formal investigation through proper channels. I suspect he is also concerned a formal investigation would set off leaks so that any incriminating evidence could be lost, strayed or stolen."

"Are you sure that's all he wanted?"

"Yes."

"Who is it?"

"Don't ask."

"Who is it? Is it any one I know?"

"Can't tell. That's my professional credo."

"Are you sure daddy didn't talk to you about me and Lucky?"

"Yes, I'm sure. Why do you ask?"

"I think he thinks Lucky and I aren't getting along. A few times he has done his famous question-through-innuendo routine about my marriage. You know, no children, weekends at separate locations; the usual stuff that would set off his old fashioned alarm. Are you telling me the truth about your conversation with daddy?"

"Yes."

"For some reason, I don't think you're telling me the truth. So I'm going to force you to tell me by putting you through a modern trial by ordeal. You must remain still and stoic. I am going to torture you until you either tell me the truth or . . . or . . . something else."

Melissa places her once-sipped drink on the table and slides over to Tony's side. Her hands cradle his cheeks more gently than a mother's touch. For ten seconds or so, she stares deep into his soul through optic portals. Then, she leans into his face, but her lips do not touch his. Two partially opened mouths are a sixteenth of an inch apart.

"Now, what did daddy really talk to you about?"

"Digging into an alleged scandal."

The rhythm of exhales and inhales is more intoxicating than the single malt. The alternating warmth and coolness of air passing over lips and into mouths is erotic. Slowly her parted lips move to his left ear and the tip of her tongue flicks the lobe, then his neck, jaw, and is finally back to his waiting mouth. The delicate kiss lasts a fleeting moment.

"Now will you tell me the truth?"

"Sorceress, I have spoken the truth. There are no lies in my heart or on my lips."

"I see you are strong of will. I must subject you to the ultimate test of truth. We must abandon this place and go to the chamber with the rack. Arise and meet your fate."

"I'm already up."

Tony leads the way to the plane of pleasure. As he enters the bedroom, he hears the sound of a zipper and the subtle cascading of fabric onto the tile floor. Hands are on his shoulders. Then as the hands snake around to his chest and down to his boxers, warm breasts press against his back. Wet lips plant precious baby kisses all over his neck and shoulders. He turns to face this loving aggressor. They lock in an embrace, which precedes the feverish groping and grabbing at the final vestiges of clothing. She will not be taken as the passion of another might dictate. She will be loved and will love in return. The dynamic tension created by delicate intimacy heightens and prolongs the pleasure. The rhythm starts imperceptibly and slowly becomes waves. Droplets of emotion . . . sweat and saliva are exchanged on naked torsos. Light, split by the slats of shutters strobes the pale and ebony bodies as they entwine in a horizontal dance. The magic, as always, is theirs to enjoy. The relief is nearly torture. A quizzical thing this; something so prized as the culmination of this act results in an immediate collapse, physical and emotional. Plus, there is such a rush to get to the pleasurable ending. Only the foolish or teen rush to the end. The lovers hold each other and the tender kisses don't stop. He knows she will be leaving. He just doesn't know when.

"I know you are wondering, so I'll tell you. Lucky is at an all night poker game with five of his cronies . . . or so he said. My driver took Tracey, Megan and me to *le Club* for a night of dancing . . . or so I said. The driver went home. The girls stayed. I came here. They know I booked, but they don't know to where or with whom. In a short time, I'll take a cab home. Lucky will arrive about an hour after I am asleep. He will sleep in the den so I cannot detect the smell of the other woman. And he will not be able to detect your cologne. Tomorrow will be a new day. We will both be satisfied."

"I don't like to pry, but you know how I feel about you. I don't want us to get you hurt. An irate husband could do a dumb thing. So, I worry. And, I'm not satisfied yet."

Tony's hands and mouth begin exploring the many curves and hollows that are Melissa's body. She is the goddess to whom he owes reverence, and she revels in the attention. The ultimate response is her acknowledgement of his worthiness. As he drifts into slumber, she clings to him for emotional sustenance. He never feels or hears her leave his side. He doesn't hear the telephone at 5:05 AM either.

Coffee, Tony's other socially acceptable drug, is ingested with gusto every morning. He is as particular about the coffee and how it is prepared for consumption as he is about his Scotch whisky. Blue Mountain beans are kept in a hermetically sealed container until they are ground fresh each morning. The fine dark particles . . . three rounded table spoons for the two six-ounce cups . . . are poured into a paper filter and covered with water heated to a near boil, but not boiling. After seeping, the elixir of the AM is poured over a tablespoon of clover honey in the bottom of a fourteen-ounce mug. Just enough room remains for cream . . . not milk. After two drafts, he is ready to retrieve the Daily News and The New York Times, which are resting in the box by the building door. On his way back into his apartment, he sees the blinking light on the answering machine.

You have one new message . . .

"Tony, it's me Jimmy. I need your help. Pam's been killed. I don't know what to do. Detective Hinton at the 34th precinct, who caught the case, wants to talk to me, but he won't tell me any more than she was killed in a robbery. It's now a little after five. I'm on my way into the city from the farm in Connecticut. Can you meet me at the precinct? I should be there by 7 or 7:15 at the latest. Please, Tony, I am fucking desperate. Call me on my cell at 287-393-3218."

Tony hadn't heard Jimmy's voice in nearly nine months. Hadn't seen him in over a year. Their busy schedules kept them apart. The mantle clock tells Tony it is now 6:51. He calls Jimmy.

"Jimmy, I'm really sorry. I'll meet you at the precinct. Don't do anything or say anything until I get there. I maybe a few minutes late. I'm going to pull the materials filed by the CAT squad that did the crime scene gathering. I'll have that when I arrive. Again, say or do nothing."

"I'm at my wits' end. But, I'll wait for you. Then can we go to the crime scene and see what really happened."

"I'll do whatever I can to help. Until I get there just remain calm. Keep that notorious Ranck temper in check. That's very important. Do you understand?"

"Yes. Hurry."

Tony fires up his laptop and gets onto S.L.A.N . . . the police department's **S**ecure **L**ocal **A**rea **N**etwork. Entry requires two general passwords. Entry to any department requires another, personal password. Access to data and information about anything within the department requires the access code and a fourth password. None of the four passwords may be the same or related in any way. At each step of the entry process, the system initiates what are called acceptability traits, to confirm that the PC is permitted to be on line and may proceed to the next level. Finally, Tony is in. He searches for CAT reports of Friday. Three forms with addenda for Case #201-05-34 submitted by Team B (Chris Wills, Jamie Lanno, and Brendan McLaughlin). Tony downloads to paper without reading the report first. He will have time during the thirty-block cab ride.

Pamela Jackson Ranck, WF, age 46, 346 East 61 Street NYC . . . three shots to the head. Lisa Raymond Williams, BF, age 27, 527 West 154 Street NYC . . . four shots to head and upper torso. Alphonso Bellon Netter, BM, age 35, 2378 Amsterdam Ave NYC . . . two shots to the back of the head. Rufus Jennings Fulton, BM age 38, 286 East 131 Street NYC . . . three shots to the head.

Detailed descriptions of body situations and physical environment. Blinds drawn. Furniture over turned. Too much gun fire. Real rage. Safe open and empty of cash. Memory tower destroyed. Door to storage room open. PC monitor destroyed. Back-up destroyed. Shells abound. Fifty-caliber Desert Eagles. Cannons. These guys were real killers with vicious streaks The destruction of the technical hardware indicates they were looking for something not physical. But what? The cab pulls up to the 3-4. Tony exits and enters the shiny edifice of community protection.

"Excuse me Sergeant; I'm here to see Detective Robert Hinton."

Before the black desk sergeant can question the white intruder, Tony flashes tin.

"Yes Lieutenant, Detective Hinton is upstairs."

"Thank you."

On the second floor, he spots Jimmy sitting on a bench. He looks like hell. The inexplicable tragedy has taken its toll on his body and countenance.

"Where's the Detective?"

"Taking a pee."

The locker room door opens and the doorway is filled with mocha humanity.

"Detective Hinton, I'm Lieutenant Tony Sattill. I'm here to assist you in any way you wish."

"What is you connection with this case Lieutenant?"

"I head up the CAT squads in Manhattan. Therefore, I am responsible for the gathering of all on-scene information relative to the crime. I came to review the scene and be sure my people did their jobs properly. Second, Mr. Ranck, whose wife was murdered, is a long-time friend. I will not cramp your investigation. Nor do I seek to gain any publicity. But, because of my personal connection with one of the victims, I feel an obligation to double-check the work of my team. If any new information were uncovered, it would become addendum to our files and therefore your investigation. I can also assist you, without getting in your way, by making sure that all reports are expedited to you."

Tony knows the flip side of the offer is the threat of slow down. He knows Hinton knows he knows.

"Fine, ride along. Just don't get in the way."

Detective Robert Hinton moves like a large cat. Gracefully and with purpose. His hands and feet are surprisingly small . . . almost delicate, given the size and of the man. He obviously spends ample time in the weight room. His head is shaved, and he has no facial hair other than eyebrows. After he defined the territorial responsibilities with verbal urine, he smiled slightly. Tony knows how to play the game of deference.

"If it's all right with you, I would like to accompany Mr. Ranck."

"Are you a lawyer, too?"

"No, but I am."

"I am sorry for your loss. Sir, you are not under arrest. I just need to get some information, a few facts to help in my investigation. We can sit here, if it's all right with you."

Tony sits on the bench outside the Detectives' bullpen. He studies the reports and listens unobtrusively.

"Mr. Ranck, where were you yesterday between 9 AM and noon?"

"I was driving to the farm my wife and I own in Connecticut."

"Can you confirm that?"

"Yes, check my toll pass. You'll see the time I headed north on the Connecticut Turnpike."

"Do you know any reason why the four people were murdered?"

"No."

"Any unhappy former employees?"

"None."

"Anyone holding a grudge against you or your wife?"

"I'm a lawyer. I worked in the corporate arena for ten years. I defended criminals. Some were guilty and some were not. I'm sure I made my share of people unhappy. But, not so miserable that they would kill. And if they were to seek vengeance on anyone it would be me and not my wife. Besides, I heard the four people lost their ears. Isn't that a trademark of the gang known as Los Hores?"

"Yes."

"I've never had any dealings with or against anyone openly connected with the gang. And I doubt they deal in checks that need to be cashed."

"How much money do you think was in the safe?"

"About $50,000."

"Why so much?"

"We are in the business of cashing checks for those who have no banking relationship. Friday was the 30th . . . payday for just about everybody. On a regular Friday, we cash about $20,000 worth of checks. On a regular payday, which is not a Friday, we cash another $20,000. Yesterday was a going to be a double whammy."

"Sir, if you are able, I would like to take you to the crime scene. There I'll ask you to examine the space and determine if anything is missing or significantly out of order. Do you think you're up to a visit?"

"Yes."

"This is where you come in, Lieutenant."

The three drive to 2867 Amsterdam Avenue. *Neighborhood Financial & Legal Services* is properly designated with yellow crime scene tape and a patrolman. Detective Hinton's badge of entry hangs over his jacket pocket. He cuts the tape on the door.

"Watch your step. There's blood everywhere. Mr. Ranck if you could just stand next to the door way and scan the room looking for irregularities, it would be helpful."

Jimmy's face goes blank, his eyes don't blink, but his shoulders slump. No tears. The ducts are dry. He tries to imagine the last few tortuous moments of his wife's life.

The chaos and screaming. The gunfire. Bodies contorting to the floor in pools of their life. Jimmy bites his lip. In his mind he sees the bad guys entering the office, subduing the security guard, Alphonso, and closing the window blinds. That triggered the turmoil. The next actions could have been confronting Lisa in the cage, threatening Pam with Lisa's death if the safe were not opened, taking the cash, destroying the VCR and PC, and then killing the four where they had stayed during the ransacking. They were executed and their ears sliced off to let everyone know who was responsible for the robbery. A sign of who is the muscle in the neighborhood.

"Nothing seems to be significantly out of order considering this is the scene of a robbery, pillage and four murders. If I could look in the storage room, it would help?"

"I'll go with you. Lieutenant, please stay here."

"Detective, it doesn't look like anything is awry in here except for the battered equipment. The office supplies are intact. Why would they destroy the equipment? They erased everything then destroyed the equipment so the police could not find even a trace. They were viciously thorough."

"Real rage. For a real statement of power."

"OK. I'm done in here."

"I appreciate you coming over here today, sir. I realize how difficult it must be, but it was a big help for my investigation."

"Damn. I forgot. Pam kept her purse and some personal stuff in a filing cabinet in the storage room. Would you mind if I went back and got them?"

"Not at all. We'll wait here."

"What did you learn today, Lieutenant?"

"That the CAT squad's assessment of the information was spot on. The abundance of the particular shell casings and the wanton destruction of the electronic hardware seem odd. True pros don't do it this way. Psycho pros, maybe. Psycho pros looking for something unseen, for sure. But, that's your bailiwick. Mine is simply the collection of facts. The lack of witnesses outside the store is not strange. It's just sad that people are so frightened that they won't speak up."

"They have to live in this neighborhood. They face the real threat of retribution. We get to go home to other, safer neighborhoods. Excuse me, Mr. Ranck; I must check what you retrieved from the filing cabinet so I can inventory the contents. Sorry, it's just a formality. Three photos of you and your wife. One purse, lipstick, face powder, emery board, tissues, ball point pen, eyebrow pencil, breath spray, hand lotion, address book with a Doctor's card and appointment date of next Tuesday, and a congratulations card. Your wife was pregnant. I am truly sorry."

Hinton's eyes glisten.

This was a bad day.

News

Manhattan Private Trust Opens European Operations

New York. Latchazar Razdarovich, V, President and CEO of Manhattan Private Trust announced the establishment of an office of the bank in London, England effective May 15. Stressing the new facility "is not a branch office" but "will provide private banking services" for those in Great Britain not yet receiving the high level of service afforded discriminating New York families. Mr. Razdarovich went on to say that the bank would open with sufficient clientele and deposits to ensure smooth operations without the need for a capital infusion from New York. The two offices would operate autonomously yet in concert, allowing customers to have ready access to superior private service regardless of their location. Mr. Razdarovich dismissed the rumors that Manhattan Private Trust was a takeover target, in that his family controlled over two-thirds of the voting stock, and they were very happy with his performance as CEO.

Big news indeed. If this is Lucky's definition of 'blow the roof off the personal banking business' he must live beneath a thatched roof. The dismissal of the 'take over' rumors does not rule out merger/purchase by some big player who wants Lucky's customer base. The banking vultures have been circling for the last two years, because rumor has it that Manhattan Private Trust has been generating double digit net profits and that the officers' bonuses have been multiples of their base salaries. This fat piggy bank may get cracked open soon.

CNN Reports
Tel Aviv, Israel

Rockets Rain Down on Jewish Settlements in the West Bank.

At 5:00 am local time residents the in the new apartment buildings in the West Bank region were shaken from their beds by the explosions of rockets and mortars. Authorities determined that more than forty shells hit the area, killing at least twenty, including eight children. As the local fire and police departments sift through the wreckage of the several destroyed homes, they believe they will find more bodies, as there are still fifteen adults yet unaccounted for. Israeli military jets and helicopter gunships combed the desert for fifty miles. Speaking on the condition of anonymity, one army official noted that in their search, they discovered the site of the firings. The officer went on to state that the site was now in Israeli military control. As of now no organization has claimed the attack. A government spokeswoman was quoted, "We will find the killers of the innocents and we will mete out swift justice". This is a breaking story. More to follow.

"I called this meeting to discuss the multiple homicides on Friday. I want you to know that I visited the crime scene last Saturday. I went there as Jimmy Ranck's dear friend. Jimmy is . . . was married to Pamela Jackson, manager of the check cashing business who was killed. I was best man at their wedding. They owned and operated *Neighborhood Financial & Legal Services*. While at the scene, I reviewed your reports and found them to be detailed and accurate. So, you did your job in an exemplary manner. Just as I had expected. Thank you. But, that was not the real purpose of my visit to the crime scene. What I want to discuss is anything you might recall that was outside the forms you completed. Do you have a sense of anything strange or just not right? So I open the floor."

"Lieutenant, I think is strange that Los Hores took ears and took the surveillance video and destroyed the equipment. There is something that just doesn't sit right. It's almost like they wanted the police to know who did the crime, but not know exactly why they did it. If they were trying to conceal their identities with destruction, they probably didn't wear masks. If they didn't wear masks, somebody passing by on the street could identify them. I mean that's a busy street during a Friday mid-morning. There's a Pathmark on one corner and a Shop Rite down the block. Somebody had to see the bad guys with masks on entering and leaving. Somebody also had to see the escape vehicle and driver. If the guys are local, they could be identified. I doubt the gang will feel safe and secure, if they are counting on nobody talking. So, I would expect the gang would soon get out the threat of silence or death in the neighborhood. And, if there is no threat of silence sent to the neighborhood, the crime may be committed by others outside the neighborhood. Then Los Hores will really be pissed. I mean coming onto their turf, mimicking them and taking their bread. Not good."

"Jamie, you may have hit something. Suppose the bad guys were not Los Hores at all. Suppose they were just trying to put the heat on the gang by slicing ears from the dead. That would explain the disappearance of the discs, the absence of masks, and the fact that nobody will step up to identify the bad guys. No one knows them, because they're outsiders. If this is the case, Los Hores will seek revenge. If they don't exact revenge, they will admit they can't defend their turf. And, that just won't do. I think we might be in for a range war."

"Brendan, any thoughts?"

"Sir, I am surprised they shot the customer while he sat in the chair. They shot the clerk in the face while she stood against the wall. They shot the guard from in front as he stood against another wall, and they shot the owner as she knelt at the safe. They faced all the vics except the customer. The customer, who had his back to the bad guys and their actions, was shot from behind. Why did they let him just sit there while they went about the robbery, and then kill him? Or did they shoot him first? If we could see the video we could determine if they shot him first, second, third or fourth. My guess is last. And that is strange. Maybe he was collateral damage. Maybe not. Maybe he knew them."

"Chris, if you have the time, I would appreciate your digging into the customer. Who was he? Why was he there? He is the one out of the ordinary."

"Shell casings. Los Hores uses 9mm . . . Glocks. Owning that gun is another badge of the gang. These guys used fifty-caliber cannons. The holes in the vics were fist sized. The guns that other street gangs usually use are not that special . . . 25's or 32's. And they drop them after a shooting anyway. We found no guns near the scene. I think we should re-canvass to be damned sure there are no weapons within two blocks. But, what if these guys wanted to keep the weapons. Or had to keep them, because the guns were issued to them and they had to be returned. My take away is that these guys were not street thugs. They were special. It's just the why and who that are left open."

"Brendan, do you realize what you are saying?"

"Sir, you asked what we thought."

"Good for you. If you can, follow that idea with the M.E. Get a reading from the slugs, if you can. And re-canvass."

"Jamie, do you know Carlita Brown?"

"She heads the Gang Task Force in Manhattan."

"Talk to her about Los Hores. Their turf, their connections, any conflicts with other gangs. Also find out if they have moved up in gun power."

"Yes sir."

"Now, two important issues. One, this investigation is extracurricular and off the books. There is no pay for this volunteer project. So, if you want to out, say so now. And two, your digging has to be on the Q-T. Detective Robert Hinton caught this case and he is very testy about outside help. If he gets wind that we are pissing in his garden, he will go to his Captain, who will call Captain Sanchez. If I get a call from Sanchez, it will entail carving multiple sphincters about half way up my back. I'll take as much of the heat as I can, but you three may also receive reprimands in your files for doing what I asked . . . not ordered . . . and not reporting this activity to our boss. Most likely, you'll get rips of a week. So if you want to stop here, I'll understand."

"Lieutenant, how many rips to you have in your file for not following orders and for doing what you thought was the right thing, or for doing some extracurricular work to solve a crime without telling the boss?"

"Several."

"Well, I'm a virgin."

"Chris, I would not let any other adults know that."

"Not that way. The reprimand way."

"One other item, sir. When we find anything of importance, how does it get reported back to Detective Hinton?"

"I'll just tell him that, I was disappointed in your work, so I had you rework the details. I'll take heat from him for having a sloppy team."

Tony knew he could count on his team. Discretion and intuition are two hallmarks of great Detectives.

"Crime Analysis Team, Lieutenant Sattill."

"Tony, Jimmy. Can you come over to my place tonight? I want to show you something. I'll spring for dinner."

"What time?"

"You name it."

"6:30?"

"See you then."

Paper work seems to have grown exponentially with the computer revolution. Like a fungus in a dark damp room. Now there are forms to order the forms to answer questions about form ordering. Each borough has a Lieutenant First Grade in charge of the CAT squads. There are two squads per borough. Each has three Detectives. Tony developed the structure. One squad member, referred to as V, is responsible for the details of the victim or victims. A second squad member, known as I E, is responsible for gathering the facts about the immediate environment around the victim or victims.

This area is within a circle fifty feet in diameter. With the exception of sniper killings, the hot murder area is almost always in this size circle. The third team member is known as EE and is responsible for gathering all the facts in the external environment, outside the hot area, normally outside the fifty-foot circle, or outside the room or building. Each member serves in his or her area for two years and then is rotated out of the borough and to another area of gathering. After six years, the P.D. hopes to add two squads to each borough. The borough Lieutenants report through their precinct Captain to a Commander at One Police Plaza. The level of CAT Captain was left vacant as the carrot to the Lieutenants. Jarel Wojevitcz, Lieutenant in Brooklyn, solved the biggest issue with the CAT squads. Time. He instituted the system-wide use of S.L.A.N. and downloading reports from the scene. This has stepped-up the dispersal of information from eight hours to two hours. Investigating Detectives now can be on the case with an armload of information before the bodies are taken to the Medical Examiner. Tony knows Jarel is first in line to become Captain. Unless he screws up or Tony does something dramatic. Like solving a multiple murder.

"Thanks for coming. Want a drink?"

"Scotch."

"Help yourself."

Jimmy looks like a shadow of his former self.

"I retrieved something from the store when we were there on Saturday."

"That's tampering with a crime scene and could put you on the list of suspects."

"Bullshit, I was retrieving the personal effects of my murdered wife. Besides I'm going to give this personal item to the police to aid in their investigation. I'm going to be a good guy."

Jimmy's smirk was mixed with a touch of pathos.

"What is this personal affect?"

"Other than the purse and its contents, which Hinton saw, I have a video disc of the crime."

"The bad guys took the discs and destroyed all the equipment."

"They never looked for the DVD compressor. It's new and we kept it hidden. Pam and I decided that because of the sensitive nature of these stores . . . people's finances and legal matters . . . it would be very smart for us to have a back-up for our historical records. To make storage of the voluminous material feasible, the only answer would be compressed discs. We figured we could also store the visual activity for a month on each disc. Each disc would be stored for three years then pitched."

"What is this DVD compressor?"

"It's a device for the business markets. It allows the user of a video system to convert all his recordings to a special DVD. Not the regular ones but compressed ones the size of a very small coaster. Pam got one from the first run off the line from her contacts at Sony. The unit won't be introduced at the fairs and expositions for about a year. So we don't own it . . . we volunteered to be part of the in-use test so we could use it for free. All we had to do was keep a complete log of our activity. The damned thing will cost over 100K when it is introduced, but we paid nothing. However, we had to make damned sure no one would steal it. We hid it behind stacks of paper and boxes on the double shelf on the storage closet. The people in the office knew about the computer tower, but only Pam and I knew about the DVD."

"What was on the DVD?"

"Activity and faces from the week that includes Friday. Let me show you. We have three cameras in the store. One faces the customer at the teller's cage and the door, and two cameras face the room from opposite walls. The system switches from camera-to-camera every five seconds. That way we get constant panoramic coverage of the space. I'll go to the beginning of the day, when Pam arrived. The system is time coded. You can see the security guard over by the teller's cage. It takes about twenty minutes for Pam, Lisa and Alphonso to get ready for the day. Pam and Alphonso are always on time. Let me fast forward to the first customer. This is Rufus Fulton. He has come to talk to Pam. Obviously, he has some legal matter he wants to discuss. See, there she is inserting a disc to get his vital data into a file. Once that is accomplished, she can create a working document for him, based on what he wants to do. It was my idea to create the files of basic legal documents. Most of the programs are for civil issues like divorce, name change, tenant-landlord dispute, marriage, adoption, bankruptcy and the like. We even have some misdemeanor programs, but nothing heavy. That's an area of long-term growth for us."

"Is there anything you can find about why Mr. Fulton was at the store? According to his driver's license, he lived forty-five blocks away. That seems like a long distance to come for some legal help."

"Not really, we're the only fair game in town. We do a complete file, get a date with the courts, and notify a client of their appearance for $200. That's about one-tenth the cost of a cheap lawyer. And, we can do it in much less time than legal aid. We are the alternative between fast and expensive, or slow and cheap. And, our forms are court approved."

"I see a woman with a baby carriage come to the store next. She goes right to the teller. Can we get any information on the paper she handed to the teller? Was it a check?"

"The Detective has the piece of paper. He indicated it was a note."

"The three bad guys come into the store about ten seconds after the girl. Mr. Fulton is seated. Look they aren't wearing masks or anything. Good mug shots. Now we know who they are, we'll just have to find them. All three go to the baby carriage for their guns."

"If you don't want to watch the rest, I'll view it."

"I've already seen it three times. I watched the hoods push the guard against the wall and shoot him. I've seen the thugs grab Pam and force her to open the safe to protect Lisa. Then they held the money up like a trophy. I watched the hoods shoot Lisa as she leaned against the wall. I've seen Pam die. The snapping impact of the shots. The blood and bone shards spreading out like chunky mist. The crumpling of her gentle body on the floor. I watched as they shot Mr. Fulton in the back of the head as he sat frozen at the desk. It seems as if he was waiting to be executed. The others were assassinated. He was executed. I watched as they removed the disc from Pam's computer and smashed the hard drive. I watched while one of the hoods went into the storage room, and another urinated on Mr. Fulton. I've seen it all, and can't make reason out of any of it. Maybe you can. I'm going to the kitchen for another drink."

Jimmy seems to shuffle from the room. Tony views and rewinds. Views and rewinds. Views and rewinds.

With each sequence, he sees a little more. But, he can't see what he is looking for, that one thing that tells him the why of the carnage. With each new pass, he studies body language, hand movements or something he did not view before. There is so much going on in such a short time and in such a confined space, he knows he cannot see all of it the first night. The five-second jumps of the cameras cause his brain to adjust constantly to each new perspective. Before he can settle into the specific point-of-view, it changes. This is unsettling. He will have to have someone edit the material into three different angles so they can be watched as three separate continuums. Then lay the three onto one screen to get one view of the events without the jumps. This will take time and raise red flags if done by the department. He will need someone at a studio. Someone who will work silently for cash."

"Jimmy, we've got to get this to Detective Hinton. But, without raising his hackles. Plus, I'll need two versions. Next question, do you have any history of Mr. Fulton coming into the store?"

"I went back over the week and no one fitting his description is visible on the tapes. This was the first week for the compressor test."

"The disc has to get back to the store. My team can take care of that. Then you must call the good Detective and tell him about your back up. But not the back up's back up. Wait until the day after tomorrow to make the call."

"Why do you need two copies of the tape?"

"One for me to study and one for my team. I asked them to volunteer to help my friend. We will use the pictures of the gang to dig into their past and connections with Los Hores."

Jimmy starts the transfer.

"Four lives for $50,000. Five when you count the baby. That's too fucking cheap. My wife and child were worth a helluva lot more than that. Someone has to be held responsible. Someone's gonna pay me with more than cash. I want to kill the all very slowly, very painfully."

Jimmy is trembling.

Rave

Tony's pager and telephone ring simultaneously. The electronic cacophony snaps his eyes open. Reflexes raise his head and turn his body toward the two noises. Hands grasp the origins of the aural discomfort. He squints at the pager and answers the phone.

"Sattill."

"Lieutenant, there's been a big shoot out. You'd better come."

"Where, Chris?"

"Nite Lites. A warehouse or club on Barrow between Canal and Sentry. 4-2-1 Barrow."

"I'm going to put you on speaker, while I get dressed. Give me details. Why do you need me?"

"We're getting pushed around by some Feds. We're having a tough time doing our job, and we're not getting full support from the precinct. We need nasty muscle. No offense, sir, that's you. This is the location for a regular Rave. The NY Drug Task Force working with the DEA decided to close down the dealing. They raided the place about thirty minutes ago. All hell broke loose. Bodies are all over. Both CAT squads are here. I thought we needed all the help we can get. We're trying to collect the evidence; there is something that just doesn't seem kosher about this whole thing. I'll have more on that when you get here. I took the liberty of sending a squad car for you. Blinking lights and a screaming siren will speed your trip."

"Stay steady. Stay calm. Take no shit and do your job. Who's the top precinct dog there now?"

"Lieutenant Martani."

"I know Ray, he's a good man. I'm sure he's just trying to cooperate with the Fed narcs. He understands the politics of territory."

"That may be true, sir, but the lords of drug discipline are pushing him around."

"I'm on my way."

Tony is dressed, armed with all the electronic and military appurtenances his position affords, and waiting at the curb for the squad car. The trip in the noise wagon will take fifteen minutes. He dials his phone.

"Lieutenant Martani. Good morning, sir, this is Lieutenant Sattill of the CAT squad. I want you to know that my guys at your site called me due to what they perceive as the substantial complexity of the crime scene. I fully understand that this is your crime scene and that I am coming there to assist my troops. We are all there to assist you and your precinct people do your job. Cooperation is our way of working. My ETA is twelve minutes."

"Tony, thanks for calling. We can use all the friends we can get. I won't go into the details now. We'll talk when you get here. We had a helluva fire fight inside the building. Bodies, blood and bullets everywhere. By the way it's Ray."

Tony sees the glow of car lights and the multi-colored blips reflecting off the buildings before the car rounds the corner. He spots Lieutenant Martani in his flamboyant green and yellow short-sleeve shirt and bright orange pants. He's dressed for either the psychedelic drug scene or a vacation in Hawaii. The two shoulder-strap holsters packed with silver Colt 45's are very out of place. He is noticed by street punks and he likes it that way. Unfortunately, the Feds, who don't know his serious dedication to his job, must think of his street attire is a clown's costume. They're dressed like cookie cutter cops: black jeans, black airborne boots, light blue shirts, black jackets with the yellow DEA on the back, and matching baseball caps. Tony flashes tin to get through the perimeter.

"Ray, how can I help?"

"Make sure your guys get all they want. There seems to be some dispute about jurisdiction. But, CAT has priority regardless of where the crime scene is. I'll make sure that no one gets in or out of the perimeter. My guys will do the questioning."

"Who are you and what are you doing here?"

The commanding voice makes Tony spin around.

"I'm Lieutenant Anthony Sattill in charge of the Manhattan CAT squad. The CAT squad is solely responsible for gathering and logging all pertinent information about the crime scene, and getting that information in its appropriate format to the precinct captain, Detectives who caught the case, and Borough Command. You are standing in my world, and if you don't do as I say, I will have you forcibly removed and taken to the precinct in a sector car in front of the news media. Now, who are you and what are you doing here."

Tony's monotone whisper has the force of hurricane wind. He does not blink and he does not smile or frown. The Fed's response is filled with the emotion of a braggart.

"I am Field Supervisor Frank Lehey of the DEA and this is my crime scene. I'll say who comes and goes."

"I'd say you fucked up the operation, and you need damage control to keep a smiley face on your department. My CAT squad can either help exonerate the actions of your posse or drive very rusty spikes through their hearts. Besides, the press will be arriving momentarily. Ah, they're here now. As you skulk into the shadows, what would you like Lieutenant Martani and me tell them about how your department instigated this unfortunate firefight? Here's what you are going to do. Your men are going to turn over all their weapons so our forensics can cross match the slugs. Then you are going to order your men to give statements to the Detectives under Lieutenant Martani's command. Then you are going to dismiss your men and you will make whatever statement to the press you want. The precinct and CAT squads will stay out of the limelight. We'll cooperate with you, if you cooperate with us. So, you can be the heroes, and we're just the mop-up crew. If not, we'll tell the press whatever we need to so we can be assured the NYPD comes off like heroes, and you guys look like rogue shooters. This is our sandbox and you just pissed in it. Now we have to clean it up. *Capice?*"

"And I get to make a statement to the press?"

"Pictures, too, if you want."

"Fine. It's a deal."

Lehey leaves to give the orders down the chain of command.

"Ray, get the same agreement from our Drug Task Force. Tell them they can make a joint statement with the Feds. That way, the department will be assured of getting some credit. Also, we better find out why the hell they never notified you or the Borough they were coming to your turf."

The bully from the other neighborhood was bested. At last count there were four dead and six wounded. Three were critical. Tony's two squads went about collecting the minutia, which was immediately dispersed to the interested parties. He watched their efficient attention to every facet of the scene in admiration. This was the way it was supposed to work.

"Ray, I'm going to leave now. Call me tomorrow . . . er later today if you need me for anything."

"Tony, I owe you."

"I was just doing my job. It's called teamwork. The Feds don't seem to understand that concept. See you later."

Tony's sleep is fitful. Dreams come in bits and pieces.

Melissa is naked and running toward him. Her face shows fear. She has no breasts. Ominous forces shift in the shadows. Bodies are lying on the street bathed in spotlights. They smile at him. He sees their mouths move, but they have no tongues or ears. Piles of paper. Six or eight feet high. The paper is blank. What is he to do with it? On his laptop, the e-mail bell rings and an electronic voice calls his name. Guns are everywhere. Old. New. Hand guns. Automatic. Street sweeper shotguns. Derringers. Tony is running in the carpeted halls and up and down the rickety staircases of a massive Victorian structure with hundreds of doors. He tries all of them. They're locked. He is being chased by a black shark that is growling at him. The e-mail bell rings again and again.

The alarm brings a reprieve from the fitful rest. He must rise and do battle in the real world.

"Have you read the Post? Look at this."

Drug Bust Crushes Rave
4 Dead 7 Injured

Early today the Federal DEA working in cooperation with NYPD Drug Task Force and local precinct members raided Nite Lites a local rave club and broke up a major ecstasy drug distribution center. Four members of the drug gang, Los Hores, were killed in a ferocious gun battle that left seven club attendees injured.

DEA Field Supervisor Frances Lehey stated: "We worked closely with local police department members of various disciplines in this comprehensive effort. We are pleased at the level of teamwork. New Yorkers should be proud. Approximately 20,000 units of the ecstasy were uncovered in the club. A major distribution ring was broken today. Members of Los Hores, the dealers, chose to try to defend their illegal goods and a gunfight ensued. Unfortunately, there was collateral damage. One of the innocent bystanders was killed and several were injured. We have been told none of the injuries are life threatening. No law enforcement officers were killed or injured. Because this is an on-going investigation on both a local and national level, I am not at liberty to discuss the matter further."

"Good props to the locals."

"Brendan, make sure you check the photos of the dead gang members. We need to see if any of these guys were at the store. It seems strange that Los Hores was so far downtown. Strange, like their presence or non-presence at the store robbery. I don't like any coincidence, because it always turns out to be non-coincidental. By the way, how are you and Carlita Brown progressing"?

"She is almost scary. She looks at me as if I were filet mignon."

"Poor bunny. I asked you to learn not date."

"Chris, do the same with the slugs found in the bodies and all over the scene. See if there are any matches with the robbery."

"Jamie, did you get the compressed disc to Detective Hinton."

"I discovered it on my second visit and handed it over to the good Detective. I am sure he has called your friend by now and is viewing a transfer."

"What do we know about the customer?"

"Nothing yet."

"Take a trip to his residence. See what you can learn."

"Lieutenant, I don't mean to be presumptuous, but where will all this investigation lead. I mean, assuming we uncover something that will impact Detective Hinton's case, how do we get the information to him or to anyone without violating department procedures? How do we make him look good and keep him from jamming us with the bosses? How do we not look like cattle rustlers?"

"That's my problem. I'm working on it. With last night's episode, your workload has doubled. And, I want a complete review of everything at lunch on Friday. For sure, I want to see the reformatted store surveillance at that time. I need to be damned sure we haven't missed anything. I'll buy the Chinese, if you give me your order by Thursday."

"Good morning, Rosita, is Mrs. Razdarovich at home?"

"No, sir she is not."

"Fine, please tell her that Tony Sattill called. Would you ask her to call me when she gets an opportunity? Thank you."

His squads are functioning smoothly on both tasks.

"Tony, Jimmy."

"How ya doing, Jimmy?"

"I am on a mission. The mission is to find out who killed my family. I am calling in all the favors outstanding. From everybody. But, mostly you. I want to be involved in the investigation. I demand to be a silent member of your team. To hell with Detective Robert Hinton. Pam was my wife and she was carrying our child. This whole mess is personal. And, time is critical. So, do I have your word that you will share with me everything that you learn, and include me in your entire decision making?"

"Yes, you have my word. But, I want to be very clear that whatever I do is strictly confidential. Any digging I do must be well below Hinton's radar. If I learn anything, it will be very difficult to feed him the information without exposing my efforts. If the bosses learn of my efforts, and the fact that my squad is working on this as an extracurricular venture, will get me censured at best or suspended at worst. But, I'm willing to take that risk for you and Pam."

"Thanks. And, besides if you get your ass handed to you, we can hide out at the farm in Connecticut until the storm blows over. Great fishing in the ponds. Better whisky in the larder. I want to thank you for the kind words you spoke at Pam's funeral. They meant a great deal to me as well as her sisters. I know I will grieve from time to time, but now it's time to press on. I've uncovered something that may or may not help in your investigation. I need your counsel and time is critical."

"What do you mean . . . time is critical?"

There are twenty seconds of silence.

"Tony, I have pancreatic cancer. It is inoperable. Pam and I discussed this when she knew she was pregnant. The child was my legacy. She was prepared to raise the child without me."

"What do you mean inoperable? What about treatment?"

"It's too late for chemo or radiology. The damned thing is beginning to spread throughout my internal organs and is devouring me from the inside out. As of this date, I have four painful months to live. I was supposed to see the baby. Now I want to get the killers."

"Jesusfuckingchrist. What can I do?"

"Include me in everything you do. I won't get under foot. Toward the end I'll be bedridden."

Tony was numb.

"I'll do whatever you ask."

"For now, listen to what I have. In addition to the visual back up, Pam was very conscientious about back up computer files. She wanted to install a secure data storage system like the one they had used at her bank in Philly. But, on a much smaller scale. She was trying to convince her vendor that if the system worked on a one-store scale, we would be in the market for multiples. She was hoping he would be willing to install a single leg for free for six months. Everything that was input at the store went on the C drive and on a disc. That's standard. But, what Pam wanted was to have all the input placed in files stored at a central point. I thought she was in the final negotiation stage, but she seems to have gone beyond that and gotten the system installed. I discovered that the black box in her den is functional. The box had been gathering dust in a corner for three months. I assumed it wasn't hooked up. I'm sorry I didn't think of it before. I guess with the funeral and everything, it never crossed my mind to look."

"That's fine. What did you find in the files?"

"A pot full of glitches. Obviously, Pam and her vendor were still working out the kinks. That's why she didn't tell me about it. She wanted to wait until it was fully operational so she could take credit for it. The electronics aspect of our business was her area of expertise. It all had to be perfect before I could see the new toy in action. But, I did see fragments of Mr. Fulton's file. It seems he had been in the store two weeks before the murder. He was filing for divorce from his wife. Her name looks like Amanda Balfor Fulton. All the vitals for him are almost readable. Amanda's vital data is greatly degraded. I can't make out a damned thing except parts of her name from the fragments of letters and numbers. I'm not even sure if that is her name. The remainder of the Petition for Divorce contains some reasons, facts and dates. Again, these are broken up. Only bits and pieces of letters and numbers and lots of code scratching. My guess is that Mr. Fulton had come back to complete the form. He had the bad timing to be there when the bad guys arrived."

"Was there anything else readable in the store file?"

"Just test letters, some personnel and financial files for the store. All of it with broken letters and numbers. Just a lot of degraded data. I can e-mail it to you. It's not a big file."

"Sure, send it over. Make sure Detective Hinton also gets a hard copy of the material. Call him tomorrow and fax the sheets to him, too. And, for God's sake don't tell him I have the data. I'll see if I can make anything out of the data. How about dinner next week?"

"Tuesday."

"Melons?"

"7:30?"

"See you then."

Why are the dying so cavalier about their fate? Maybe we should all be that way. Live like we were dying every day. Jimmy's mission is now Tony's mission. The driving force. The e-mail is downloaded and looks like some transmission from a SETI lab. Lines, boxes, partial replications of some language that may or may not be Martian. The data confirms Mr. Fulton's name, address, and telephone number from other sources. His Social Security number looks like it start 219-35-#@#^. Tony is unsure. The digits could be any combination of three's, eight's, nine's or zeros. Jimmy was right that the information for the other party was more difficult to decipher.

"Chris, could you include these sheets of paper as part of your investigation. The information is very sketchy. I can barely read a complete line. But, I want to confirm the details of Mr. Fulton and the other party in the civil action. Let's focus Mr. Fulton for now."

"Lieutenant, Mrs. Razdarovich on line two."

"Hello Lieutenant, I am returning your call. How can I help you?"

"I was wondering if you and your husband would like to join me for dinner on Friday evening. Other than the galas, I never get to see you two. I thought some catching up would be enjoyable."

"That's very thoughtful of you. But, I'm sorry that my husband is extremely busy lately. I'm sure you read about the new bank he is opening. He's taking a very important bank business trip to Europe on Friday. During the preparation, he leaves the house before sunrise and arrives home after ten. I barely see him myself. So, I'm afraid he would not be able to make dinner on Friday. However, if you don't mind half a loaf, I would enjoy dinner with you. Will you be alone?"

"Yes. It will be the two of us, then. How does Café Argenteuil sound? At 8?"

"That will be very nice. I'll see you there. And thank you for the kind invitation Lieutenant."

Analysis

The three windowless walls of the large meeting room at the Twelfth Precinct are covered with sheets of paper ranging in size from 3 x 5 cards to 19 x 24 drawing paper. Each wall has a section dedicated to one of the CAT squad members, Chris, Jamie, and Brendan. The purpose of this meeting is to present all the material to all the members, and seek input and questions. The process will produce some basic assumptions and conclusions, as well as dictate appropriate actions to resolve the outstanding issues. Conversation is freeform and notes are taken furiously. There are no right or wrong answers at the beginning, but everyone must agree to the conclusions and actions. A dissenter is required to seek additional information to confirm the counter point-of-view.

"The guns at the store robbery are not the guns of choice of Los Hores. The cartridges were pre-fragged to ensure maximum destruction. As if they guys were sending a message. This is compounded by the fact that the loads were most likely hot. Fifty-percent more powder. The shot entered like quarters and exited like softballs. The shooters were definitely not Los Hores or dime store cowboys. They probably had some major backing. If all this tracks, they would have to give their godfather a cut. The rule is at least half. The take was 50 large. The video shows us three shooters and a woman with a baby carriage. That's four plus the driver waiting outside. A total of five. That means each of the perps gets five grand, at most. Frankly, that's not enough cash for such a brutal robbery murder. Five grand for life or the needle is a bad trade. Unless this was the way they were to earn their bones. That could explain it all. They commit the slaughter of four innocents and pick up some chump change all to prove they are worthy. That could make them Los Hores wannabes. Very dangerous, because they are out to prove something and are willing to take extreme risks to do it."

"Nice job."

"That's not all."

"Stand back gents, she's on a roll."

"The M-E removed fifty caliber pre-fragged slugs from three of the victims at the DEA rave raid. We know the Feds use 9's, and we found those casings. So, I am willing to bet a week of your salary, Lieutenant, that the same guns used at the raid were used at the firefight. Unfortunately, because the slugs at the robbery and those dug out of the victims of the DEA raid were pre-fragged, it is impossible to get a match on the weapons. But, I think it's more than coincidence."

"Much more. I got the mugs from the video and ran them through the files. One of them came up. Wilson Torque. He's Jamaican. Not Hispanic. All Los Hores that we know of are Hispanic. Maybe Wilson was trying to be the first brother in la casa. Maybe he has nothing to do with the gang. The girl and the two others in the store are clean according to our files. And, we don't know crap about the driver. I'll check the Feds' files. When I went to see Lieutenant Brown about current gang activity, she advised me there was nothing happening with Los Hores. She could be covering an on-going investigation or she could be telling the truth. When she is staring at me, I couldn't tell."

"Don't be a poor bunny, Brendan."

The face of the young man from the farm near Troy, New York turned crimson at Chris's jibe. He pressed on to overcome his uneasiness.

"I examined the photos of the victims at the raid and bingo . . . matches. There is Wilson Torque and the two unidentified, dark-skinned black males, who just happen to be on the video at the robbery. Why were they at the rave? It's really far from their uptown turf. What is their turf? Is it the entire island of Manhattan? This is a mobile society, you know. Why were they shot? Who shot them? I know this. All three were killed with pre-fragged 50s, and each was hit four times in the back and side. These guys were not killed by the DEA. Most likely, they were killed by multiple shooters already inside the building. All of this doesn't get us any closer; it just points us in a direction. But, I have a theory that the shooting of these three had nothing to do with the raid. Maybe they were just in the wrong place."

"Shot in the back and side proves the DEA did no damage here. But, suppose the shootings were some kind of execution and the raid was called to cover it. When the guys arrive, someone calls the Feds and the NYPD Drug Task Force at the same time. The narco-cops come in, make their presence known and the shooting begins. But, no one shoots at the narco-cops. Just the three dark skinned blacks. They were slaughtered. Why? Brendan, we've got to find out who the other two guys were. Pull the LUGS on the payphones at and near the store front and the rave. Canvassing neighborhoods will be tricky given Detective Hinton's parallel investigation. Ask our local street snitches. See if that turns up anything. But, stay out of Hinton's way."

"An execution is a bizarre idea, but it could happen if these three guys were killed by the two remaining perps from the robbery . . . the girl and the driver? We never saw the driver. Maybe he and the girl figured to really make their bones plus some more bread. When I looked at the tape, I noticed she is wearing a disguise. The others showed their faces. She has a long thick coat on and a scarf around her head. Plus, she has a large Afro that looked like a wig from the sixties. And she was wearing large face-hiding sunglasses. So she could be anybody of any age under all that. Or, maybe she wasn't a she. It could be any gender beneath all that. Twice she accidentally banged the baby carriage. No one who knows a mother would do that with an infant inside. I assume the carriage was empty except for the guns. Plus, as the gang was leaving, the guy, who was apparently the leader because he had the money, put the cash into the carriage. And they all dumped their guns in the carriage. What we don't know are two things. Who was waiting in the getaway vehicle? And, where the money went? Did it stay in the baby carriage and did the she-male take it somewhere while the shooters and driver went elsewhere? If she kept the money separate from the others, did she ditch her scarf, wig, and carriage somewhere near the robbery and just blend into the crowd? Hide in plain sight. It's too late to go back and look for the discarded disguise if it existed at all. She or he probably dumped the items in an alley dumpster. City sanitation and private carting companies have picked up since the robbery."

"So far, we need to find out who the dead guys were and if they could lead us to the shemale and the driver. Does anybody have a guess how Hinton is going to play this?"

"Depends on his case load. He may just take the opportunity to close the case based upon the death of the three guys at the rave. Or he may push it to the back burner, knowing there are a few inconsequential loose ends that he can hide from the brass. We can't go public. We must somehow make him want to keep the investigation open. I'll take care of that."

"Jamie, what do we know about the customer, Mr. Fulton?"

"His address checks out. I went there and it's boringly average. I saw a few old pictures of him and a woman. I assume she was his wife, Amanda. The pictures look like they were taken five to eight years ago. Clothing styles and hairstyles were different. I learned Rufus Jennings Fulton was some type of a computer clerk for a mid-town investment firm, Whyte, Molina, and Dorsch. I checked with them. His work record is spotless. Got the usual merit raises and bonuses. Liked by the partners. Always put in the hours to get it right. He was trustworthy and diligent. Like a Boy Scout. They never knew he was seeking a divorce. They had run a background check and he was solid. Faux marriage. Faux divorce. Strange. Cover-up? He came to them from a similar firm in Seattle."

"Did you call them?"

"No, but I will today."

"You studied the fax from Jimmy Ranck? Was there anything of note on the sheets of scribble?"

"I deciphered multiple Social Security number possibilities; twelve for Rufus and at least forty for his wife. I've asked a friend in the Federal system to cross match the numbers against the names and descriptions we have. I also asked if she could search other combinations. I asked for a favor, because I didn't want to expose our work to Hinton if he goes through official Federal channels. And because this is a favor, my friend will do her work over the weekend. So, I won't have the information until Monday."

"Has anybody studied the re-formatted video?"

"Brendan, Jamie, did you see anything out of the ordinary?"

"No, Sir. Pretty cut and dried. They came in. Got the money. Killed. Did a lot of damage. Left the store. Frantically methodical. They looked almost like pros except for the damage. I think they felt safe that their identity would leave with them on the tape. So they went mask less. Maybe the taking of the video means nothing more sinister than they wanted the event to look like Los Hores, but they were not part of the gang."

"Would you run the tape for me, Brendan?"

Eight eyes are glued to the screen. Jump cuts from camera to camera have been almost eliminated. The screen is divided into thirds. The ebb and flow of the basic action is seen from three angles. The stars of the performance dominate the stage. The four bit players are like pictures on sets until they are brought into the action. Then they are killed. The fluid spray of each bullet's damage paints a faint outline of everybody on the surface behind it. The body's strength dissolves. The osteo-superstructure and outer wraps of flesh and fabric collapse in a crumpled heap. The tape is rewound and re-viewed thrice. Movements of the perps, as well as their lethal consequences are etched in the four minds of the viewers.

"Can we go back to the point before Rufus is shot? See. He's sitting beside the desk. He is not moving. Now rewind a little bit. He seems to be bringing his right hand and arm back to resting on the desk. Now go back further. His right hand and arm are by his side. They're not on the desk. At some point while the perps were focusing on Mrs. Ranck opening the safe and then shooting her, Rufus extends his right hand and returns it to its original position. It is safe to assume he was told not to move by the perps. Then why did he move? Why did he risk harm by moving? He had to figure he would get shot if they saw him move. It must have been very important for him to take the risk of motion. If nobody had been killed at the time of his arm motion, he was not sure death was imminent. Or did he know he would die? What did he do during the move? I don't think he was just getting comfortable. I think he was doing something important."

"Whoa, guys and girl. Slow down. Yes, Mr. Fulton's arm moved while the perps were distracted. Was the move intentional or was he just getting comfortable? I think Chris is right in ruling out a comfort-seeking move. So, let's assume for argument's sake that the movement was intentional. Was he reaching, taking or placing? You guys didn't find anything out of the ordinary on the desk. Detective Hinton and his men didn't find anything out of the ordinary on the desk."

"I believe there are drawers on that side of the desk. I never removed anything in the three drawers. I never noticed anything out of the ordinary. Maybe there's something he left for us to see."

"Why would he do that?"

"We'll seek the why after we learn the what. I'd like a follow up of this analysis on Tuesday morning. People in the pictures. The people we never saw. Mr. Fulton's previous employer. All the material in the desk drawers must be inventoried. I'll call Detective Hinton to get a temperature reading. And I'll call Detective Brown to see if she'll be more forthcoming. Maybe, I'll just have to sacrifice somebody to the gang goddess to get information. Have a nice weekend. Don't work too hard."

Homework assignments build character.

Café Argenteuil tres magnifique. The food is perfect. The wine list is unparalleled. The service is impeccable. Melissa is fashionably twenty minutes late and makes an entrance to entrance. This incredibly beautiful, high cheek-boned, fashionably thin, and perfectly tailored vision stops conversation and draws looks from all diners. While men lust, the women shoot icy glances of envy. They do not stare. She deigns to acknowledge others in the room. She kisses Tony on the cheek with the affection of old friends. Much less affectionately than lovers. Her greeting will not make the papers.

"You look wonderful."

"Thank you Lieutenant. And I add that you are dashingly handsome as always. I'll have Gray Goose on the rocks. My friend will have Balvenie and two ice cubes, in a tall glass."

"Assertive tonight."

"Always. Now tell me. What is the occasion? Why are we dining so elegantly public?"

"As I mentioned on the phone, I had hoped to spend the evening with Lucky as well. It's been so long since we had a chance to sit and just talk. Old friends from Brown and all that. Your husband and I are fast approaching our 25th Reunion. And if he and I are going to lie for each other, we better get the stories straight. Plus, I was hoping to make this a semi-business event with him. But, that can wait. I'm pleased you could join me. Tell me, what fills your busy days."

Melissa leans into Tony and whispers.

"You can be so fucking condescending sometimes. Just like Lucky. It makes me want to slap you."

She leans back and commences the epic saga of her socially visible days. He knows she is uncomfortable with her photo op events. Charities. Gallery openings. Programs for the poor. But, he also knows that she knows these see-and-be-seen days are expected from the daughter of the borough president and wife of a bank president. Curiously she is never out in public on Mondays. Tony basks in her beauty.

"Armand, we'll have the rack of lamb and asparagus. Please select another vegetable for us . . . something exotic to balance the delicate nature of the lamb and asparagus. And an appropriate salad. For the wine, we'll have a '92 Merlot. Or something else that is not too sweet. I would like to start with escargot. My guest will have pate. And, a second round of drinks before it all. Thank you."

"So, I'm your guest. You like control don't you?"

"I like being assertive. I hate another's control over me and my life. Let Lucky pay for this evening. It's his bad luck he can't enjoy it."

Small talk fills the time between sips and bites. Her father's health. Her mother's new hobby, fly-fishing. Her old hobby was nagging about grandchildren.

"I have never understood what you do? Tell me."

"It's a combination of bureaucratic tap dancing, technology, wizardry, and old-fashioned digging. We gather the information at vicious crime scenes . . . homicides. We process the information on appropriate forms and disseminate it to the Detectives who will sustain the investigation up to the resolution of the crime. We're the gathers and hunters who interface with everybody . . . from street cop, to Chief of D's, to the M.E. Sometimes the Detective who caught the case asks that we go back and review the crime scene. At the beginning, the CAT squad was hated by the old timers. We took some of their job. But, we were better schooled and trained, and more focused. And they knew it. Now our biggest two hurdles are constantly infusing the latest technology and not stepping on the feet of our brothers and sisters on the job. Many of them couldn't find their own ass with both hands."

Melissa pays. Big tip. She doesn't need to be remembered, she is known. As we exit, she takes Tony's arm.

"Let's have a nightcap or two and listen to Billy Tripp."

As we enter the Doyle, Tony realizes she is known here, too. The table for two is in the corner to the right of the piano. Tony can't beat Melissa to the order.

"Two, Armagnacs please."

"Billy will be out anon, Mrs. Razdarovich."

"I feel a lot like a kept man and it's becoming uncomfortable."

"I know how uncomfortable it can be. I'll release the velvet chains if, you tell me the truth."

"What truth?"

"The truth about my father's conversation with you at the R.E.A.C.H. fund raiser."

"I told you. He wants me to do a little digging into something political."

"Bullshit. Now the truth. You owe me that at the very least."

"Ladies and gentlemen, Mr. Billy Tripp."

The Eastside elite are almost raucous. The icon of café society entertainment acknowledges numerous regulars. Particularly, Melissa. His first song is "Luck Be a Lady" followed by "Better Luck Next Time" and "Old Black Magic." Tony smiles at the homage and wonders why. Ten songs later, the gentle maestro takes a break.

"Now no more bull shit. You owe me the truth."

He's trapped between his lover and a politically powerful man. The candle flame flickers across her glossed open lips. The refracted moistness beckons him to taste. To enter and experience her. He is the deer in the headlights. She awaits his reaction to her cue. He leans forward and kisses her on the left cheek. Melissa flinches. The room is dark enough and they are off to one side so very few people even notice the flirtatious instance. Besides, keeping social secrets is currency of the realm.

"Ooh."

"Sorry, I didn't mean to hurt you?"

"My cheek's a little tender. I bumped it in the bathroom last weekend, and the tenderness has not completely gone away. Now what were you going to tell me."

"The truth? Your father is worried that a senior member of the City Council is taking bribes from all the local, state, and federally funded construction. The mobs are threatening physical retaliation. Deconstruction of the construction and several fatal accidents. Apparently, this guy is taking more than the mobs are, and the capos in each borough want this rectified. Your father is hoping to nail this bastard and, at the same time, have the Feds get the mob's role in the construction industry greatly reduced. That's really all I can tell you or I'll have to do something physical to silence you. Like take you to my bed and cover your body with hot gypsy kisses."

"Why don't you demonstrate the consequences of telling me before I decide if I want to know any more details?"

Bill paid. Taxi ride is eight minutes. Her twitching to his kisses indicates discomfort in her abdomen and rib cage. Melissa leaves in three hours. She wants to think what she'll have to endure to learn more.

Team

Before Anthony can make the first call of the day, the light on his telephone lets him know somebody wants him.

"Tony, Ray Martani. For your help the other night, I'm going to pass along some interesting information. I know your friend Jimmy Ranck's wife was killed in a robbery by some Los Hores. So you have a personal and professional interest in seeing the killers are taken down. My guys determined that three of the vics from my narc raid were the same mugs who are responsible for her murder. My guys checked pictures from both crimes. Detective Hinton put the mugs' faces on our Intranet. I just called him and relayed the connection. I suspect he is ready to close his case, 'cause he's got his shooters. He has never been one for dragging out investigation, and closing a public killing like your friend will look good on his record. It will increase his total closes and close percentage and push him toward the next grade. Here's what my guys learned from interviewing the people at the scene. The three mugs were not shot by the DEA or NY Drug Task Force. They were killed by two black dudes, who were at the bar. We believe the three mugs were in the way. They were standing inside the entrance to the club, when the DEA entered. I know the DEA was looking for dealers. We don't know if the two black dudes were the dealers or just muscle for the dealers . . . or just bad ass guys. Also, we don't know who shot first . . . the DEA or the bar dudes. Regardless, the firefight started. The DEA shot 9's from the entrance all over the walls of the bar. Hell, they hit more booze bottles than anything else. And the two black dudes returned fire. My guess is that the three guys from the robbery were standing in the wrong place at the wrong time. They were in the line of fire, but they had no guns on or near their bodies. They had all the drugs. Just damned bad luck on their part."

"Did your witness give you any description of the shooters?"

"Tall. Over six foot. Mid-twenties to thirty. Very black skin. Bony facial features. Dressed in dark suits and white shirts. The no-button long collar type, like the Euro-trash wear. And they wore grey leather shoes. They stood out from the crowd. No regular at any club dresses like that. We're going after them."

"One more thing. Were you able to identify any of the three vics?"

"Yeah, one was Wilson Torque. A local guy from my precinct. Never been in trouble. Never any hint of trouble. Lived with his sister, Amber. At least everybody thought they were brother and sister. She had a small baby. No parents anywhere to be found. He worked as a Stocking Supervisor a Pathmark down here. Good record on the job. My guys spoke to Amber and she had no idea why he was even at the club, because he was pretty much a stay-at-home. She said they were saving money to get out of the city. He was taking care of her and the child. Don't know why he was caught on video up in Harlem. Obviously, his sister didn't know everything about them. Or she lied. Nonetheless, his part in the robbery murder investigation is over."

"Anything on the other two?"

"Nothing from our street people. Nothing from Wilson's sister. Nothing from the store. We'll keep digging, but only for a while. Our real priority is to find the two very black very bad-ass shooters."

"Thanks for the information. I guess I'll see what Hinton does and then figure out what to tell Jimmy."

This is Tony's day for dialin' and smilin'.

"Lieutenant Brown, this is Lieutenant Sattill of Manhattan CAT Squad. Do you have time to talk? Thanks. As you may know I have a personal interest in the robbery-murders that occurred recently at the check-cashing store on Amsterdam. I don't want to get in anybody's way, but I was wondering of you had any further information on Los Hores involvement."

"Lieutenant Sattill, I did some digging and I'm convinced that Los Hores were not involved in the robbery, but that the people who robbed the store and killed the four employees were attempting to disguise their identities by sloughing off responsibility to Los Hores. We have checked our sources and no one will confirm that anybody was even trying to make their bones with the gang. So the episode is not gang related. Just a simple, but bloody and badly disguised robbery. I have relayed that information to the riding Detective, Hinton, and he told me that that the three shooters were killed in a DEA bust at Nite Lites a few days ago. So that ends the investigation from my stand point."

"Thanks for your help, Lieutenant."

"By the way, Lieutenant, when are we going to have that drink you avoided the last time we were together?"

"How about tonight?"

"Six at Clarks?"

"See you there."

What is she saying? Nothing. Sometimes there is only dirt under the rock. N bugs and no snakes. Tony decides to go to the gym after he finds his desk beneath the paper.

Mindless exercise: the Stairmaster, and weight lifting. Three purposes: body tone for that youthful look . . . a little too little a little too late in life, cardio-vascular exercise and cleansing for physical well being, and stress relief to promote clearer thinking. This is the credo of the over-40 crowd. Tony always feels better after the sojourns to the PD gym. But, he is constantly reminded of his impending mortality, by the young hard bodies that seem to live in the clanking, humid rooms. Despite his maturity, Tony has yet to lose completely the competitive edge that drove him to wrestle at Brown.

"Hey, Sattill, wanna go on the mat?"

Kurt Strabel, two-time NCAA champ at 184, will never lose the edge. At 44, he is in incredible shape and competes in Masters Tournaments. Rumors are that he is on ephedrine and steroids, which may explain a lot.

"Thanks anyway, Kurt. Every time we venture into the circle, I fear one of us will get hurt. And, I'd feel guilty if I kept you from a tournament."

There are hoots from the guys in the weight room. And Kurt's body stiffens. He just dropped the glove and Tony just peed on it.

"Come on 'ol man. Let's see what you've got. Balls or BB's?"

"I'm glad you respect my superior maturity, but I must decline your kind invitation. I'm at the end of my work out and, unlike some others I have a real job awaiting my attention at the house."

"Trust me, 'ol timer, mat time won't be long. I'd guess less than twenty seconds, unless you back pedal."

"Kurt, with all respect to your challenge, the answer remains no."

As Tony exits to the lockers and the showers, the tension lifts and Kurt is huffing and puffing with his buddies. Confrontations on personal time are disquieting. There is enough confrontation on the job.

"Lieutenant, we learned some interesting stuff on our visit to Amber Wilson's apartment, cousin of the deceased."

"Talk to me."

"Well, first of all there was no visit, because there is no Amber Wilson. She's gone. Went to the apartment and it was damn near clear of humanity and personal possessions. Nothing but furniture. No clothes or toilet articles. No baby stuff, except a crib. We asked the people in the building and two neighbors on the street, and learned that Amber and a boyfriend had left yesterday with the baby in a large white van."

"Do we know anything about the boy friend?"

"Neighbors describe him as tall and thin. Very black, with a bony face. Neatly dressed . . . white shirt, dark pants, and gray shoes. He had been at the apartment a number of times before, but no one knew his name. Oh, and he was not the driver of the van. There was another guy behind the wheel. The driver and the boy friend look like brothers . . . maybe twins."

"So, two days after the shooting at Nite Lites, and a day after Martani's men talk to the sister, she leaves with two guys, who may resemble the shooters of her brother."

"Or, she just decided to split with her main squeeze, given the tragedy she just went through."

"I like my scenario better."

"So do I."

"Then find them."

More mindless paper work. The walk to Clark's takes twenty minutes. The place is jammed with bodies and noise. Carlita Brown is sitting by the entrance to the dining room. A special table for two, who wish to be seen.

"Hello, Lieutenant. Please call me Carlie. May I call you Tony?"

"Good evening, Carlie. I see you've ordered. I better play catch-up."

Tony goes to the bar.

"Hello, Sir, it's nice to see you again. How long has it been? Six months I wager. Your drink is waiting in its bottle wanting to be poured Two ounces of Balvenie with one piece of ice. Sad thing about Mr. Ranck's wife. He's such a good man. Tell him I hold good thoughts. Haven't seen him for a long time. You two used to be regulars. I'm glad they caught the bastards that did the crime."

"Dennis, it's nice to see you again. I'll tell Mr. Ranck you send your best."

Bartenders never forget. They earn their living from this. But, their real stock in trade is not remembering what they have been told and then told to forget. The memory of a good bartender at a place like this could get husbands divorced, politicians impeached, and wise guys dead.

"I'm glad we have this chance to get to know each other."

Carlie leans forward in a manner of introductory intimacy. She is dressed in a pantsuit . . . gray with light blue stripes. Her blouse matches the stripes, and is open to reveal the work of a pushup bra. A round iridescent medallion with an emerald in the center nestles in the cleavage. Her dark hair is too precisely coiffed. She is attractive, but smiles too much in an unreal way. The pleasantries of life outside the force lead Tony and Carlie to the second drink.

"Carlie, I'm asking you to facilitate my talking to Los Hores about the incident involving Pam Ranck."

"You are free to do what you wish, but I understand that case is closed. Besides I told your Detective McLaughlin that my sources confirmed Los Hores was not involved."

"Yes, I know, and we appreciate your assistance. But, I have a few personal questions that I need to have answered. You know, Pam was a dear friend."

"So, if this is not official, why not let me get the information for you"?

"I don't want to jam you up with the gang by putting you in the middle of my inquiry. I just wanted to give you a heads up."

Tony noticed that Carlie was sitting upright and her blouse had closed to cover the cleavage. She had adopted a defensive-don't-piss-on-my-territory posture.

"I appreciate the heads up. Would you let me know what you learn"?

"Of course. I don't mean to be abrupt, but I have a lot of work awaiting me at home. Can we do this again"?

"Of course."

During the ride uptown, Tony thought about what Strabel's reaction would be if he learned about this evening's social interlude. He was fairly sure that Carlita and Kurt were an item. Kurt would be jealous and then pissed. Insecurity in others who were mean made Tony smile.

Sleep was fitful. Tossing and turning to find the right spot, kept Tony in that uncomfortable place between slumber and awake. The more he fought to get comfortable the more he gravitated toward awake. Something was bouncing deep in his brain. A conundrum that had no ready answer, because he knew only a small part of the problem. Or, was it something out of synch? Some fact not in line with others? The only way he knew to settle the issue was to forget it and let it bubble up from the depth of his subconscious to become clear. Now it is only a chimera strong enough to inhibit sleep. Nights of shitty sleep make the next days really long; they have 24 hours in them before noon. Particularly, since he goes to his office before six.

He uses the time to deal with the paper dragon; forms, reports, and correspondence. He tries to clear his desk before the first of his crew bounces in. All bright-eyed and bushy-tailed. Ah, youth.

"Lieutenant, my friend sent me the information about the Social Security number possibilities. She delivered a total of 137. She apologizes for being late with this information, but she wanted to dig for all the information, erase her path, and then send the report from her personal PC at home. She listed the names, addresses, and any other pertinent information about the individual to whom the number was assigned. She eliminated those of women and the deceased. But, here's the real interesting thing; there is no listing for a Rufus Jennings Fulton. Maybe we got a number wrong. A digit misread. Anyways here is the list. If you want I'll go back to my friend and ask her to run other numbers."

"Not yet. I'll narrow down the list by checking all the names. A fresh set of eyes, and I'll go over the list with Jimmy. You contact your Federal banking source and ask her to check for any account activity under the name Fulton, anywhere. Tell her we will treat to a night on the NYPD in the Apple. Airfare, dinner, theater, and a night at the Plaza. The only hitch is that you will have to escort her as sort of an ambassador of the city and force. Would that be OK with you?"

The young man beamed.

After eliminating the obvious by age and ethnicity, the list is pared to 68 living males. Tony ruled out those males with present addresses west of the Mississippi. Now there were 48. A further geographic refinement to the metropolitan area cut the total to 24, with eight in the city. There were still 7 with no addresses. These could not be ignored. So, Chris would have to find them. The devil is in the details, and Chris was going to have a devil of a time. Hours on the computer cross-matching names and addresses. Maybe even some leg work. Pound the pavements looking for the ghost known as Rufus Fulton. The buzzer on the telephone breaks Tony's wool gathering.

"Sir, it's Jimmy Ranck."

"Jimmy, what can I do for you?"

"I don't know if this has anything to do with anything, but I once had a client named Fulton. Benjamin Fulton. A black guy, who shot up a liquor store. It's just that I became pretty attached to the guy. He was broke. Needed money for his wife and kids. He didn't kill anyone, but he was a two-time loser, so he struck out and is doing life in Ossining. He claimed to have family of his own. A brother, I think. I realize I'm grasping at straws, but how about a nice drive upstate."

"Hey, Jimmy, my crew is devoted to your situation. Above and beyond their normal duties. If this could be something, we had better look at it. So, you and I will go. Can you call Sing Sing and set up a meeting with his lawyer, that's you and a cop, that's me? We should be there in two hours."

"Thanks for indulging me."

"No thanks needed."

Tony picked out an unmarked squad car. Swung by Jimmy's place, rang the door bell and waited. Slowly the once proud, upright male beast took halting, short steps to the door, down the steps and to the car. Up the West Side nightmare, to the confusing intertwining that passes for transportation planning. Jimmy stares straight ahead and his head begins to dip, only to be jerked back by the innate fear of missing something. The spittle is only slightly apparent.

"Here we are, Jimmy."

He sits upright and begins to look like the angry lawyer, he once was.

We show our credentials to the gate guard, park the car, and show our IDs' again to the two guards at the main entrance.

73

"Good day, sir, I am James Ranck, attorney for Benjamin Fulton. I called for an appointment. This is Lieutenant Anthony Sattill, of the New York City police."

"Yes sir. Please come with me."

The guard, who looks like Pa Kettle, except for the 9mm Glock strapped to his skinny waist, leads us down a very brightly lit hall to the Office of Superintendent, John Stimac. During the entire trek, Pa Kettle's shoes squeaked on the freshly polished tile floor. His shuffle was barely faster that Jimmy's pace. Obviously, this man is working toward retirement with a nice fat state pension.

"Gentlemen, please be seated. I'll tell Superintendent Stimac you're here."

He goes through the one other door in the ante room. This door reopens and two men exit. Pa Kettle seems to drift back to his post, and the other man ushers us into a large well appointed office. John Stimac looks like he spent most of his money on grooming and clothes. My bet is that the Porsche in the parking lot is his. His hair is perfect, and the same color everywhere on his head. Not a hint of gray for a man most likely in his early fifties. His suit looks like it cost a grand, and the shirt was obviously tailored to his trim, yet buff body. He wants everyone to know he works out. I guess that's good advertising in a place like this. His tie and matching foulard are either strangely retro or very *avant garde*.

"Please be seated. We need to talk."

The softness and modulation of his voice are camouflage for a fierce inner fire. Controlled power. The denizens of this den know this.

"Superintendent, we drove up here from the city to see my client, Benjamin Fulton. May we see him?"

Jimmy was countering the soft-on-the-outside-hard-on-the-inside of the Superintendent with his own direct-on-the-outside-hard-on-the-inside approach.

"May I ask the purpose of this visit?"

"You may, but I am not going to tell you, because he is my client."

"I find it strange that Convict Fulton has not had visitors for eight years, then he gets two visitors in six months; his so-called brother and his attorney."

"I don't know about the other visitor, but Benjamin Fulton is my client, and I want to see him. I've already shown you the file with docket and case numbers, as well as my credentials. Now, if you please."

The silence was palpable. Neither of the pit bulls even breathed. It was time for me to mediate.

"Gentlemen, I'm not sure what this is all about. But, we all know that James Ranck is Mr. Fulton's Attorney, and by law he has the right to visit his client. So, Superintendent, why don't you just have someone take us to the visitor's room?"

"Well, it's not as easy as that. You see, Convict Fulton is in lock down. He has been in lock down for three years. Seems he took umbrage to the comments of fellow convict, and shoved a broom handle in the poor man's mouth. The force of the blow tore the man's throat and larynx. Now he can't say anything at all. If you really want to see Convict Fulton, you will have to wait while we retrieve him and make sure he is safe for visitors. It may take an hour. Will you wait?"

"You're damned right we'll wait."

Jimmy is pissed.

"You may wait in the outside office, if you like."

Pleasant chairs, no magazines and a digital wall clock. Thank God, Tony brought the Post. He even reads the classifieds. Jimmy slumps and catnaps. Then jerks awake.

"Jimmy, if it this difficult for his lawyer to see him, how difficult must it have been for a family member to get in?"

"Something is very strange here."

"Gentlemen, please follow me."

They both perked up at the thought of activity. We followed Superintendent Stimac down the hall. The hall has no windows, yet is very bright, and smells of disinfectant. We follow with purpose through two sets of guarded gates to a forbidding door with a window slit. The Superintendent scans his ID on the box to the right of the door, and the door opens slowly as if it were for the handicapped. Then I see the video camera and mirror reflecting the two men behind and above us. They are in a guard house monitoring the population at eight different stations.

"This is where I leave you. I have other matters to attend to. Just follow Mr. Jenkins and Mr. Leach. They'll take you to the interview room. Have a nice day."

The door closed behind us with a thud of permanence. The two dour guards turn and walk down the hall. They make the first right and the second left. These guys are big. The Kevlar vests help with the appearance of girth that sits well on 6'3" frames. They do not converse or smile. Their perfunctory nature is calculated to control.

"Here you are, gentlemen."

They open another steel door with a small slit for observation.

"When you are ready to leave, simply press the red button here by the door. We'll come back and lead you out. Please be seated."

Jimmy and Tony enter and sit at two chairs facing a two-inch thick shatterproof glass floor to ceiling wall. There are microphones and speakers on both sides for sterile and taped conversation between prisoner and visitor. Illegal, but routinely done. There is a door on the other side. Another wait. Finally, the door opens and a medium built 5'10" black man is propelled into the room. Two new large guards are attached to the man by poles at his waist. He is manacled and shackled. The guards are gripping the poles attached to the leather cummerbund. With one final shove, they click the handles and retract the poles. Then they step back through the door and it is slammed shut. The man staggers to the shatter proof glass wall. He seems to be crumpled. His frame is stooped so he looks shorter than when he entered prison twenty years ago. His face is distorted from years of abuse, and one eye is closed permanently. As he looks at us, he seems to squint and peer upward.

"Who the fuck are you?"

"Benjamin, it's me Jimmy Ranck. I was your lawyer. Don't you recognize me?"

"Recognize you. Why should I? I ain't seen you in years. Besides I got only one good eye, and it is nearly blind. Prove to me you are who you say."

Now the black man is pressed against the glass wall. He can't move his hands.

"I have your case file right here. And, Benjamin, I remember your children's names, Sara and Avram. And your wife is named Bethany. You lived at 134 West 98th

Street in Manhattan. The liquor store was at the corner of 125th and Amsterdam."

"OK, you've read the report. Big fucking deal. You read the newspapers."

Jimmy's memory and mind were as sharp as ever.

"I know you have family of your own. A sister. She lives in Mississippi. I think you have a brother, but you never spoke of him except once."

"That don't mean shit. What do you want?"

"I need to know the name of your brother."

"Why the fuck do you want that?"

The moment of truth: Jimmy was going to show Benjamin his, hoping that Benjamin would show Jimmy his.

"I think he knows something about the murder of my wife."

The black man's countenance morphs from defiance to pity, then to serious.

"I'm sorry to hear that your wife was murdered. But, if I help you, what will you do for me?"

My turn to play.

"Mr. Fulton, if you help us with the murder investigation, I can assure you I will get you out of lock down. And maybe more."

"Like what more."

"What would you like, other than freedom?"

"I'd like to see my children. Make sure they are all right, and tell them I love them face-to-face."

"That can be arranged. Now what will you do for Mr. Ranck?"

"Do you promise you can get me into the general population and for me to see my children?"

"I can and will get you out of lock down. And I will contact your children and let them know what you would like. If necessary, I'll even help them get here."

The convict's countenance has become hopeful. There is near warmth in his tone.

"Jimmy, I'm sorry about your wife. My brother's name is Rufus Fulton. Really he's my half brother. Same daddy. I am the criminal. He works for the Fedril Gummint. We're opposite sides of the same fence. That's why I don't speak of him. And, I'll bet he don't speak of me. My brother came to see me a few months ago. He came to make peace with me. Like something was going to happen. We chatted for a while then he asked me what your name was . . . you know the name of my lawyer. He said he was going to get a divorce. He knew you did right by me, and he wanted your name so he could go and see you."

Stunned, Jimmy and Tony stared at each other then Benjamin.

"He just looked real serious, almost scared. Like when we were kids and the thunderstorms came in the summer. He'd climb into my bed. Now he needed me for information."

Jimmy sits. More like plops into a folding chair.

"Are you all right Mr. Ranck?"

Yes, thanks. Just very tired."

"Now how soon can you get me out of lock down?"

"When we get back to the city, I'll fill out the paper work that shows how much you helped with the investigation. I'll make sure the DA's office makes this a priority. The entire process will take about ninety days. Then I'll make sure we find your children and go from there. We will let you know of our progress as we go along."

"Ya know, the whole thing was strange, 'cause I didn't think Rufus was married. Anyways he wasn't married when I was on the outside. Said he was married to his job and would never expect any woman to understand his devotion to the other woman. Maybe he found someone who understood then stopped understanding. Maybe that's why the divorce. But, I can't understand why he came all the way here just to ask for your name. There are lots of divorce lawyers in the telephone book"

"Benjamin. You have been a big help. Now, we want you to take care of yourself. We'll start the process."

Jimmy and Tony both knew the part about the children would be up to them. The red button was pressed and the two were escorted out.

"Jimmy, why did Rufus really go to see his brother? Did he want us to know he made the visit? If that's right, then he must have known something was going to happen to him and that you would uncover who was responsible."

Jimmy was asleep and slept the entire ride back to the city. Exhaustion and relief. The trail seems to becoming clearer.

Pyre

The bodies were contorted like so much steel in a demolished building. The charred remains still smoldered. Bits of flesh and fabric emitted a stench that made living eyes burn and tear. Even through filter masks, the disgusting odor triggered the gag reflex. The tires that were beneath and on top of the bodies still contained small pockets of flames.

"Talk to me."

"Lieutenant, there are five bodies; three adult males, one female, and an infant. Two of the adults, a male and female, were bound with tape . . . hands, feet and mouths. It looks like the female held the infant while they burned. That's a sin. To kill a child like that. The other two adults appear to have been shot during the process. Not sure if it was before, during or after. The ME will be able to tell. Since they were bound, my guess is that they were shot after they were set afire and burned. Like insurance of death. And, both of these adult males had their hands cut off. Hopefully, we can find their hands or the remains of them. Again, my assumption is their hands were cut off, and then they were torched and shot with the others.

Regardless of the sequences, it's not clear why. But, it is ugly and brutal nonetheless. It is going to be a while before we have many details."

"We'll let the investigating detectives determine the who and why. Just down load the facts, make sure the ME jumps on this one. The news is gonna have a field day. That means the brass will be all over this to get the news off their collective asses. I want everything to be better than squeaky clean in your reports. I'll see you back at the house."

On the ride back to the precinct, Tony mentally talked his way through the preliminary questions. He was doing the job of the investigating detectives. He always did. Mentally. The hands or lack thereof, were the keys to all the answers. Why were they cut off? The when doesn't matter except to the handless who are now dead. To hide the identity of the two adults? No fingerprints. What about dental records? If they were foreigners, chances are there would be no dental records. Or, if the adults had a poor record of dental hygiene, there would be no dental records. Or, if they were from out of state, it would be nearly impossible to trace the dental records without knowledge of who the adults were. But the condition of the teeth could tell domestic or foreign. What if the hands were cut off to send a message that someone did not sanction the fact that these guys took something that did not belong to them? A big, ugly message. Then they were torched. The news would print the grizzly details, and the message would be pronounced loud and clear across the land. Why tires, except that were handy and had a long burn life. Was it an African necklace party? How would they know this, unless they had done it before. Or, seen it done. Was it a funeral pyre? Was it a formal or ritual killing? Sacrifice? These must be powerful gods to require that humans suffer this much. And, why the infant? WHY?

Tony's message light is blinking and there is a hum in the squad room like an engine that is starting. The internal bureaucratic grilling begins

"Yes, Captain. No, sir, we have no identities. We are in the process of gathering the information, getting the bodies to the ME, and down loading our evidence and reports for the investigating detectives. I don't know who the team is. The cutting off of the hands. I think that's the key. Yes, sir, if I learn any more at the debriefing, I'll let you know."

Captain Sanchez is the command's best manipulator. He holds out the carrot of favor leading to promotion so he can extract more work or information than anyone else has. It's his way of controlling. Once the rules are understood, the game is simple. A message from Jimmy.

"Tony, I've been thinking about the Fulton brothers and I need to talk. Whenever you have ten minutes, call me. Thanks."

"Lieutenant, Lieutenant Carlita Brown on line 3."

"Hello. What can I do for you?"

"It's not so much that as what I just did for you. I just got off the phone with Diego Seville. He, if you are not aware, is heffe of Los Hores. I convinced him to have a sit-down with you on his turf. I told you wanted to clear his name and that of Los Hores of the horrible murders at the check-cashing place. If you go to the bodega at 235 West 167th Street at noon today, he will sit down with you,"

"This will be a big help. I owe you."

"Yes you do."

The morning fills itself with paper work.

"Lieutenant, we have the preliminary finds of the torching for your review."

"Talk to me."

"Four adults. One infant. On two adults, one male and one female, and the infant, ME noted carbon in the throat and lungs. They were all burned alive. There were small fractures of the skulls on all three. The guess is that they were hit, taped, and burned, while they were alive. That way they could suffer the most. The other two adults were treated differently. Both males had their hands were cut off and then they were shot in the head. Maximum pain. A lesson to others. In either case it was a show of some kind. Here is something interesting. The male, female, and infant were African-American. The ME guesses that the two other males were true African. She bases this preliminary point-of-view on their bone structure development and some dental indications. She said that when they were alive, they were tall and thin. She can't say where in Africa the guys came from, but will have a better idea by then end of her shift. She will give all the information to the riding Ds."

"Who wants to take the quantum leap?"

Tony always looks to train speculative powers. He has his entire crew in the conference room.

"I'll guess that the couple and the infant were Amber Wilson and her boyfriend or brother, or both and their baby. And, that the two other guys were the two who hustled them off."

"What if the two guys were the same as the two shooters at the rave?'

"What if the guy and girl were from the robbery murders at *Neighborhood Financial & Legal Services*? That would explain the baby carriage, the empty baby carriage at the first murder."

"If that is accurate, that could explain the dead guys at the rave. They were shot to keep them quiet about the robbery murder. Then the two guys, who shot them in the back, went after the couple. Didn't Lieutenant Martani say that witness indicated the two guys, the two shooters, were dressed like Euro-trash, and that they were very black, tall and thin? It could be them."

"But, who killed them and why?"

"What if the four worked for somebody or some group who saw the robbery as a way to make real money? Like leverage the fifty grand into something much larger. What if this other person or group wanted all the money from the robbery? Didn't want to share? That could explain the whole mess. That could explain Los Hores. Hire the stooges and then eliminate them so there is no involvement on their part."

"What if the pyre was a revenge act by Los Hores for sullying their already dirty name? Teaching a visible lesson for pissing onto their turf. That would mean that Los Hores was not involved, but vengeful."

"The pyre is not their style."

"But, a great disguise."

"If someone hired the two Africans to put together a gang to rob the store and the gang went stupid and did a Los Hores copycat, then who ever hired them would want to be damned sure that Los Hores did not seek revenge on them. So the hiring boss shows his good faith to Los Hores by cleaning up the complete mess."

"And keeping all the money."

"Some or all of which Los Hores will want as an homage payment."

"So far so good guys. Over the next few hours keep working your theories. Lets meet again at three . . . after your shift. Oh, yes, the money . . . follow the money. Where is it now? Who has it?"

The drive uptown at this hour took an hour. Conveniently there was a parking space in front of the Bodega right beside the fire hydrant. Tony checked his weapon and put in back it the holster. There would be pat down, and they would want him to give up his gun. He would not. Diego knows this already. Posturing. Out of the car and into the shop. The rich and exotic aromas and noises are of daily food commerce. Tony spots the door at the rear of the single large room. He also notices the three men playing dominos at the table by the door. Guardians at the gate. As he approaches they rise.

"May we help you?"

"Yes, please tell Diego Seville that Lieutenant Tony Sattill is here at his request."

"Diego Seville? We don't know any Diego Seville."

"Would you be so kind to tell who ever is behind that door that Lieutenant Carlita Brown sent me to see him?"

"There is nothing behind that door except boxes and cans."

"Look, friend, I am here to do you and Diego a huge favor. If you don't want what I have to give, I will tell Lieutenant Brown that you would not let me help. Then we will have to proceed in the other direction as discussed."

"Sorry, we could not help you help us. But, we don't know what you mean or who you want to see."

"If I leave here now, I will have to call the local precinct commander and have this place raided for commerce violations. If they find any other violations during the investigation, good for them and bad for you."

The silence is quite pregnant and two minutes long.

"What is it that you want?"

"I want to have a friendly sit-down with Diego Seville. Now tell him I am here."

The door opens and the doorway is occupied by a man in his thirties. Obviously Hispanic.

"Please, come in. How can I help you?"

We walk down a short hall, turn left and enter a nicely appointed office with six video screens displaying the building's exteriors, and two on the inside of the store.

"Please sit. Would you like some coffee? Or something to eat?"

"Thanks no. I just need to ask you a few questions so that I can clear up any misunderstanding the police may have about the recent murder homicide at the check-cashing establishment."

"You may ask what you want. But, I am confused as to your purpose. You are not the investigating detective. Just what is your interest in this matter?"

"The murdered manager is the wife of a good friend. I am trying to help him come to grips with the situation."

"And make some points with the brass down town?"

"No, all of my asking is on my time, and I have promised to stay in the shadows of the investigation. If I learn anything, I must turn the information over to Detective Hinton. Or not, if what I learn has no bearing on the case. It is my understanding that Detective Hinton is about to close this case. He loves a quick clear. So, I would not want to interrupt his schedule and ruin his glory. But, I have to be damned sure whatever I learn is important enough to convince Hinton it is in his best interests to keep the case open. Or that I have enough to go to the brass and they will make Hinton keep the case open. Then he will be very pissed at me, and anybody that has upset his plan. And I mean anybody. That said, I am asking you to help me help my friend."

"OK, say I believe you are not here to implicate me. Ask away."

"As you know, the murder had some of the trappings of a Los Hores event. Location, money, and ears to mention three. What can you tell me about any involvement of Los Hores?"

"First I don't know what or who this Los Hores is, so I can't tell you of any involvement. But, my guess is that this murder and robbery were done by outsiders to the neighborhood. And, whoever the Los Hores are might be very angry that some punks came into the neighborhood and pissed on the sidewalk."

Although Diego's eyes became passionate and they danced from screen to screen and from Tony to the door, his voice never rose above a gentle monotone.

"So, is it your guess that this murders and robbery were committed by people not of this neighborhood? Some interlopers. And that if there were Los Hores, they would seek revenge for such a transgression."

"You could say that, yes."

"Why would this gang of intruders, mimic the actions of Los Hores?"

"Maybe they thought it would throw off suspicion."

"But, why Los Hores?"

"You mentioned that Los Hores seem to be very powerful in this neighborhood. It could be that this little stupid gang is planning to start a turf war and wants to take over the area."

"If that's true, how do you think Los Hores would react?"

"If I knew these people, or if I were a member of Los Hores, I would guess they would be very, very angry and would defend their turf with all their might. They might even go after the little punks and hit them first. Ya know, send the message that invasion and taking are not a good ideas."

"Sir, I appreciate your candor. I am satisfied that investigating the mythical group know as Los Hores would be futile to this case. I have nothing to report to Detective Hinton or the brass downtown. Thank you for your time."

"Do you have to leave so soon? I was hoping we could have lunch after our business meeting."

"I have to leave get back to my squad. You know how a squad will not stay in line if the leader is not around."

"Yes I do."

Walking back through the store, Tony feels the eyes of man and machine. The eyes of man cease their stare as he reaches his car. All during the ride back to the precinct, Tony keeps visualizing the office interior. Something is trying to be seen or remembered. The screens. The desk. What the fuck is it?

"Jimmy, let's have dinner. My day has been filled with this torch job, so let's make it 8 at Melons. Look forward to seeing you."

Voice mail is the impersonal communications mode of the present. Soon it will be thought waves, and we will no longer have to speak face-to-face.

Three fifteen and the gathering of eagles.

"Before we start, I want you to know that I met with Diego Seville. Beyond the arrogant disclaimer that there is no such thing as Los Hores, he admitted that if there were such a group of community-minded citizens, they would seek revenge on the outsiders who came into his neighborhood and quote 'pissed on the side walk'. So, my guess is that he knows of the torching and is taking credit for it. Posturing for the neighborhood and the department. I am convinced that he or his group had nothing to do with the robbery-murder. And equally convinced that they had nothing to do with the torch job. The ME said nothing about missing ears. Besides torching is not the style of Los Hores. I think he is accurate, in that he is angry that some outsiders did the deed on the sacred turf of Los Hores and that they are powerless to defend their turf and the people who pay them protection. This could signal the beginning of the end of their power base. We'll keep this chapter open for a little while longer. Now who want to play show and tell?"

"All I have been able to extract from the ME is what she told me this morning. But, she is convinced that the two hand-less males were African. And, the hands are nowhere to be found. So they were taken as trophies. Just the way Los Hores takes ears. They're never found near their victims either. The newspapers are going with this aspect, so it will have the desired educational effect. Whoever was to learn of the punishment for transgression will know. That means there are more of these African types or other people associated with a boss or organizer. So we're up against a gang. Probably substantial. Now the question is why was this gang interested in the check-cashing place? The answer is

$50,000 in untraceable bills. Fifty large is clean and can be converted into drugs and multiplied by five in two weeks. It is the fuel for the engine of gang commerce. Thus, they want to send a real message as to how important the fuel is to them and what they will do to protect the pipeline. That's my take on the money. If we can learn who has a large new supply of drugs to take to market, we can find the killers, who now are responsible for at least eleven bodies."

"OK, where is the fifty large? Obviously the two guys at the rave and couple with the baby don't have it. The two Africans don't have the money. So my guess is that the money moved up the chain the day of the robbery. The couple with the baby carriage had it, the two Africans got it from them, and the people above the Africans took the money from them. Now do we know of any recent incursions by African gangs? Are there any new kids on the block?"

"I'll talk to my friend in narcotics and get a temperature read."

"I'll talk to Lieutenant Brown again, about any new African gangs. OK, boys and girls, that's it for today. See you tomorrow."

Tony heads for the gym to stretch his body and exorcise his demons. Thank god, no Strable. Some weights, a brief run and thirty minutes in the steam room. Shower and off to meet Jimmy.

Melons is crowded with the usual, whomever they may be for the season. Jimmy sits way in the back. As Tony approaches, Jimmy smiles and nods.

"Have you started without me?"

"No. The medication works with the single malt to really hammer me so I wait for others to start then have one light drink catch up."

"Then I'll start and you can tell me what you know."

"Well, I called some old friends in the federal offices and got some very diverse answers to my questions. I tried to find out exactly who this Rufus Fulton was. The FBI was little help. My guy accessed records and came up dry. I trust him to be honest. He may simply be out of a loop. The CIA was no help. Treasury would have to get back to me, and the DEA told me to submit my request in writing under the Freedom of Information Act. All that said, I think I learned more than I was told. I called a guy, who retired from Treasury last year, Tim Martin. He owed me big time. He told me there might be some connection between this man Fulton and an international gang of gun runners and munitions dealers. My guy had heard that Treasury was in some kind of deep cover ops. Something to do with infiltrating this operation and learning where the money was coming from and going. National and international money laundering and movement is big business. And if they could stop it, it would be a huge feather in their cap. He had heard that they were using a team or teams to get into the system. The mole digging started a few years ago. He said the big boys at Treasury had a five-year plan. And here is the typical Chinese Wall; the guys at Treasury were telling no one. There was no coordinated attack on this issue. The jealousy factor among the departments and sub-departments is fierce, because they all live on the dole from the government. The more successful they are, the more money they get so they can be more successful. My God, we are paying for a testosterone laden street fight for territorial value. It's almost as if the more they share the less they get. Now I'll climb off that soap box. Also, my guy had a suspicion that Treasury felt that they could not trust the other departments. He said that they might believe the money operation was getting some inside help. If that were the case, then Treasury could be investigating one of its own or at the least a fraternity brother. So, regardless, they didn't want to tip their hand. Now I'll have a drink."

"No offense, but you probably set off every alarm in the Federal Government."

"None taken. It was intentional. I want them to know that I know something and that I want answers or I will answer my own questions with the noise of their silence. Besides they can't do anything more to me than the disease will do. The worst case scenario is that I die before we learn the truth and they come looking for you."

"Thanks a bunch."

"You're welcome."

"Allow me to go down the path of teams. If Rufus was a team member, who are the others? Where are others? How does Amanda Fulton fit into all this? Were they the team that was under cover and could not show itself? So, they are no help. Assuming for the moment that he was who we think he was, why was he coming to your store? Ostensibly to file for a divorce from a woman who may or not be his wife. Where is his theoretical wife? Do we have an address? A name? And, why your store? We know he went to see his brother, who told him you were a good guy. It is safe to assume, that he wanted to get in touch with a good guy for something other than a phony divorce. Why? What did he want to tell you or relate to you? What could he tell you of his theoretical wife? Did he want you to get in touch with her? I believe he went to see his brother to find you to deliver some kind of message or to push you down a trail. You are an honest officer of the court with no debts or connections to the Feds, or so he hopes. That might mean that he knew someone in the Federal viper nest was dirty, and that this someone knew that Rufus knew. It very well could be he wanted you to know of his activities, of his pursuer, and wanted you to protect him. But, from who or what? Too many questions that don't match answers. Like an improperly buttoned a shirt."

"How can we find his wife?"

"Let my team go back to his apartment and sift through everything one more time. Plus, now that we know who the mystery guest was, we can take a fresh look at the dyslexic scrabble that you sent us. Plus we know the importance of his wife, or whoever she is. I am hungry. Shall we dine?"

After London broil and home fries and two beers. Tony walks Jimmy four blocks to his home then drives to his own. Force of habit drives him to turn on the TV to catch the late news. He falls asleep watching the Discovery Channel's episode of fishing in the Pacific. The water is a round iridescent pool with an emerald-like cluster of leafy growth in the center. He sits up in a start. Where has he seen that? Of course, the large piece of ersatz art hanging in Diego Seville's wall. Now he can sleep in piece.

Money

The day begins with a review of Tony's calendar. Meetings and conferences are placed on his calendar by those above him, and he is obligated to attend. The puppeteers determine how much of his daily skin they want, and therefore, how much he can devote to his squad. This process very often means taking the job home. No wonder so few Lieutenants stay married, if they are married at all. Police work was not supposed to be like the corporate world where you got jerked around in constant rites of passage. Police work is a 24/7 affair with an uncompromising mistress. But, the modernization of the force and the high level of college educated officers have made the NYPD nearly a corporation for all those not in uniform. There it is; the monthly Homeland Security presentation. Another two hours of stats and boredom held downtown with the borough commanders. The Federal guys come in and play show and tell. They show the police brass all the things that could go wrong and tell us what we are not doing according to their procedures and standards. Hell, they are still working out the procedures. How are we to know what they want if they don't know themselves? Plus, they don't know a damned thing about what we have to do to keep Gotham safe for all. Bitch, bitch, bitch. The good news is that he can head home after the presentation. Like the last class at school. But, he will do homework tonight. Now, to the reams of memos and paperwork.

"Lieutenant, I think we may have found out something about an Amanda Fulton. That is we found out nothing."

"Enlighten me."

"Well, the best we can determine is that the address on the file Mr. Ranck sent us is 2844 West 138th Street. That is either in the Hudson River or over in New Jersey. So, the address is bogus. We even looked at possibilities using numbers that could resemble 2844 West 138th Street. You know the eight could be a five or a three. And with all the combinations, nothing works. We even looked at the city grid books for 138th Street and found nothing but empty lots and abandoned warehouses. Sorry, sir, we came up empty so far. There must be other ways to find her. We'll keep digging."

"Thanks. Did you ask your friend about the possibility of Amanda Balfour?"

"No. Sorry. I'll get right on that."

"Thanks."

"Lieutenant, Carlita Brown on line 4 for you."

"Good morning, what can I do for you?"

"Just closure on Los Hores. I spoke to Diego Seville. He spoke of your visit, and was agitated about the robbery-murder, because his people had nothing to do with it, but were taking a hit. I assured him that he would not take a hit, and that you were satisfied he and his people were clean. Was I correct in this point?"

"Yes. I don't believe Los Hores had anything to do with that mess. And, I hope they had nothing to do with the recent funeral pyre. I will assume, unless told otherwise by you, that they did not seek revenge for the robbery-murder by torching those people."

"Diego mentioned that and he was concerned that someone would think he and his people were the burners. It is not their style. Plus, they are working hard to stay clean on both events. He promised to reach out and try to help us with the torch job."

"That's public spirited of him. Well, I guess that road less traveled is a blind alley. I'll let you know if we need to re-contact Diego. Thanks for your help."

"Tony, I thought our meeting of the other week was productive and I was wondering if we should meet again to get a little deeper into the details of the situation."

What the hell did she mean? What kind of code was this? Was her phone tapped? If so, this moth should stay away from the fire. But, all little boys like to test the fire to see if it is really hot.

"Sure, we need to get more details on the table. What about the same place tomorrow at 7? Is that good for you?"

"That works with my schedule. See you then."

"Have a great day."

This is deeper and murkier than Tony wanted, but it fascinated the hell out of him . . . like swimming in a very strange river. He heads out of his office to his crew.

"Can we meet in my office for ten minutes?"

The troops obey.

"What do we know about the money or drugs?"

"Well, I learned from a Detective in Lieutenant Brown's Department, that a large amount of Ecstasy is about to hit the street via the clubs, schools and corners Bodegas. She told me this in confidence as an unnamed source. She says that distribution will be so wide that no single spot can be traced back to the original source. Like a big wave hitting the beach. The whole thing will go down in the next week or two."

"That pretty much ties in with our assumption that the robbery was for money to buy drugs to make a whole lot more money. The investment of capital and a quick turn will harvest substantial profits. The 50 large from the check cashing place might buy up to 250 thousand pills. This would require a big pharmacy, or access to some new inventory somewhere outside the metro area. They could get more pills if they went right to the manufacturer. Two hundred and fifty thousand pills could generate two million dollars or more on the street. Subtracting the middle men, the originator could easily net a million. My guess is that the net will be closer to a million and a half, and could go as high as two million depending on the base cost, the chain of distribution and pent up need at the street level."

"If that is directionally true, that quantity of pills will have to be spread out to other markets, like Newark, Philly, DC, Baltimore, Boston, Pittsburgh, Hartford and New Haven. Otherwise that quantity of pills in one market would flood the market and dramatically lower the price. People, get in touch with any friends you have in those PD's. Give them a heads-up. I'll confirm what we think with the Drug Task Force. Although I'll bet Lieutenant Brown's Department has already alerted them. Everybody be careful not to tell anyone why we think all this will happen, just that it may happen within the next two weeks. Reliable unnamed source and all that crap. One more question. Did your source tell you who was going to be the distribution arm of this event?"

"I asked her and she said that it was none of the regular gangs that she watches or that anybody in her department watches. That's what puzzled her. This was a new gang. She had no ID on them. But, my guess is that she got information from Los Hores. They are either trying to act like choir boys and put some credits in the bank. Or they are pissed, and want us to clean up this mess so they can be heroes."

"Ok, everybody dialin' and smilin'. We are short on time and long on questions. Make damned sure that your questions and any answers you get are off the record. And most of all we don't want to be highlighted as a command center for this mess. Whatever we learn, we'll turn over to the Drug Task Force and let them tell the DEA."

The rest of the day is just that except there is no rest. Rumors and hints come back from Boston, Philly and DC. At least, they are talking about something big going down real soon. The other PD's act as if this is news to them. Either they are sitting on the truth or they are deaf to their streets. With all the info in hand, Tony calls an LT friend at the Drug Task Force. Yes, they knew about the X explosion. Yes, they had alerted the counterparts in major East Coast cities. Yes, they had spoken to the DEA. So, it was all under control. Why was a CAT squad LT getting involved, and how did the CAT squad hear about the deal? Tony had to do a little back peddling to keep the whole truth from sight. Damn! He actually got scolded and told to keep his hands to himself. Another day. Another holler.

"Tony it's me."

"Jimmy, what's going on?"

"I think I found Rufus Fulton. Remember, his brother said that Rufus worked for the Federal Government, yet you told me all public indications were that he worked for a financial services company . . . a stock broker in mid-town. There it is. Either he lied to his brother, and went to Sing Sing to make amends. Or he was undercover for some reason. I believe the latter. I don't know the reason or for whom he was undercover. But, it all ties together. He was on to something really big, but couldn't go up the chain of command, because he knew there was a break. So he took the risk of exposing himself, by trying to contact me and give me his information. Your guys didn't find anything out of the ordinary on the desk. Neither did Hinton. But, did any one look *in* the desk? If they did, how would they know what was ordinary or out of the ordinary? I would be the one person who would know. I would be the only person who would recognize the clue. You have got to get me back into the store. Now!"

"Jimmy, you are so hot shit. I'll pick you up in twenty minutes."

The store is no longer guarded by foot patrol. Just the telltale yellow ribbon and the official Crime Scene notice glued to the door and door jamb. This confirms the purity of the scene. The seal can be broken by the police, but must be replaced by another. Tony carries a small supply of these seals in his squad car. The original seal is carefully sliced apart, and Jimmy's key still works. The room is a frozen moment of death and destruction. Blood, overturned furniture and paper strewn on the floor are signs of mortal chaos. The lights still work.

"Now, Rufus was sitting here at the side of the desk."

"That's on the video. Plus, one of my team noticed that he moved his arm when the killers had turned their backs. There was nothing on the desk top to indicate he had left a message. But, we never looked in the drawers that are on his side of the desk."

Jimmy had already seated himself in the dead man's place. His right arm on the desk. The hand drooping over the edge.

"This is how he did it. Now to find out the what. Nothing strange or different in the top drawer. Just pens, paper clips and a few rubber bands in the half drawer that slides over the paper and note pads."

Jimmy wrestles with the drawer, extracts it from the tracks and empties everything onto the desk top. He looks angry, as he tosses the drawer into a corner. The second drawer is a double and it contains forms for client input at home.

"Help me get all this shit out of the drawer."

Jimmy's hands dig at the paper as if he were digging for treasure in the desert. Tony takes hands full of paper from Jimmy and cascades the sheets onto the floor. Something hard hits the floor.

"Tony, what was that?"

"A disc."

"Let me see. Not one of ours. Not our brand. And certainly in the wrong place. This is what Rufus was trying to deliver to me. This will tell us what he knew and what he wanted the world to know."

"Jimmy, give the disc to me and I'll have my team get the information."

"No. The disc was meant for me, and I shall have it. I'll do the opening. I'll do the learning. Pam was my wife. She died, while he hid the disc."

"I understand how you feel, but this is a critical piece of evidence in a criminal investigation. The police need to control it, and to advise Hinton when appropriate."

"When appropriate! When appropriate! Tony, for God's sake. Pam's dead. Our baby is dead. I am dying. When will it be appropriate for me to find the killers? When will it be appropriate to put my soul at ease?"

"OK. I'll compromise. We will do the opening with you, but in our office."

The silence lasts for as long as the two have known each other.

"OK. When?"

"Tonight at 7. I'll send a car for you at 6:30. Hell, I'll even spring for Thai."

"Not Thai. I hate that shit and the spices are ruinous to my system. Pizza."

"Pizza it is. Now give me the disc, please."

Being a cop to your friends is no fun. Particularly, when your friend is in need. But, Jimmy was an officer of the court and deep down he understood.

"Boys and girl, in my office please. Today, Jimmy Ranck uncovered a piece of evidence at the store. Evidence that we would have found given the keen perception that Rufus Fulton moved his arm. He was just ahead of us. In the bottom drawer of the desk amidst the forms and paper of the work place was a disc. Jimmy says that he and Pam did not use this type of disc. So we can deduce that this stray item was placed or planted there by Mr. Fulton. What we don't know is what is on the disc and why it was planted. At 7 tonight Jimmy is coming to our house and we all will examine the disc and its contents. He has requested pizza. My treat. Now go back to your everyday. And thanks."

"Sir, my friend in DC is digging into Amanda Balfour. She should have something for us tomorrow. And, something else. All of the Feds in DC are atwitter . . . her word, LT, not mine . . . about the big X splash. But, no one seems to know more than it will happen. At least that's the party line. With all this chatter, she can work on our requests at ease. Everyone is digging and probing on their computers. So everyone assumes she is in the pack."

The next few hours seem to be the better part of a month. Then he appears at Tony's door. Jimmy looks older than he just a few hours ago. He is ashen and slumped as if he were fading away and falling down. How much time remains for this once great fighter for truth?

"Hey Jimmy, you're early. The pizza won't be here until seven thirty. How did you get here? I was going to call for the car to pick you up until six thirty. But, enough of me scolding you. Come in and sit."

"May I close the door?"

"Sure."

"Tony, remember I told you I contacted the Feds a few days ago and got the stone wall treatment?"

"Yeah."

"Well, I think I am being watched. Followed by three not-very-good teams. I don't think they want me to see them. It's just that my experiences with the Feds and even you guys make me a little paranoid. And as we both know a little paranoia is a healthy thing. So I scope out the surroundings everywhere I go. Over that past few years I have trip routines. Grocery store. Dry cleaner. Deli. Liquor store. I am aware of every parked car, delivery van and civilian in the neighborhood. Suddenly these eyes, a man and a woman in each vehicle or in a place where I shop, are new to my world. Then this afternoon, as I was leaving the store, many blocks from my neighborhood, I recognized a familiar van. This is the same grey van, which was parked around the corner from my brownstone this past week. No markings, just a plain gray van. The license plate is J65-EA1. I am absolutely positive the couple inside tailed me to the store and back to my place, because I saw the van in a different spot when I left to come here."

"Shit. Here is the first step. We'll run the tag. That will tell us something. The second step is to be sure your place is not bugged and your telephone is not tapped. You can't be moved into a hotel, or whoever is watching will suspect something is amiss. They will know that they are being watched."

"What about a hospital? My Doctor has been threatening to check me into Mt Sinai. He wants to run about a week's worth of tests and start me on a regimen of chemo, which I know is futile. He holds out some slim hope. If I were in the hospital I could sneak out to help you."

"It's an idea. A bad one, but it is an idea. You are to maintain your routine. Once we know who is looking and how extensive are their efforts, we can control them by feeding them what we want them to hear and see."

"OK."

Jimmy's shoulders sump further. He was getting geared up for adventure and Tony said no.

"Brendan, can you come in here for a second."

"You've met my friend, Jimmy Ranck"

"Yes. Sir, it's nice to see you again, albeit under these circumstances. We are doing everything we can to solve the heinous murder of your wife."

"Thank you. I appreciate that."

"Brendan, I want you to run a plate for me. Tell no one of the team. Just run the plate and report back to me. And do it now, please."

"Yes, sir."

"Jimmy, if you would like to go up to the crib and sack out for an hour, we'll come a get you when the house has emptied and we are ready to dig into the disc."

"There is a part of me that just got angry at you for treating me like a sick person or some doddering senior citizen. There is a larger part that understands why you said what you said, and knows it was out of friendship. I'll take you up on your offer."

Jimmy shuffles out of the office and up two flights of stairs for a power nap. During the laborious ten-minute trip, he has to hitch-up his pants every so often due to unplanned weight loss. Impending death is not the diet of the healthy. It is Wait Watchers. Wait and watch the pounds leave. Tony immerses himself in being a manager.

"Sir, I ran the tag and it came up belong to R&B Construction in Queens. I checked R&B and learned that the company does work in brownstones and co-ops. Light work. Some plumbing, electrical, renovations. Stuff like that. They are located at 1418 Northern Boulevard and owned by Arnold Roth and Angelo Bustelli. R&B. Is there anything else?"

"Yes, call them to verify they exist and plan to take a trip out there early tomorrow morning for an on-site visit. Before your shift. Thanks."

The desk calls and the pizzas have arrived. Better get them before the night crew smells them.

"Would someone go up to the crib and wake Jimmy and someone else take this money and liberate our pizzas from the desk Sergeant? We'll meet in the conference room."

"Sir, I can't waken Mr. Ranck. He's not dead, just unresponsive."

Tony streaks upstairs two at a time, catches his breath and enters the open door to the crib. There is his friend. Still except for short, shallow breaths that barely move his chest.

"Get a bus. I'll try to find out his doctor's name."

Searching Jimmy's wallet, Tony finds a laminated card entitled In Case Of an Emergency. Beneath Pam's name is that of Dr. Norman Strate and his telephone number.

"Yes, I understand this is Dr. Strate's service. This is Lieutenant Anthony Sattill Shield Number 4852. I am calling about one of Dr. Strate's patients, Mr. James Ranck. Mr. Ranck appears to have fallen into a coma. He is resting at the 27th Precinct. I want to get Mr. Ranck to a hospital, and wonder if Dr. Strate has a preference. Please contact Dr. Strate immediately and have him call me, Lieutenant Anthony Sattill at my cell phone number, not the number showing up on the screen in front of you. Here is my cell phone number for Dr. Strate. Please repeat that number back to me. Thank you. This is a dire emergency. We are ready to transport."

Two minutes later Tony's cell phone vibrates alive.

"Dr. Strate. Thanks for calling back so quickly. Where would you like us to take Mr. Ranck? Mt Sinai. Yes, Sir. We will arrive in fifteen minutes. Will you call ahead? Thank you, Doctor."

The paramedics load the still body into the EMS vehicle. Tony leads the way. Multiple Sirens and many flashing lights cut a clear swath through the early evening traffic. 82 blocks and 82 traffic lights in eleven minutes. Tony is soaked in sweat.

This was a very bad day.

R&B

Car Bombs and Rockets Level Hotel

*A*t 2 am local time, four strategically placed car bombs exploded at the Islamabad Crown Hotel. The explosions were followed immediately by a hail of RPG rocket fire. Estimates of the rocket explosions are as high as thirty-five. As the hotel was collapsing from the structural damage caused by the car bombs, the rockets, some incendiary, inflicted the death blow to the crumbling structure. As of now it is assumed that all guests and employees of the hotel, who were on duty at the time, were killed. If accurate, the total death count could be as high as 240. Shops and small residences on the side streets were also demolished. This fact could bring the death total to over 300. Fire and police officials have cordoned off an eight-block radius so they can assess the damage and search for survivors. Dogs have been brought in to the site for the human remains search. While no one has claimed responsibility for the destruction and carnage, Reuters has informed officials that the local branch received a message around 1:55 AM stating, "Remember Mumbai." This appears to be a reference to the tragedy inflicted upon that city by Pakistani *religious zealots. Pakistani Government officials have reached out to the Indian government. There is no indication of the dialog between the two entities. This is a breaking story. More to follow.*

"Good morning, Lieutenant. I called R&B Construction yesterday and got an answering service. The woman wanted to know if my call was an emergency. I said no. Then I went out to the Northern Boulevard address for a face-to-face before four. I was early, because I thought that construction crews start at their assembly point well before the job. I noticed three vans in the parking lot. All had the company name, telephone number and the state license number on the side panels and numbers designating the trucks on the door panels, #18, #27 and #34. But, the information was not painted on the trucks. It was on magnetized panels that can be slapped on and taken off at will. I felt the hoods and each was warm as if each van had been driven within the hour. As if driven to the site. I waited until the first car arrived, around five-thirty. Upon entering I met a receptionist, who sat behind a service counter and in front of a wall with a single door off to the my right. There were the usual decals on the windows . . . PAL, C of C, Local 3451, and the like. On the counter were various wholesale supply books for plumbing, electrical, and hardware. There was a single telephone with multiple buttons, but it never rang nor were any of the line lights lit. I guess it was too early. The receptionist was surprised to see me. The entrance area had all the trappings of a construction business, but none of the activity and none of the dirt. There was no noise coming from behind the wall behind the receptionist. I would think that at nearly six am there would be some activity of workers getting the orders and material ready for the day. But, it was like there was nobody back there. I asked to see Mr. Roth or Mr. Bustelli. I said that the driver of one of their vans may have witnessed a hit and run accident in Manhattan, and I'd like to talk to the driver. The receptionist asked if I knew the number of the truck, and I told her no. I just knew the company's name and address. That is why I was there. I asked to see a manager or foreman. She said that all four of the men I mentioned were out. She was minding the store. If I would leave a card, one of the owners would call me today after lunch. I left my card. Before I got back into my car, I noticed there were no windows on the side building beyond the entrance. Strange, I have never seen a warehouse or work building without windows. Most of them have windows very high in the walls to allow for some sun light and ventilation, but to discourage entry. Sir, my general observation is there is something amiss with R&B. One of the owners will call after lunch. Maybe I'll learn more."

"Good job, Brendan. Take the call and repeat your story. You and I may want to pay a nocturnal visit to 1418 Northern Boulevard."

"Can you all come to the conference room for shared updates?"

"This is what I know about what is new in the investigation? Jimmy Ranck is in the hospital. So our efforts take on a greater urgency. Jimmy mentioned to me he thought he was being followed and got the license number of the van. Brendan did some good street cop sleuthing this morning and learned that all seems not kosher with R&B Construction, the company to which the van's plate is registered. More on that tomorrow. I am meeting with Lieutenant Brown again to learn more about Los Hores. Anything else?"

"Sir, my source in DC came back with a match on Amanda Balfour. She is a black woman, a graduate of Brown University, Class of '90. Your alma mater. She has a law degree from Harvard. Worked for two three years for the IRS. Then Justice. Then she disappeared. No job, no home, no income. She is off the grid. But, she could fit the profile of the wife of Rufus Fulton. I am going to compare her picture with the one in the Brown Year Book. That will lock it up one way or the other. Then we'll just have to find her. I doubt of the other Feds will be as helpful as my friend."

"LT, I did some digging into the ritual of hand removal as part of an execution. It is prevalent among the Colombian Drug culture, the old-style Mafia, the Russian Mob and some tribes in Africa. I doubt if this is an old-style message whacking, so I rule out the Mafia. Given that there appear to be drugs at the root cause, the Colombians may be involved. Except that their drug of choice is cocaine and we're worried about X. So, I put them on the back burner. That leaves the Russian Mob. They are vicious enough to want to leave this message and they will get into anything that makes them a lot of money, but they favor the illegal. That's X. Then there are the tribes of Africa. We know nothing about them on this side of the Atlantic. They don't seem to be a force. But, they do lop off hands and they use tires to burn their vics. A burning tire around a victim is called a necklace. It was a big deal in South Africa before, during and after the collapse of apartheid. But the necklace concept has been part of the warring culture in Somalia, Ethiopia and parts of Western Africa. My gut is that we are seeing the calling card of a new mob not the Russians. Further, if this mob is from Africa and the cultural roots carry over from wherever, they are not cowboys, but they hold a strong allegiance to a central council headed by a tribal chief."

"Good hypothetical. Now get the facts. Speed is of the essence. We don't want to let Jimmy down. With all the turmoil, I have not looked at the disc contents. Tomorrow at 7 am we'll meet to look at the disc Jimmy found in the desk drawer."

He felt like he has let Jimmy down. The afternoon jets by. Most of the tedium called forms and procedures completed. Time to meet Lieutenant Brown.

"Sir, you mentioned a possible nocturnal visit to Northern Boulevard"

"Yes, Brendan. Meet me here at 10:30. We must look like thieves, who strike after most people are in bed. So dress accordingly. No tassel loafers or button-down shirt. See you then."

Clark's is a constant. The people may ebb and flow, but the saloon remains.

"Good evening, Lieutenant Brown."

"Good evening, Tony. I told you, call me Carlie. We are both off the clock. I ordered for you. The bartender was very helpful."

Taken aback is a good expression. Time to be still. The tigress is on the prowl.

"I want you to know that after having met with Diego Seville, I am convinced, as you said, Los Hores had nothing to do with the robbery and murders at the check cashing store. But, I also feel they are angry that some cowboys came onto their turf and did the deed. Further, this anger may have manifested itself in the recent burning murders of five people. This might have been some kind of very visible retribution."

Just enough yet not anything she didn't already know.

"Tony, I can assure you, Los Hores had nothing to do with the funeral pyre. Now relax and let's get to know each other better off the job."

How could she assure Tony? What does she really know?

"Sorry, I am just so wrapped up in the case, because of my friend Jimmy Ranck that I can't let it go even for a pleasant evening with a beautiful woman."

A little flirtation, response to her overture, may get her to lower her guard or take a misstep. The push-up bra is working overtime.

"What do you do for fun, Tony?"

"Sorry to say, not much. Time at the gym just cleanses my spirit. I do love to go to the library or Barnes & Noble, sit in a fat chair and read British history. The expansion and contraction of the Empire from all sides. Then I take tangential trips into the histories of the countries, empires and tribes directly impacted by the governmentally capitalistic force of five hundred years. I guess that all sounds boring, but it is a mind expansion for me. Unfortunately, I don't do enough cultural expansion."

"I meant real fun like clubs, trips or weekends in the country."

"Nope. I can't stay awake long enough to go to clubs. The last trip I took was to a wedding in Pennsylvania, and I can't afford a weekend getaway cottage."

"Get us another round, and we'll discuss your hermit-like existence further."

Looking in the mirror behind the bar, Tony watched as Lieutenant Brown made an animated telephone call then stuffed the phone into her purse with a vengeance. He placed his order to go.

"OK, so I am a city hermit. Big deal. Who does it hurt?"

Lieutenant Brown's countenance had changed from stalker to attacker.

"It hurts no one but you. As fellow cohorts of the NYPD, why don't we try to give you a life?"

"What did you have in mind for this Pygmalion-like experiment?"

She looked at Tony as if she didn't understand the reference. She didn't, but she would not ask him to enlighten her, because she would check it out when she got to the computer.

"Here is an initial game plan. This week end when you can stay up way past your normal work day bed time; you and I will go dancing."

What a snot.

"I can't dance"

"I'll lead and you'll learn. You can come by my place, I can come by your place, or we can meet at Caliente, Friday at 11. I promise to have you home before 2 am. So, it's a deal. Not a date. I will consider this my community service hours for the month. And you can consider the time spent with me as enriching cross-departmental relations and cultural expansion."

"Caliente is where?"

"333 West 166th Street."

"OK you have sufficiently shamed me that I will meet you there at 11 on Friday. Sorry to be abrupt, but I have some police business to attend to. I ordered a sandwich to go and I see it's ready."

"See you Friday at 11. I'll pick up this tab and you can pick up the tab Friday."

There is no experience as awkward as a male being led around by his nose or other appendage.

———◎———

The drive to Queens, is a drive to Queens.

"Brendan, park here. We'll go to the building on foot. If during the investigation we become separated, find your way home. Leave the car if need be. We can get it tomorrow. OK?"

"Yes. What do you mean separated?"

"Well, we don't know what is here and we don't know what we're looking for and we don't know who might be here. That said, we may have to book very suddenly. We both can't go the same direction of we have to flee. It's just safer that way. This is not police procedure; it's something I learned playing very mean-spirited and destructive Halloween pranks as a teen."

"I understand."

As they approach the fenced lot with the vans parked at angles, Brendan noticed the unmarked van amongst the other six. He pulled Tony's sleeve and pointed. Tony acknowledged the anomaly. As they got to the gate, they heard the growls. Pit Bulls are favored deterrents of auto parts and other hard-scrabble retail outlets with parking lots. For now they were only growling. They had not reached the snarling, barking, jaw slamming mode of full protection. They were warning Tony and Brendan. Like a shot across the bow. Tony reached into the bag and withdrew two large hamburgers. Dropping to the sidewalk, he reached in his inside jacket pocket and removed a small bottle and spilled its contents between the burgers. He waited about thirty seconds for the liquid to become fully immersed in the ground meat. Then he gently placed the doggie treats inside the gate.

"Let's go back to the car. I forgot something there. Something we will need to continue our investigation."

"What did you put on the burgers, Lieutenant?"

"Just something to help the dogs relax for about an hour. In a few minutes they will be more mellow than a stoned hippie."

"A what?"

"Never mind, I'll explain later. Ah, here we are my night goggles."

Returning to the gate, Brendan noticed both dogs splayed out as if they had been hit on the top of their heads with a hammer. Their breathing was deep.

"Since I wore sneakers and you did not, I'll climb the fence with your help. You stay here and watch for real intruders, the owners or, heaven forbid, the cops."

"Won't you set off alarms?"

"That's what the dogs are for. They keep people out of the parking lot. The electronic security and surveillance at the building entrances, keeps those lucky enough to get by the dogs out of the building. At least that's the theory. Now give me a boost."

Clamoring over the chain-link fence makes a small racket. Nothing to alarm the neighbors, if there are any within two blocks. The dogs continue their naps. Brendan was correct; there are no windows visible from the front or side. Tony walks to the back entrance. Two doors, each large enough for a van. Each door has a window at the top, like the old-fashioned garage doors. Now to find something to make a stand. Two 55 gallon drums. Perfect. Moving them into position is not easy and it is time consuming. The drums provide the right height to allow Tony to look through the small windows in the door. Putting on his night vision goggles, he peers through the dirty windows and sees nothing like he had expected. No tools. No equipment. No hardware. What he sees is very curious. His small light-enhanced night camera clicks away as many angles and points in the large room as he can click in three minutes.

"Time to boogie."

Back over the fence and to the car.

"I want you to take the images in the camera and download them at the house. Make multiple sets of pictures at three different sizes. We need all this done with no fanfare and by noon tomorrow."

"What did you see in there?"

"I am not sure, but we'll know tomorrow. Would you drop me at my place? I need to change out of these dirty clothes before I visit Jimmy."

———◆———

Hospitals have always seemed to be sterile warrens of pre-death. Super clean hallways that twist and turn and become open areas only to twist and turn into the horizon. Mt Sinai has color coded the lines on the floor. The sign at the front door tells the visitor that red is for ICU, green is for X-ray, yellow is for Obstetrics, blue is for surgery and white is for Outpatient. The sign goes onto warn the reader that there will be different colors on other floors. The lines lead to specific elevators. Tony is struck by the ironic similarity of prisons and hospitals; very clean and well lit halls and lines that lead the walker in the right direction. Hell, they even smell the same, except in the rooms or cells. The two major differences are that hospitals have larger rooms off each hall, and not all the people are in some form of uniform. Oncology is on the third floor. There is no line for cancer The ward is the entire floor.

Tony hears someone or something that sounds the cereal leprechaun very angry or a drunken Barry Fitzgerald. The words are not distinguishable, but the chatter is notable. At the nurses' station he asks to see James Ranck. After the usual dance between after visiting hours and Tony's gold shield, the young nurse points toward the noise and tells Tony Room 345.

"I would appreciate it. The entire ward would appreciate it if you could quiet him down. Most of our patients need their rest."

"I'll try."

"And who is this laddie-buck standin' in the darway?"

"It's me Jimmy?"

"It's me ye say. And who might ye be?"

"Lieutenant Anthony William Sattill of the CAT Squad in the 27th Precinct."

"Jaysis bye, you don't have to be so fookin farmal. I don't know a Lieutenant Anthony William Sattill of the CAT Squad in the 27th Precinct. But, I have a dear friend name o' Tony. He is a damned good cop. I love him like a brudder, and he loves me. He loves me wife, too. Have you seen her? She's not been to visit me. I am all alone in the unhealthy health hell."

There is a frail man with tubes in each arm and one running to his nose. He looks like an ill-constructed marionette. His eyes are glazed and red rimmed, and his hair, normally clean and combed is matted with sweat and disheveled. Stubble of a beard is beginning to show. He has sweated though the regulation night clothes. Tony sits beside the bed. Tony leans into his friend and whispers. Jimmy is a tad stinky.

"Jimmy, I came by to make sure you were being taken care of, and to let you know we are making progress. We're about to open the cookie jar. I learned at you were right. You had some strangers embedded in your neighborhood. When we traced the license plate, we found R&B Construction Company in Queens that has no construction equipment."

"Tony, have you looked at the disc. I am sure all the answers are on the disc. Who was Rufus Fulton? Why was he really there? What did he want from me? Why was he murdered?"

The rasp of Jimmy's voice and the odor of his breath spoke of the nearness of his termination. The accent and behavior had morphed into quiet seriousness. The lawyer is back.

"We are going to look at the disc tomorrow morning at 7. My entire team. Plus, we're going to examine the photos I took at R&B. These two sources will give us what we need, I'm sure."

"Damn it bye. What the fook have ye bin dooin? Ye shudda open that disc the minute I gave it to ye."

"I am sorry, Jimmy, but something more important came up. Getting you here."

"Fook it. I dinna matter. The information on the disc is all dat matters. I'm gonna die soon. The information will lead you down a long path. It's me legacy to ye. To find the truth, ye got ta start with the disc. Now what are ye waitin' far."

"I'll call immediately after we open the disc."

"I hope I am still alive when you call."

"Jimmy, what is the matter with you. You're in the best hospital, getting the best care. You'll be around for some time to come. I'll bet you'll be out of here in a few days. Back to your cranky self."

"I'm not walking out of here anytime soon. And my behavior is drug induced. Not my drug of choice, but it really works to distort my thinking and emotions while it suppresses the pain. Tony, if I go off the drip, the pain will knock me out. If I stay on the drip, I bounce in and out of reality. It's a great existence. Promise me that whatever happens to me, you will get Pam's killers. No matter what. You'll kill 'em all. Kill 'em all. Do you swear?"

Jimmy had a grip on Tony's arm. Incredibly powerful for a man who looks so weak. Real desperation in his eyes and raspy voice.

"I promise. Now promise me something"

"What?"

"Cut out the Barry Fitzgerald routine at such a loud level and so late at night."

"I can't promise all of that. I'll tone it down a little. But, it's one of the things that helps me endure the shame of my condition and my impending demise. I love you."

"I love you, too."

Tony nearly runs down the hall to the elevator. He wants to get out of this place and away from that man's condition as fast as possible. He can't save Jimmy. He can't help him now. Could he have helped earlier? Tony does not want to be Jimmy's killer because of a failure to act. He feels guilty that he is letting his dear friend down. Most of all he wants to simply get away from a dying man. A man being eaten alive from within. A man with no hope. Is this man Jimmy or Tony? One thing is for sure. This will be a three-drink night. Maybe the booze will help him sleep.

Dance

"**N**othing. Chris, how the hell is that possible?"

"Sir, the file was encrypted. And, frankly, it was a damned good job. I don't recognize any of those symbols. Obviously, Mr. Fulton did not want just anybody to have the information. He wanted the Rancks to have the information and probably encrypted the information based on what he assumed was their level of encryption expertise."

"How the hell could he have known *their level of expertise*?"

Tony's frustration had turned to anger, and that anger was being vented in a very sarcastic attitude.

"My guess is that he came to the store several times before, deduced from his conversations with Mrs. Ranck that she was computer sophisticated, encrypted the file, and delivered it."

"OK, let's say you are correct. How do we unencrypt the SETI-like symbols? I don't want to go through channels. Too many forms, too many eyes, too many questions, too much crap."

"I have a friend, not with the department, who can probably do the job. He is discreet, but expensive."

"Give me a ball park for quick and thorough work."

"I'll show him what we have and find out if he thinks he can do what we want. If he can do it, he'll ask for $2,500 in cash up front."

"I'll get you $2,000 in fifties by ten. Offer him $1,500. See if he bites. But, we need the clean information yesterday. We're close, so time is too precious to piss away. Too many innocent people have died."

Tony would front the bread for a good cause, and get it back from the department. With the normal speed of reimbursement, he could expect the money within three months.

"Now to the pictures of last night. Brendan, what did we see?"

"No construction equipment, hardware or building supplies. The pictures show what looks to be a ton of electronic equipment; microphones, tape recorders, parabolic dishes, and cameras of all sizes and shapes. The warehouse is the supply room for very extensive surveillance activities. Who runs the room is what we don't know? After I dropped you off at home last night, I came back here and dug as deeply as I could into who really owns the building. Three shell corporations are so intertwined that no one could ferret out true ownership. What is interesting is that the names of Roth and Bustelli don't appear on any of the ownership papers. I even checked for their spouses names. Nada. The names that do appear are Smith, Brown, Jones and Wilson. These sound obviously phony. This leads me to conclude that someone at the Real Estate Commission is in on the fraud or was simply told to do the deeds and remain quiet. The common name from the Commission on all the leases is Moe. I checked on this name and it does not exist on the Commission's roster. This is a government screen. City, state or Federal. I don't know. But, given the amount of equipment, my guess is Federal."

"Good job. Now we have to find out which branch and specifically who. Jimmy mentioned a Tim Martin, recently retired from Treasury, who might be helpful. I'll call Jimmy after this meeting and get Mr. Martin's particulars. Then you can call him."

"Sir, I finally found Amanda Balfour. She was not in the senior pictures, but she was a member of a social club, Zeta Psi Alpha, and the Middle East Peace Club. Here are her pictures. I'll have them enlarged and cleaned up for our work."

"Good job . . . so far. We need to track her through Harvard Law and know all about her before she dropped off the grid in DC. Let's get to work people. Chris, come with me to the bank. Bring the disc and then find your friend. I have to call Jimmy before we leave."

Why was Jimmy being followed? Who were the followers? Where is Amanda Balfour? What is on the disc? It's going to be tough to concentrate on administrative minutia with all the important loose ends dangling in the front of Tony's mind.

<hr>

The line in front of Caliente is six wide and stretches a half a block and around the corner. Tony stands across the street with several other on-lookers; dealers plying their trade.

"Watcha need.?"

"Nothing. No thanks"

"Hey homes, you can't have a good time in there unless you have a good time out here. Know what I mean?"

"I do, and no thanks. I am waiting for somebody."

We're all waiting for somebody. A girl with a killer body and soft lips. Or maybe you are waiting for a . . ."

"Don't go there my friend. Just leave me alone and do your business somewhere else, like ten blocks away."

"You tryin' to muscle in on my territory, homes. That could be dangerous."

"I am not trying to muscle in. I am here to meet someone. And I am the man. See the shield. I am not a narc, but I am someone who will make your life a living hell if you persist. Now do yourself a favor and either shut up or walk away. If you don't do one of these, I will advise Senor Seville that you are a public nuisance illegally interfering with his club."

Sudden silence means the message has been received. Why are women always late? It's already 11:15. Tony was early, because he wanted the evening to be over quickly. Now he is feeling the anxiety of abandonment. Not an un-common emotion. Left alone in a strange place. Was this like the bars of his childhood? Was Carlie like his mother? Why did he go there? Then he spots her working the crowd as she approaches the entrance. He steps smartly across the street.

"Well, you made it. I was not sure you would show. I mean this is way out of your world and comfort zone."

"I came because I said I would and because I am curious how this would play out."

"Play out! God, Tony we're off the clock. Just two people trying to get to know each other better. Just that. We'll see where it goes from there. OK?"

"OK."

"I hope you're not carrying. The door personnel do pat down hard. Some people just come here for that. They get their jollies being massaged by strong people."

"I am not carrying."

Sometimes you have to lie. His shield is safely tucked in his left shoe beneath the sock.

"By the way stay very close to me until we are seated. After one drink at the table, all appropriate eyes will have scanned you with me and determined that we are OK."

The regular and the rookie pass through the second door. The noise and lights explode into Tony's senses and psyche. He feels overwhelmed, almost frightened. Carlie takes his hand as they follow the hostess to a table up front. Her hands are surprisingly soft. The hostess deliberately bounces on the path. Her buttocks and breasts, all four nearly visible, seem to follow the music's beat. Carlie whispers in the hostess's ear.

"I think I forgot to tell you. But, Caliente does not take credit cards or checks. Strictly cash. Hope you can cover that tab. It would be an embarrassment if I had to chip in. I ordered our drinks. Your usual from Clarks."

The noise, strobe lights and dervish-like activity create an atmosphere of total disarray for Tony. The men are all smartly dressed in the fashion du jour. Not cheap. The women, all of whom seem to be ten years younger than the men are exposing as much flesh as possible to outshine each other and to attract the best male beast. Mating season evenings/365. The drinks arrive and the waitress, who looks like a clone of the hostess, just younger, hands me a card. On one side: Club Caliente #3, on the other side the date and time.

"When we are dancing, if we order drinks from the bar or another waitress, all you do is show this card and our order goes on you tab. Seamless, as they say in the corporate world."

Quiet conversation is impossible, and yelling is out of the question. That means that Tony and Carlie have to nuzzle to speak. Or, not speak at all. That seems to be the MO of couples at other tables. No speaking while seated. Like the long-time married and suffering Jewish couples at a Catskill resort except younger and better dressed.

"Well, what do you think?"

Carlie has leaned toward Tony's ear as he leans down and into her he sees the iridescent medallion with the emerald is nestled on her breasts, which are being pushed from their natural resting places. The same pendant she wore at Clarks. Now, the epiphany. This is the same design as the piece of art in Diego Seville's office. This is Los Hores art. A sign that guarantees safe keeping on the streets. A badge that signifies a bond stronger than just cop to criminal. A gift from a lover. He stifles the gut reaction to pull away. Now that he knows the players, he can better play the game.

"At first it was overwhelming. Now, I think I am getting used to this place and the activity."

"Let's dance."

"Are you sure you want to risk my two left feet?"

"I have been dancing in places like this for years. I know how to avoid being stepped on."

"Another warning. I can't lead, because I don't know this music."

"Just observe. You know how to do that don't you? And follow my lead. It will be fun."

"What about our stuff. Your wrap?"

"Trust me, we could leave cash on the table and it would be here when we returned."

Tony has no doubt. They insert themselves into the pulsating, churning humanity. Tony observes the men. They seem to be doing little or nothing. An occasional spin, a hand cross over, a two hand cross over. The women, on the other hand, are whirling and swirling up to, onto and around the men, and even other women. Temptation by display of goods offered and reinforced by soft contact. Tony follows; mimics the actions of the men, and follows the lead of Carlie, as he was instructed. She glides and undulates like an upright serpent. Hands over her head to partially exposed her breasts. Hands by her sides as she shakes her body. She takes his hand, twists his arm around her waist and slides into him only to twirl his arm over her head and holding onto his hand goes beyond him. Tony can't hear the music. He feels it. It is good. He brushes against other dancers and they against him. All part of the ritual. He begins to move with the throng and the throb. Legs and hips now form a team that tries to dance on its own. Awkward at best. A valiant effort nonetheless. Carlie twirls into him again. This time she takes both his hand and they perform a double cross over. She quickly twirls back into him. She stares at him for the first time since they entered the dance arena.

"Let's take a break."

"Good idea. I need to review my notes on what I was doing."

"You were doing fine."

"For an older white guy."

"No really, you are a quick study. A few more trips to the floor and you'll be dancing like one of the boys. Order us another round. I have to go to the ladies room."

As he watches her disappear into the morass, Tony sees the tribal gathering. The dance floor contains those who are eligible to mate. The first circle around the floor is comprised of the mating-wannabes. Younger, older, not as good looking or not as well dressed. They just don't make the cut. This group stands and watches. Very occasionally some wannabe goes onto the mating space. They are not rejected. They are ignored. There is no eye contact between the interloper and the chosen as there is amongst the chosen. That subtle form of rejection is enough to discourage them so they return to their outer circle. Around this circle of wannabes mills a small but distinct population of older couples. They acknowledge the existence of each other and chat occasionally. Their eyes are homed in on someone or some couple on the dance floor. Perhaps a child or younger sibling. Did this population meet on this dance floor and mate for life? Or at least more than weekend? Beyond this older, established group are couples sitting at tables on platforms that overlook everything. They are here for the show beneath the strobe lights and in the surrounding circles. Tony notices plates of food and champagne glasses on the tables. These are the heffes. Carlie slides into her chair and moves toward Tony so they can speak. As Tony leans down to her voice, she kisses his ear.

"Did you miss me?"

"As a matter of fact, I did. I realize I have been less than enthusiastic about this evening. But, I am having a great time. Cheers."

They tap glasses. She blows him a baby kiss before she sips. He winks. The chase is on in earnest. She leans in again.

"Are you ready for your second dance lesson?"

Tony notices a few small white flakes on the emerald. She is high.

"I am more than ready."

The second lesson goes well. Tony is at ease and becomes adventuresome with his steps and moves. Carlie guides them to another couple and the four dancers switch partners. No introductions, just a simple hand off. Carlie briefly speaks to her new partner and he to her, but Tony's new partner doesn't make eye contact. This has all the feeling of a business transaction to which Tony is not privy. It is not part of his evening's game. After a few swirls, twirls, waist wraps and even a dip, the diversion is thorough. The exchange is temporary. Carlie returns, because her business is complete. Her smile seems pained. Her seduction of Tony intensifies. The hand holding is firmer, her body clings and rubs in all the right places and her eyes are focused on his. Tony is not aroused, but he is intrigued.

"Enough.?"

A strange surrender from the dancing queen.

"Order another round of drinks while I go to the ladies room."

This is not small bladder syndrome. A new waitress brings the drinks and hands Tony a note.

Welcome to my club. I hope you find it enjoyable. DS

Tony scans the room for his communicator. How the hell could he expect to find THE heffe who is hiding in a sea of heffes? Look for the body guards. There they are. The center table on the main platform. He can't see

Diego, but he can see the backs of two very muscular males and the profiles right and left of two more. No acknowledgment from either party. As he sips his drink, he notices that it is 1:30. He has a big day tomorrow. So this is has been a very informative and somewhat pleasant evening.

"Sorry. But, there was a line to get in and a line to use one of the two stalls. I promised that we would call it a night by 2. It's a little before the bewitching hour. Why don't we finish our drinks and go our separate ways. If that's OK with you? I mean, we can leave, but we do not have to go directly home."

The seduction's turning point.

"Let's finish our drinks and leave. I'll call the waitress for the tab."

The tab arrives and it is noted as *Paid in Full*. Six drinks for $150.00 plus a $100.00 cover charge the compliments of the owner. Tony leaves a $50.00 tip. No piker, he. As they head toward the door, Carlie has gone from holding his hand to clutching is arm. The walk is circuitous, because they have to transverse the dance floor and squeeze between wannabes in the outer circle. Finally the portal to the real world. The line seems to have slightly thinned and shortened in the past few hours.

"Let's walk around the corner to catch a cab."

"There are cabs here."

"Tony, indulge me, please."

There is fear in her voice. As they turn the corner, Carlie pulls Tony onto her and kisses him deeply.

"Let's go to my place."

"Carlie, we . . . I can't.

"Why not?"

As she speaks she slides her right hand down to Tony's crotch and begins to rub. Then she discovers the hardness that is not flesh.

"What do have down there?"

"A small gun that makes a big noise. I never leave home without it."

"How did you get it passed the door staff?"

"They are reluctant to feel deep into a man's crotch."

"OK. I'll accept the fact that you were carrying the whole time we were in the club. But, I don't understand why you won't come home with me for a night cap."

She continues to rub him.

"Stop that. You want reasons. First, I have a bitch of a day tomorrow. Second, I just don't think it's right for us to start something. Third, I am seeing someone very seriously."

"Fuck number one. You're a big boy. You can handle a tough day. Besides, I'll put a smile on your face. As for numbers two and three; I'm not talking about moving in. I'm talking about another drink then exchanging some bodily fluids as part of a fun event or two."

Tony pulls away and steps into the street. His whistle is effective. As his dad used to say the whistle is great for calling dogs, kids and taxis. Tony knows about dogs and taxis. He opens the door.

"Carlie, your chariot."

"Damn you."

As she slides in, Tony notices her pained smile again.

A second whistle is equally effective and Tony is at his door in eight minutes. Not much traffic at 2 AM even for a Saturday. The alarm is set and he is asleep in five minutes.

The noise is disturbing, as it is mean to be. He hits the alarm, but the intermittent ringing continues. Eyes pop open driven by fear and a call to action.

"Yes, Lieutenant Sattill here."

"Lieutenant, we caught one that you will want to see before all the bullshit starts. Lieutenant Brown has been murdered. It's really bloody. I sent a car for you. Come quickly."

There was urgency in Chris's voice that went way beyond the emergency commonplace in the job.

———◈———

He spotted the flashing lights before he was out of the car.

"Sir, over here."

Tony lifts the cover. The sight is appalling, even to a veteran of horrific murders.

"I count twelve stab entries. Front and back. Top and bottom. This means that the killer wanted to inflict a lot of damage both before and after her death. But here is the worst part of the crime. See these shreds of flesh. The killer used a serrated knife. Serrated on both edges. After these frontal stabs, the killer twisted the knife when it was inserted and then sawed the blade as it was being extracted. This is more than a crime of passion; it is a crime of demonic rage. This much rage goes way beyond the level found in murdered caused by spouses and friends. She did not struggle much. I suspect the first two or three blows to the back rendered her nearly helpless. But, she was a fellow officer. I found a few defensive wounds. Also, a little bit of flesh and fabric under two nails. The killer cleaned well under the other nails. He or she just didn't do a thorough job. The perp knew we would look. Maybe a pro, who wanted this to look like a crime of passion. Or, someone familiar with our procedure. A cop? Someone, not a cop, who is connected to Lieutenant Brown."

"What about her personal stuff?"

"The purse was empty except for two vials of coke. If it were a robbery, the thief would have taken the coke. I think it was planted to besmirch her reputation. A sign for the public. Or maybe for us."

"Get prints off the vials."

"Already lifted two sets thumb and index finger prints. We'll run them through the system for the riding D."

"What else?"

"She was first assaulted over there. The perp must have hid in the short ally away from the street light and then pounced when Lieutenant Brown appeared. What I don't understand about the waiting part is how long would the killer wait? Or did he know when she was coming home? After the first few strikes, the perp dragged her over here. See the scuff marks. She was not dead at this point, because she began to struggle, feebly. See the broken shrubbery and how the scuff marks become crazy as if she and her shoes were tossed around. See the blood drops in a spray pattern of emanating from a central source."

"Good job, Chris. Did you find any jewelry?"

"No rings or watch and no indications that she ever wore a ring or watch. But, there is this tear of neck flesh, as if a necklace were ripped off. The tear is deeper in the back of her neck indicating that the necklace was violently removed when she was down face up. Most likely dead by then."

"Be thorough and try to grab an hour of rest in the crib. Get out of here before the media vultures arrive. See you at 8."

Reveal

The Post carries a front page shot of the crime scene with the headline:

Officer Butchered on West Side

Great way to start the day! Tony will get coffee and a bagel at the precinct. His troops always pick up food for the white soul.

"Good morning. Has everything been turned over to the Detective assigned to the case of Lieutenant Brown's murder? Who is it?"

"James Oxee. He has a good rep as a straight shooter,"

"On to the business at hand. Let's see that disc."

Eight eyes are glued to four computers as the contents of the disc spill out from the central entry. Eleven pages of single-spaced-no-margin text with numerical sequences.

"Damn. I can't follow this. I prefer to read the text on paper."

"I printed you a copy, LT."

"There is nothing but wall-to wall words. Look, there is a short shopping list; chicken, broccoli, sweet potato. This list is followed by the number 2.5336. Is that money? Or drugs? Or the key to a larger puzzle? Then more text about wires. Some initials. This mode of writing is repeated throughout the entire three pages. Did this guy ever think of punctuation? Or spacing. These are the ramblings of someone, who was very disturbed. Or someone who wanted to keep his message hid from prying eyes."

"The text runs without interruption. There are spaces between some words and then there are words which run together, like 'fighttheevilsatan'. There are numerous references to 'Satan', 'master' and 'holy'. Here is another cryptic number, 3716287743. And another, 2512356729

"I spotted the number sequence, 56800 or similar sequences at least eight times. No ten. What the hell does that mean? It is different from the other numbers. There is no decimal point. Did anyone find pi?"

"Apple or boysenberry?"

A laugh is good when being confronted by such an arcane situation.

"There is his to do list for the day. Which day?"

"The numbers are a code. Decipher it. That's your job?

"Sir, he was under a lot of pressure. He had uncovered something, and he knew others knew he knew. He feared for his life. What I don't understand is why Mr. Fulton was attempting to get this information to Mr. Ranck."

"Jimmy was recommended, by Rufus's brother. Jimmy was deemed to be honest and caring."

"Jesus, look at page two. It's just one long word."

"And on page five there are three references to a 'fortress'."

"The same on pages seven and nine."

"Another puzzle is why he came to the store at least once before he delivered the disc? Suppose he came to the store a few times just to set up the cover that he was seeking a divorce, only to return one last time to deliver the disc. I think Mrs. Ranck's file indicated that Mr. Fulton had, in fact made a total of three visits. And that these visits were logged into her appointment file we found on her computer. Before and after they occurred with notes of the meetings. Suppose someone recognized Mr. Fulton on one of his earlier visits and knew of the upcoming visit. Suppose this someone knew vaguely of Mr. Fulton's activities and that he was some sort of a threat. Then this someone alerts the perps, who arrive just after Mr. Fulton. He was the only target and the others were collateral damage. If that is true, it is very sad. They wanted to stop him from something, which I think we now know was getting the information to Jimmy and maybe others."

"That is an amazing conspiracy theory. It requires that someone in Jimmy's office was in bed with the perps. And that they shot this employee to ensure that the secret connection would die. And how did the perps know to look for Jimmy?"

"Well we got to Rufus Fulton through his brother. It would not be too difficult for another, say agency, to know where Rufus's brother was. They watch the brother. Rufus goes to him. The brothers converse. The conversation is taped. The information is provided the agency. The agency now knows who, that is Mr. Ranck, they know the what, information, and they know the where, the store.

Where else would Mr. Fulton try to slip Mr. Ranck the information? The agency then provides the how. They reach out to a gang. It has to be disguised as a robbery. That way the investigation goes one way and the truth another. Somebody contacts a gang of thugs to do the wet work. The gang reaches out and lays some bread on the insider. Or, maybe a threat. The deed is done, and the NYPD goes off in at least three directions; Los Hores, a gang of recent African immigrants, and anybody else we can find. With the shoot out at the rave, Hinton closes the case and all is well that ends well."

"That's a lot of ifs and suppositions. It stretches the mind."

"The mixing of evils has happened many times before. One evil decides that the ends justify the means, because he enjoys the money and the ensuing protection from other evils."

"That could explain the new Porsche of the Prison Warden. But, we must get into the Federal rat's warren for more details. Mr. Fulton's department, the IRS, is out. They can't know we suspect anything. If he was a rogue they will want to cover their ass. If they were watching him, they don't want the world to know they slipped up and he got dead. They also don't want us pissing on their turf. We also have to find out the name of the rotten apple in Jimmy's office. If we can learn who, we can follow the trail back to the perps, and maybe the proper agency."

"LT, we don't have to go to the IRS to get a lead. The IRS is part of Treasury. Treasury has more doors than the IRS. So they may have some inkling of what one of their children is doing and mother might be willing to share, because she cares enough about herself not to sully her skirts in the media. Can't go to any other department because of the Chinese Wall syndrome or worse. If they are investigating the IRS internally, they don't want us pissing on their territory. Or, both the department and the sub-department simply clam up and mom isn't embarrassed in the media"

"OK. I'll get Tim Martin's telephone number from Jimmy. Tim used to work at Treasury and he may be willing to guides us. What else do we think?"

"LT, I see initials, but I don't see the specifics. Are these notations of cash? Why the decimal point? Are they thousands, millions or billions? These amounts are too big to be carried in a shoe box. And any movements of these sizes between financial institutions would raise a domestic red flag."

"Unless Oversight at the Department of Banking in New York or someone in Treasury was on the payroll. It keeps coming back to Treasury"

"Frankly, sir, I don't see this amount of money to be big deal. The Russians got nailed three years ago trying to launder $50 million a month. These amounts, if they are amounts, total much less than that. And that's over a six month period. Frankly, I doubt it is money. The numbers mean something else. Maybe they are part of a code."

"Suppose this was the test period for a much larger operation about to start up and Rufus stumbled onto it. He could have been trying to nip something before it grew too large. There could be other money transfer operations like this about which no one knows?"

"Chris, are you confident that your guy can unencrypt the information exactly as it was on the disc? No special alterations or augmentations. He is legit."

"I'd stake my career on this guy. He is my brother, Alex. And by the way he took the $2,000.00."

"OK. Here's what we will do. Get Alex to decipher this mess. Line-by line, page by page. Then we work to find out what was so important about this information that a lot of people have died. When you put these ramblings meant for Jimmy with the fact that Jimmy was being spooked by some very heavy hitters with the really good equipment, I'd say we have stepped in a big pile of doo-doo. The question is just whose doo-doo is it? That leads me to this: We are now entering an area of complete silence and healthy paranoia. No one and I mean no one, must observe, hear or suspect what you are doing. If you think someone is getting a little too close, or you feel your activities are being monitored, come to me and we will go deeper. Until then we have to operate in the open as if nothing out of the ordinary is being investigated."

"Sir, I have another wrinkle. I checked with Harvard Law and they confirmed that a woman known as Amanda Balfour did some course work at the school, but never graduated with a degree. She withdrew after her first year. And she went by another name while she was there. She called herself Musin Mahmoud. Although as far as they knew she never changed her name legally. She has never responded to any fund raising or reunion letters at either Brown or Harvard. I am going to track her down through her references in DC. I was told she worked for the IRS then Justice. Maybe that's a ruse, too."

"By Monday we will have gotten in touch with Tim Martin. I hope he will be a trove of information and leads. Now get your brother to work on the text, I have to see Jimmy. I'll be back around four, unless you have solved the puzzle before then. I realize how much this is draining everyone, and that you have no life outside of this place. I just want you guys to know how much I appreciate all of the work. And, I know that if Jimmy were here, he would be tearful."

"LT, I can speak for Chris and Brendan, we are proud to serve and learn. And we think we understand just how big a case this might become. So we are making big bones, right."

"Yes . . . under the radar bones."

<hr />

The warm feeling stayed with Tony the entire trip to Mt. Sinai. Then the coldness of the building and his purpose there set in. Prisons, hospitals, and morgues bothered him since he joined the force. The floor was familiar. The nurse at the desk was different. There was no noise coming from down the hall. Tony's admonition had worked. In the doorway he saw the truth. Jimmy was asleep or comatose. There were another tube and a breathing apparatus of some type. Minutes were now precious.

"Jimmy, can you hear me. It's Tony."

Two eyes opened slightly and a slight grin creased Jimmy's lips. He nodded.

"I came to tell you that you were right. You were being spooked by someone. We think they are Feds of some kind. We went to the R&B Construction warehouse and found a shit pot full of surveillance equipment. We don't know why they were shadowing you, but we are on the trail. Do you understand?"

Another nod and his grin widens.

"We finally got the Rufus Fulton disc open and we are starting to get the information unencrypted. It was written like SETI code. When we saw it in English, it didn't get a whole lot better. The commentary was of a mad man, or someone under incredible stress. Eleven pages of single-spaced gibberish. One sentence covered three pages. Words are strung together. Number sets repeated. We think we see money transfers and the dates of the transfers. Just not the people or institutions involved. He gave us some initials to research. We think he was trying to give you something really big and he was killed for trying."

Jimmy's eyes got a quizzical look then a dead stare.

"I am sad to tell you that we think Rufus was the target and that Pam and the others were innocent bystanders."

Tears well in eyes that have had no excess moisture for weeks. The new reality hurts more than the chemo. Jimmy raises his hand. Tony takes it and gives it a loving squeeze.

"I hate to be so business-like, but . . ."

Jimmy shakes his head.

"Thanks. We think someone in your store tipped off the perps. So they knew when to show up, kill Mr. Fulton and ransack the store looking for the evidence. That's why they took the discs and CDs from the back room. They didn't know exactly what they were looking for. They just assumed that the information was already transferred to you. Can you think of any of the employees, who might have been connected to the perps?"

Without losing the grip of agape, Jimmy holds his other hand up and wiggles it as to write. Tony finds paper and a felt tip pen.

Al Netter, security guard is scrawled on the three-by-five sheet. Beneath the name . . . *never trusted him never looked me straight in the eye*.

"Good. One more thing; to get a handle on Mr. Fulton's recent past, we need to dig deeper into Treasury. Do you know how we can contact your friend, Tim Martin?"

Home 799-882-8765

"Great. You are truly an anonymous source. We can quote you, but have to shield you from the public's glare. Now what can I do for you?"

Jimmy begins to whisper. Tony leans over and places his ear near his friend's mouth. Their grip never breaks

"Catch the bastards that killed Pam. Crucify them and the Feds, who spooked me. I think they're all tied together somehow. Kill 'em. Kill 'em all. Now let me be in peace."

Tony felt an eerie wave and a knot in his stomach. He left the hospital. This was not a good day.

———◦◉◦———

"Brendan, how you guys doing?"

"We're making some progress, but a lot of it is conjecture."

"Keep going. I trust you. Jimmy trusts you. Access the file of the original murder and get me the address of the Security Guard, Alphonso Netter. I think I want to visit his lair. And, tell Jamie that she can contact Tim Martin. His home telephone number is . . ."

"Sir, Mr. Netter's address is 2378 Amsterdam Avenue. Anything else?"

"No. See you at four."

Tony decides to walk. He has time and needs to clear his head. It's a nice day. Tony's eyes begin to well and he has to cough to cover up a sob. He waits and watches joggers, dog walkers and kids playing soccer in the field. Central park, like the subway system, is a great equalizer for New Yorkers. Health clubs and limos are great dividers; creators of class distinction. Walking diagonally through the park from east to west, he crosses the baseball fields. People are setting up for the league games. Cook outs, baseball and beer. All in Spanish. Crossing the park's internal road way, he has to wait for the passing of a large pack of runners all with chest and back number signs. Some sort of race. Fred Lebeau would be pleased. The ring from his cell phone breaks the mood.

"Lieutenant, this is Ronald Aylir."

"Yes sir, good day to you."

"I hope I didn't catch you at a bad time."

"No, sir, what can I do for you?"

"I hadn't heard from you, so I was wondering if you had learned anything new about my daughter and her husband."

"Nothing new. I had dinner with Melissa a few weeks back and she seemed OK except she claimed to have bumped her cheek on a door. I tried to have dinner with the two of them, but Lucky was wrapped up in the opening of his bank in London. I am due to call try to set up another dinner. I will do that today."

"Lieutenant, Lucky is out of town for a while getting the bank operations up and running. So now might be a good time to press Melissa."

"Sir, if you don't mind, please don't take offense, leave the investigation up to me. It has to be delicate. If she is in danger, she will be reluctant to rat out her husband due to the possibility of reprisal and very bad publicity for you. If she is not in danger, she has nothing to tell, and I look like I am making false accusations. She will know that I am acting on your behalf. This could anger her to the point that she will take it out on you and your wife. So, let the delicate probing up to me."

"You're right, Lieutenant. I am just very anxious and perhaps overly protective. Please, call me after you have dinner with Melissa."

"Yes, sir."

The walk on Amsterdam Avenue is a walk through the New York City of the 20th and 21st centuries. What it was during the first two generations of the 20th, what it became during the next two generations and what it was to be during the last ten years of the 20th century and now. A great deal of street activity. Buildings and stoops that are old but kept clean. Some show signs of too much wear and tear. The occasional vacant lot and abandoned building are fertile ground for a developer to risk capital in the name of gentrification and huge profits. Lots of kids. The day is warming. Soon the fire hydrants will be opened. Errands to run. Cooking for the night's parties. Languages and ethnicities blend, yet keep separate. An idyllic world if it were not for the numbers' runners, the corner drug deals, cheap booze, hookers and stolen goods for sale from the trunks of cars. Maybe the underbelly is necessary to support the public persona. Here is 2378. Tony is sweating. Al Netter 6-B. Tony rings the buzzers for 6-A, 6-C and 6-D. Then he calls Brendan.

"Can you get me the telephone number and address of the Security Service Al Netter worked for?"

Suddenly the super appears.

"Who are you?"

"The police. We are trying to get into the apartment of Mr. Alphonso Netter, 6-B. Would you let me in?"

"Let me see your ID."

Tony's badge and picture ID satisfy the older woman. They ride the elevator together. Rickety is an understatement.

"I don't think anybody is home. I have heard anything from his apartment for a long time. Normally, he plays the radio or his CDs pretty loud. But, nothing recently. Even the nice young boys who visited him stopped coming around. He is a security guard. Maybe he is guarding something important out of the city."

She didn't know that Al Netter was a murder victim. The building's absentee landlord does not seem to be in a hurry to rent a murder victim's apartment. Bad for business.

"Thank you. I'll take it from here. Please go back into your apartment."

The door is locked. But it is slightly warped and gives way to Tony's lock picks and a big shove. He reminds himself to thank the burglary unit for his tools. The stench nearly knocks him over. Sweat and human waste are a powerfully repugnant olfactory combination. He hears the buzzing of flies. The temperature has to be at least 90 inside. Entrance hall clear. Kitchen clear. Living room clear. Bedroom clear. The TV is on, but no channel is on. The DVD player is lighted. Tony creeps over to the set and presses replay. After an interminable thirty seconds, the disc reveals its contents. There are two young boys and Mr. Netter. None of them are dressed. The boys have tied him to his bed, and are torturing him. Hitting him with rolled up magazines. He is crying and smiling at the same time. One of the boys leans into Al and kisses him, while the other boy strikes Netter's genitalia with a magazine. Then he spots that boy. Rather the dried, rotting corpse that was the boy tied as Netter was in the video. The sights, the sounds of laughter and affectionate cooing and the stench of the apartment drive Tony to the bathroom to puke.

"Jamie, get your collection gear and come to Al Netter's apartment, 6-B at 2378 Amsterdam Avenue now."

Tony feels like passing out. He retreats to the hall, closing the door behind him. He waits by the front door for his team. When they arrive, he tells them to put masks on before entering the apartment.

"We'll take a crack at the evidence then call it in. Hinton will be pissed. That is, if we want to call it in."

"Hinton should have seen this. But, it was not in his final report. Maybe he didn't even check. Maybe he checked, and didn't care. That would be dereliction of duty . . . filing a false report. Maybe he's dirty."

"Not so fast, Jamie. Let's just gather evidence and then leave as if we were never here. I don't want anyone to know what we suspect."

"And, what is that LT?"

"I suspect that Al Netter was the link between the murdered people at the store and the perps. They got to him through his deviancy. And then they eliminated the connection with Al with a few well-placed bullets. I think I will visit the security firm that employed Al Netter. Have you gathered enough? Take enough photos? OK, let us all get out of here."

"LT, I think the boy's neck was broken. That's the COD. I guess Al had had enough playtime."

On-Site Security is housed in a store front six blocks from Al Netter's apartment. The overweight man at the desk is sleeping when Tony knocks on the door.

"Who are you? What do you want?"

"I am Lieutenant Anthony Sattill of the 27th Precinct. Here's my badge and ID."

The man waddles to the door and examines Tony's credentials. Sheepishly he opens the door.

"What can I do for you Lieutenant?"

"An employee of this company was murdered recently, and I am doing some follow-up investigating . . . a background check."

"You're a long way from your jurisdiction. Besides I gave Netter's file information to a big black Detective."

"Hinton"

"Yes, that was his name. He signed the file to confirm that he had read it and returned it to us. Don't you guys talk to each other?"

"May I see the file?"

"Sure, see Hinton's signature and badge number."

Tony scanned the five pages. Mostly check-the-box type of information. Some background information from a previous security service in Seattle.

"Is there anything you can add to the file? Any personal information? Did Netter socialize with any other guards?"

"Naw . . . our guards are basically loners. Their lives after their shifts are their own. Wait. I do remember Al mentioning on two different occasions that he liked to dance and had been to a Spanish club up town a couple of times. He said dancing took his mind off the pressures of the job. I never saw him there, and I am damn near a regular."

"Do you mean Caliente? Did you mention this to Detective Hinton?"

"No, he never asked about anything except Netter and his job performance."

"What was his performance?"

"He showed up on time, was well dressed and polite. He was new. On the job a few weeks before he was killed."

"Thank you. I appreciate your help."

Caliente. Home of Los Hores. Another link. And what about the necklace that was missing from Carlie's neck. If it had been left it would have been a direct link to Diego and his crew. Therefore, ripping off her neck could be a way to hide evidence. Why would they want to kill her? What had she done? She was frightened enough to try to lure Tony back to her bed. What frightened her? The guy she spoke to at the dance. Had she violated some sacred oath by bringing Tony to the club? Diego was too cool to react so violently to that social indiscretion. From whom was Tony to be protected? Would he have died protecting her? Seattle. Seattle. What is important about Seattle? Rufus Fulton was from Seattle. Big city connect or city big coincidence? Most time coincidences are not. Was Al Netter ghosting Rufus Fulton? Why? If he was new to the job, was he sent to the job? Somebody knew how to get him into the right position. Back to Los Hores. Seattle and Los Hores. Two connections. Different loci. Same focus. But somebody is pulling Los Hores' strings. Who? A feral fear comes over Tony. The forest is very dark. The hunters are numerous and well disguised. A tree is not a tree. It is a man in camouflage. He has weapons to destroy all the animals in the woods.

"OK, guys what do you have from Netter's place?"

"Nothing out of the ordinary for a sick-o. We'll just stash the information out of sight. By the way, Captain Lenz of IAD called. He just wanted to know where you were. Why did he call the precinct looking for you, LT? He could have called your cell."

"One more thing. I called Tim Martin. I spoke to his daughter at that number. Her father was accidentally killed in a hunting accident. I think it is strange that there is hunting in Pennsylvania in the summer. Hunting and fishing seasons are early spring or fall, and they last 45 days. Something is amiss. If something is amiss and he was executed, it is because someone knew that he had been in contact with Mr. Ranck. If that is true, then that someone probably had Mr. Martin's telephone tapped. Then they now know that we know. But the good news is that we are on the right path. Treasury is the mother lode. But we are at a dead end, unless we can get into Treasury through some back door."

"Lenz was checking up on the team. I'll deal with him tomorrow. Now to the text."

Tony hears, but he does not listen. Words. Paragraphs. Extraneous verbiage. Repeated phrases. Numbers. And on, and on, and on. Tony's mind is awash with names and images Diego Seville, Los Hores, Caliente, Jimmy Ranck, Melissa Aylir, Rufus Fulton, Musin Mahmoud, Al Netter, Seattle, Carlie Brown, Tim Martin, Treasury, and on, and on. Stressed driven fatigue is beginning to take its toll, but he can't let his team down. He must do everything in his power and guile to take all the heat, so they can continue to work.

Raid

"**L**ieutenant Sattill. We would like to talk to you, alone."

The commanding voice of Captain Wolf Lenz of IAD. He came to the precinct at 7:20 am to embarrass Tony in front of the team. Lenz is a twenty-year vet, most of which has been spent in the Internal Affairs Department crucifying bad cops, and humiliating those who have stepped over the line. He is the poster boy for the department. They drag him out every time there is a civil case against the force. He loves to cut the nuts off beat patrolmen, because they are the most visible. His work gives the community a warm fuzzy feeling that cops are good, and that they can clean up their own doo-doo. They are policing the police. There are two rumors about Lenz. First, he keeps a scrap book of all the fallen angels he has helped repent or sent to jail. Second, he has a godfather at One Police Plaza. His protector will never let anything bad happen to Lenz. Maybe Lenz has pictures. Tony hangs up the telephone.

"Yes, Sir. We can use interview #3."

Then Tony sees the three men behind Lenz. One with a tape recorder and two with dead faces.

"Will your friends be joining us?"

"Yes. I want to be sure that we are not disturbed. So, one of my men will stand by the door, while the other is behind the glass. Let's go. Now!"

They walk to the interview room.

"Stay here a second, Lieutenant. We want to make sure that the precinct mics are non-functional."

The three other enter the room. Tony hears the moving of furniture and other activity that can only signify search and seizure of the microphones hidden in the room. Then the three enter the observation room behind the glass and the noise continues.

"All clear."

"Now we can begin the interview."

⚫

At 7:35 am the two all black SUVs glide up to 1418 Northern Boulevard, pull into the parking lot and block the vans from exiting. The black clad masked bodies with assault rifles are disgorged. With the speed and deliberation of good training, the two teams of four divide; one to the front door and one to the back doors. At the whistle the teams smash in the doors and storm the building. The back door resists the initial hit and requires two more before it becomes an open portal. Then the pandemonium begins. The four men and two women in the warehouse reach for side arms, but they immediately realize that they are surrounded and out gunned. Their resistance fades.

"Stop. Stay where you are. Drop your guns and get on the floor. This is a raid by the Queens Organized Crime Task Force.

We have a warrant to search these premises and arrest all those within. Who is in charge?"

"I guess that would be me. And who are you?"

"My name is none of your concern. The only thing that matters is this warrant and how you are going to explain all of this surveillance equipment."

"But, I need to know the name of the asshole, who staged this phony raid and who is interfering with an on-going government investigation."

"After we confiscate and catalogue all this equipment, we will take you to our precinct. Then you can call a lawyer. Just stay where you are."

"May I see your badge and ID?"

"Fuck you. So you claim to be a Fed. Let me see your ID."

"We're under cover and carry no IDs."

"Then your anonymity will be a real hindrance to uncovering your version of the truth. What is your name?"

"Special Agent Michael Fay."

"Well, Special Agent Michael Fay, we can let you try to sort this out at our house. Just sit and be quiet, while my team checks all the goodies have here."

———————

"What was your relationship with Lieutenant Carlita Brown?"

"We had no relationship other than that of fellow officers."

"Were your sleeping with Lieutenant Brown?"

"I have answered that. Let us move on."

"Did you ever date Lieutenant Brown?"

"No."

"Did you ever meet socially with Lieutenant Brown and have drinks with her at a bar called Clarks."

"Yes. On two separate occasions."

"When?"

"You already know the dates, why ask me to confirm that fact that you were tailing either Lieutenant Brown or me."

"Did you ever go dancing with Lieutenant Brown at a club called Caliente?"

"Yes. Last Friday night."

"Was this the Friday night when Lieutenant Brown was murdered?"

"Yes."

"When you were with Lieutenant Brown at Caliente, did you use or snort cocaine?"

"No. Should I pee in your coffee cup?"

"Don't be smart with me. You are in deep water; way over your head. When you left Caliente, did you force your feeling of affection onto Lieutenant Brown?"

"We kissed good night. Two pecks on the cheek. Symbols of a pleasant evening between two adults. Have you ever kissed the cheek of your hostess when you left a party? That question assumes you were an invited guest. Big assumption. Well, Caliente was Lieutenant Brown's party to which she invited me. I was being friendly. Nothing more."

"After you attempted to force your affection on Lieutenant, did she subsequently jump in a cab to escape you?"

"I hailed a cab by whistling. I opened the door for Lieutenant Brown, closed the door behind her and the cab drove off."

"When you went to Caliente, did you know it was owned by Diego Seville and Los Hores?"

Lenz has just given Tony a way out. It must be seized and massaged delicately so it makes everyone happy.

———◦◉◦———

"Well what do we have here? Cell phones. Hand guns. Cash. But no IDs or driver's licenses. Obviously, you gentle folk were not going to drive those vans today. That would be illegal if you got stopped. Or maybe the licenses are already in the vans. Let us take a look."

"How long is this going to take? How long before we call our lawyers?"

"A while. Not too long and not too short. Just right. But we're just getting to be friends. We need to get all the details down tight before we introduce you to the general public. Alpha, check the vans. I think the keys are on the various rings we found on our new best friends. Bravo, check for wires and connections."

Alpha finds four New York Driver's Licenses in the vans. Plus, additional surveillance microphones and night vision binoculars. Bravo's electrical scanning unearths no wires or connections other than the ConEd and Verizon lines. The building was clean.

"You must be David Smith. And you, Robert Jones. And you are William Brown. And last, but not least, James Gray. What brilliant aliases. No one would ever suspect that these names were phony. Shit you guys have the same birthday. Were your parents in touch with each other on . . . let's see . . . about July 16, 1980. How serendipitous. That leaves the mouth, Mr. Fey, and another unaccounted. We'll get to you soon. OK. Now we'll tear this place apart looking for guns and the like. Like C-4. Like ammunition. We can stop at anytime. Just tell us where everything is so we can conclude our treasure hunt and get you to the house."

"There is nothing more than you have found. Everything was and is out in the open."

"Why do I not believe you? Maybe because criminals live to lie and lie to live. Everybody cuffed and locked down? Then you two tear apart the vans outside while we rip this place apart."

Out come the pry bars and large hammers.

———◆———

"Listen Captain, Lieutenant Brown and I have vaguely known each other and about each other for a year. We re-met at the R.E.A.C.H. gala, which by-the-by you did not attend. Not good for your squeaky-clean public image. She offered to buy me a drink. I had work to do and took a rain check. We were investigating the possibility that Los Hores was involved in the murders at the check cashing place a few weeks ago. I called her, and she requested we have a drink at Clarks. The second time we met at Clarks was because I was still not sure that Los Hores was not involved and I suspected that she was involved with them at some level other than as a senior member of the Gang Task Force. She invited me to go dancing at Caliente. I can't say I knew that Diego Seville owned Caliente, but it does not surprise me. We danced and had a few drinks. She made a few trips to the ladies room. We left, kissed as friends, and I put her in a cab. The next time I saw her, she had been sliced and diced between our buss and her arrival home. My team called me to the scene. Her attack was obviously planned or done by a stalker. Not me."

"Would it surprise you to know that she did not go directly home, but went back to Caliente?"

"Yes."

"Would it surprise you to know that there was extensive cocaine in her blood?"

"No."

"Would you mind taking a drug test?"

"Yes, because it violates my right against self-incrimination. However, with my Lieutenant's Benevolent Association lawyer made aware of this charming offer, I will pee in the cup for you. Since cocaine stays in the system for about a week, you have time. OK?"

"What does the name Alphonso Netter mean to you?"

"He was one of the victims at *Neighborhood Legal & Financial Services*. He was the security guard."

"Do you know where he lived?"

"I would have to check the case file."

"Have you ever been to his residence?"

"No."

"Has any member of your team been to his residence?"

"As of this moment, I cannot vouch for all of their actions."

"Who is Rufus Fulton?"

"He was the murdered customer at *Neighborhood Legal & Financial Services*."

"Who are James and Pamela Ranck?"

"Friends of mine who owned *Neighborhood Legal & Financial Services*."

"Has Mr. Ranck been an active participant in the murder investigation of his wife?"

"You'll have to ask Detective Hinton."

"Do you know why Detective Hinton closed the investigation?"

"You'll have to ask him."

———◉———

"Look what we found. More bugging devices. And weapons. Many weapons. More oomph than the Glocks you were carrying. What do we have here? A box of six 50-calibre Desert Eagles and a half case of ammo. Fifteen automatic rifles and thirty boxes of ammunition. Look, three Street Sweepers. These have been illegal for years. Ten sawed-off double barrel shot guns. Small enough to hide under an over coat or a rain coat. Enough power to take out a door or stop a car. What were you planning? World war three. I can only deduce from this cache that there are more than just you guys involved in this illegal enterprise. Wait! Here is the best part, boys and girls. There are no visible serial numbers on the hardware. And no scratch marks visible to the naked eye. Does this mean the numbers were removed with acid? Numerous passes will remove the serial numbers, but not leave the nasty tell-tale etch marks. Very professional. Almost like a Federal agency."

"Alpha, do you think we should hit the speed dials on all these phones and see who answers?"

"Roger that."

"But we can't, because we don't know the codes to activate the systems and the entry portal to each speed dial file. Do you think our new best friends will tell us?"

"No Sir."

"Then let us take the telephones back to the electro-wizards at the station house. They can sure crack the codes."

"Sir, look what we found in the vans. Small note books with dates names, addresses, initials and actions taken. Here is one with the name J. Ranck. This looks like his home address. This is, er was, the address of his legal and check cashing business. Here is an entry for A. Sattill at his home. Here is an entry for C. Brown at

Caliente, a club on the West Side of Manhattan. And here is an entry for M. Aylir at her home address."

"Gotchamutherfuckers."

"Give me that note book, and stay here with the scum."

The teams' leader heads to the lobby of the building and the copier.

"Has everything been catalogued?"

"Yes, sir."

"OK, call for the wagon to transport these bags-of-shit back to our precinct. We'll wait for them arrive."

"What do you know about the murders at the rave a few weeks ago?"

"My team covered the disturbance, the DEA and local Task Force had requested our assistance. I spoke to Ray Martani. He invited us to the party. Detective Hinton thought that the men, who were murdered at the club were the same ones that had committed the murder and robbery of $50,000 at *Neighborhood Legal & Financial Services*. My guess is that, because these were the same guys and they were now dead, Lieutenant Hinton closed the investigation. But, that is just my guess."

"What do you know about any discs or other computer software that was removed from Mr. Ranck's establishment?"

"Nothing. I suggest you speak to Mr. Ranck. I know he took his wife's murder very personally, and wanted to help Lieutenant Hinton as much as possible."

"Who is Amanda Balfour Fulton?"

"I believe she is or was the wife of Mr. Fulton?"

"Why was Mr. Fulton a patron of Mr. Ranck's establishment?"

"I believe he was seeking a divorce from his wife, Amanda."

In the IAD game of cat and mouse, the mouse gives the cat what they both know from the files, plus a taste more to send the cat scurrying off in the wrong direction. Click. The tape recorder is turned off. The sound reverberates in the stark room

"Lieutenant, let me tell you what we know. We know that you and your team have taken an inordinate, unwarranted, and unauthorized interest in the robbery murder at Mr. Ranck's establishment. We know you and your team have devoted many hours investigating the robbery murder even after the investigation was closed by a very thorough Detective. By taking this time and the resources of the department, you have improperly used the financial aspect of your responsibility. We could have your suspended, and give your team members ten day rips for the abuse of trust. And don't use that bullshit about helping your pal Jimmy Ranck. That little shit defended scum against the police. He is no friend of the department. I think you know more about Lieutenant Brown's murder, or you have your suspicions. So, what I am going to do is tell you to cease and desist in your investigation of the murders of Mrs. Ranck, Mr. Fulton, Mr. Netter and Lieutenant Brown. Because your activities have hit our radar screen, we must advise One PP. So, if you value your job and pension, stop. Now! You're off the hook for the time being."

"Yes Sir. One last thing; does the department have contingency plans to control the vast amount of Ecstasy that is about to hit the streets? I mean, I hear it will splash down all up and down the East Coast. When that happens, death and destruction will follow. Then, my team will get very, very busy. It would be a shame if we were all suspended when the drug wars began. Who would handle our work load? Would you? If the department is aware of this pandemic, we should be ready for it."

Lenz did not flinch, but his forehead began to glisten.

———◦◉◦———

When the transport wagon arrived at the Queens Borough Precinct 15, there were three camera crews waiting. The faces of the teams in black were hidden by masks. The perps' faces were not. Many questions and a lot of 'no comment' were heard. The spokesman for the department was there and announced a bust of a very important crime ring as the bad guys were hustled into the hold pen.

"Tony, we did it. You and your photos were spot on. The judge had no problem issuing a warrant, and we made a huge haul of guns and surveillance equipment. You should have seen the treasure: automatic weapons, street sweepers, Desert Eagles, sawed-off sand and enough ammunition to equip a small third world army. If they are Feds, they will stop their activities. If they are rogues, they will go to jail. In either case my team and I will get commendations, medals and maybe pay bumps. Plus, we really pissed them off by taking for ever to get them to the house, where the media was waiting. The big plus is that we retrieved a note book loaded with information that may help you. I vouchered the note book, but not the copies of the pages. I'll currier them to you now, before my shower. Oh, yeah, one last item. The bad guys all had cell phones. I will have our technical people unlock the systems and retrieve the speed dial and last called numbers. That will take a

day. I'll get the information over to you then. I'll send it to you. How did things go with Lenz? He is such a prick. Call me when you have a chance. Hang tough buddy."

———⸱◉⸱———

Sergeant Luis Morales. Tony owes his buddy big time. Desert Eagles are the same cannons that killed Pam and the rest at the store.

"Sir, it's a Melissa Razdarovich for you."

"Hello, Mrs. Razdarovich, how can I help you?"

"Lieutenant, I would like to discuss a personal matter with you. You have always been a trusted advisor to my family. And while the matter is not life or death, it does require that I seek your counsel."

"Yes Mrs. Razdarovich. What is personal matter you would like to discuss?"

"I'd rather not discuss the issue on the telephone. Could you meet with me after work?"

"Yes. Where would you like to meet?"

"I'd feel comfortable if we met at my home. Is that satisfactory?"

"Well, I guess. At what time?"

"Can you be here at 6:30?"

"Yes. See you then."

Newly installed telephone bugs keep conversations vague and stilted. For the next few hours, Tony has little time for anything else, but paper shuffling and comprehending the scheduling of his week by the brass. He calls a team meeting.

"IAD claims we have spent way too much time on our clandestine investigation. They have threatened us with harsh reprisals if we don't cease and desist. So, I can't ask you to continue. That would jeopardize your careers. In fact, I am asking you to stop, and let me do the heavy lifting. I'll take the heat and the punishment."

The silence is disquieting.

"LT, I am going to speak for only myself. But, that's bullshit. You and I know there is something very wrong with the murders and what they really represent. We are lifting rocks and the bugs are getting bigger, uglier and slimier. In for a dime. In for a dollar."

"Thank you Chris."

"That goes for both of us, too, sir"

"I am honored that you three are willing to take this risk. If we fail, maybe we can all get jobs flipping burgers."

"Now for some good news. I contacted my friend in DC, and she told me that, as of 7 am today, Treasury was stone-walling all requests about personnel files. Obviously, they know something. But, my friend was able to back-channel to a friend of hers and learn that Tim Martin, Amanda Balfour and Rufus Fulton were all in the same section, under the leadership of William Donovan. It seems that Mr. Donavan died this year in an automobile accident. So the trail ends there. We have the connection. We just don't know what it means."

"Great. There was a raid this morning in Queens. The Anti-Crime Task Force raided a warehouse on Northern Boulevard and unearthed a cache of weapons, some of which are now being tested by our ballistics department for a possible match to the guns used in the robbery-murder. The second find is a notebook, the pages of which were couriered to me and I am now turning them over to you for your expert analysis. You will see initials, dates and addresses. Jimmy Ranck was under surveillance. We need to know who else was being watched etc, etc. I believe there is a connection between the spook squad operating in Queens and this mess that includes Jimmy, Rufus, Amanda and Los Hores. But, please remember that you are not working on this work. Take the material home, work on your personal computers, create files and send those files to the entire team including me at our homes. And, thanks. Really, thanks."

The taxi ride to Mt. Sinai in the heat of summer and the frantic rush hour traffic of the East Side is a respite after the shit storm of the day Tony had. When the cabbie announces the arrival at the hospital and breaks into Tony's reverie, he is almost reluctant to exit the cab. Dr. Strate is on the floor.

"Dr., I am Lieutenant Tony Sattill."

"Nice to meet you."

"Will you tell me how Jimmy is doing?"

"You are not next of kin."

"There is no next of kin. I am as close as to Jimmy as anyone alive . . . and I am a New York City Police Lieutenant."

"Walk with me to the sun room. The cancer has spread throughout his body. He has a very short time to live and that time will be excruciatingly painful. Therefore, I have prescribed a regimen that provides nourishment and relieves the intense pain."

"Very short time. What does that mean in layman's terms?"

"A few days at most. Perhaps only hours."

"Is he able to communicate with me if I go into the room?"

"He has asked for you frequently. You may see him now."

The room is dimly lit. The pumps and pings maintain a slow background rhythm to the raspy breathing coming from the bed. Jimmy has become so small, so beaten that he appears to be shrinking into the bed's mattress.

"Jimmy, it's Tony. Can you hear me?"

The head nods slightly.

"I'll talk. You listen. Here is the latest news. We got the guys who were spooking you. My guess is that they are Feds. We embarrassed them in the press. We learned that Al Netter was the mole at your place. He may have been ghosting Rufus Fulton since they both lived in Seattle. Or he was working for Los Hores. One point. Two leads. We're still trying to fully understand the ramblings on Rufus Fulton's disc, but we will follow the money. Los Hores is deeper into this than we initially thought. I think they are connected to your spooks. We are obviously on the right path or paths, because IAD is up our ass and is threatening to suspend us. They're getting heat from somewhere, because they have never had an original thought. So the brass is aware. If they are aware, how did they learn? Not from the bottom up. The top down. That means Feds. There is going to be a big splash of Ecstasy on our street very soon. The local PDs in other cities know. But, no one at the top has set a game plan. It could be they know the place and time for the big drop and can stop the distribution before it starts. Somehow, someway I think these elements and people are all connected. The leads are so diverse and they all are collaterally connected. I just don't know how they are connected. But, we are getting closer."

Jimmy raises his boney right hand. The veins are a deep blue seem to be bulging through the skin. He squeezes Tony's hand and smiles. His lips move ever so slightly. Tony leans toward Jimmy's mouth to hear. The voice is frailer than the body.

"Kill 'em. Kill 'em all."

Silence. Jimmy's grip loosens, and Tony leaves the room. The sight, sound and smell of death are behind him. Revenge is his command.

Confession

Dateline Tehran, Iran

Bombs and Gun Fire Kill Eight Scientists

At approximately *midnight local time, car bombs and a withering hail of automatic arms fire destroyed eight homes and killed all, who were sleeping at the time. The deceased residents were all involved in the Iranian government's nuclear energy program. All eight adult males were scientists. Four of the adult females were laboratory employees. There were twenty children killed. Six guards were killed also. Somehow, some group was able to penetrate the tight security surrounding the compound in which the eight families lived, and cause the carnage. This is the second attack on people involved in the government's program, which many believe is designed to produce nuclear warheads for rockets. The Iranian government insists that the program is designed to produce energy and to fuel expansion of its nascent manufacturing sector. A spokesperson for the government stated, "We understand that there are nations big and small that wish to restrict our financial growth and keep us a third world country so that they may look down on us and take advantage of us. Their vicious attacks and the slaughter of innocents will not deter us. In fact,*

*their attacks will strengthen our resolve. We are justified in our use
of a swift and sure response to the nation or nations that invaded our
sovereign soil to kill our people. Allah Akbar." This is a breaking
story. More to follow.*

The doorman acknowledges Tony, calls to the
penthouse, walks Tony to the elevator and keys him up.

The elevator door opens onto a panorama of fine
wood paneling, oriental rugs, large potted plants, art, both
paintings and sculptures, overstuffed leather furniture,
and a huge fireplace. All of this pales in comparison
to his beautiful hostess. This looks vaguely like a high
end private men's club. Even the woman seems to fit.
Obviously, she had nothing to do with the décor. She is
the center piece. While Tony had been in Melissa's inner
sanctum, he had never been to her home.

"It's nice to see you Lieutenant. Welcome to my
home."

"Thank you Mrs. Razdarovich. It's nice to be here."

Melissa inserts a key into a panel beside the elevator,
the doors close and the car is whisked away. She spins,
wraps he arms around Tony and kisses him deeply.

"OK. Enough formalities. Would you like a drink?
You better say yes, because I already poured you one."

"Yes."

"Are you OK? I mean you look drained and sad."

"I just came from Jimmy Ranck's room at Mt Sinai.
He is dying. Very soon. And this damned investigation is
becoming wider and wider and more and more confusing.
I just can't get my arms around it."

"Care to talk about it?"

"I can't. You're a civilian. And, even if I could talk to
you about the case, I wouldn't know where to begin or

if I were telling you everything I know, because I don't know what I know and don't know."

"Well, that was convoluted."

"This drink tastes good and I like the effect. What are you drinking?"

"The same, just in a tall glass with water and a lot of small ice chips."

"Heathen. Water and a lot of ice. You obviously don't appreciate great single malt."

She got the desired response; a smile and hyperbolic anger. They walk arm in arm to the couches. She motions him to sit opposite her. Melissa is dressed in a casual, but properly tailored slacks and a top meant to resemble a running suit. Her feet are shod in some type of house slipper. Her hair is pulled back and her ears glisten with diamonds that match the very large tennis bracelet, and single pendant hanging from her neck. She is the modern Queen of Sheba. He is her footman.

"On the telephone, you said you had a personal matter you wished to discuss. That you needed my guidance. I am here. How can I help?"

"First things first. Have you eaten dinner?"

"No."

"Then let us venture into the kitchen and see what Rosita left for us before she took the night off. Black beans, yellow rice and shredded pork. All we have to do is heat and eat. What do you think, Lieutenant? Should we preheat the oven to 300 or 350? Should we cook the dinner for 20 minutes or 30 minutes? I don't often get into this room to work, so I am a bit rusty."

Tony is amused at this little-girl-lost type of flirting.

"I'd recommend 300 for 45 minutes."

"That will give us time for more drinks."

"And to discuss, what you wanted to discuss."

"Ah, yes ever the policeman. Well, here goes. I think Lucky is in some sort of trouble. I'm not sure what kind, but my gut feeling is that he is in trouble."

"How do you come to this conclusion?"

"Well, as you know. He is opening a bank in London. I don't think he wanted to do this. I think he was pushed into it. There were several times over that past year that he has bitched about the opening, and how it was sapping time away from the core clients of the bank. Those clients, who made the bank and all who manage it very rich. He seemed to fear losing these clients to one or another of the other private banks in the city. And with a break in the damn, the water would flow out of the reservoir. I don't know who or what was pushing into this international dalliance, but it was eating him up. Particularly since he had to go to London to take care of all the details. It seemed as if he could not trust anyone else with the work, not even Bob Linder, Lucky's right hand toady. Everything had to be handled in secret by the great tsar Razdarovich. And, yes I don't love my husband, but I do fear for his life."

"I am afraid that banking is beyond my ken. Have you spoken to Bob Linder?"

"Yes, and he is in the dark as usual. The man is hapless and hopeless. If it weren't for slip-on shoes, he couldn't get dressed. Can't you do something? Can't you go through channels and they say, and find out more than I suspect."

"Melissa, Lucky's bank is Lucky's bank. People bank at a private bank, because it is private. They don't want that privacy broken, and they trust the bank president to mindful of that. Lucky is used to that world. He thrives in it. I'm sure his secrecy, as well as his concern for potential loss of clients is part of his wiring. Is there anything else?"

"Yes. In the few weeks before he left for London. Lucky was becoming almost affectionate. On more than one occasion, he brought me flowers, and we shared a quite dinner before he went back to work. He never worked here, although his home office is a replica of the one he has down town. Do you want to see?"

"Why single this out? Lucky was your husband. It seems to me that he was behaving like a husband."

"But we have not slept together for over six months. When a job becomes that demanding it falls into the category of mistress. I know he did not have a mistress. I also know he visited hookers. Not street girls, but expensive call girls. He would meet them at his office at night. When his lust was slaked, he would come home and sleep in the guest room or on the couch. He claimed he did not want to disturb me. He didn't want me to smell the other woman. How do I know all this? I had him tailed and I have photos of his liaisons. Let's eat. Care for a beer. We have Rolling Rock."

Melissa's demeanor has gone from coquette to wronged wife. The meal is savored slowly due to the spices and its heat. The beer is ice cold and it burns the palette nearly as much as the food. They pick in silence.

"When is Lucky due back?"

"Not tonight."

"I assumed so, but when do you expect him to return to New York?"

"Actually, he is a few days late. He was due back Friday. He e-mailed me that he had run into a few snags and had to delay his departure by a week. So, I guess he'll return this Friday. I am sure he found someone or ones to help him relax after I hard day at the office."

"Melissa, I am not being condescending. But I think you are being overly worrisome. When Lucky returns, everything will get back to normal."

"Thanks a lot. I don't like normal with him. I like normal with you. Perhaps you're right. Now on to the long festering sore. What does my father want you to do about me?"

"I told you, he wants me to dig into his alleged corruption. So far I have uncovered nothing, as I reported to him on Sunday. What makes you think he wants me stalking you or digging into your life? Have you done something wrong or something that would make him feel you were in trouble or danger?"

The toothpaste was out of the tube. Melissa was silent.

"His probing questions and sideways glances lead me to suspect that he suspects there is something wrong with my marriage. On more than one occasion, he has grilled me about my physical condition. And he and mother have stopped asking about the possibility of grandchildren. It's not like them to give up on that subject."

"Maybe, just maybe, they love you and care about your safety and well-being. Plus, they respect your life's decisions and privacy. Heaven forbid they might just treat you as an adult. What about your physical condition?"

"Well during the past year, I have had a few nasty falls and bumps. I seem to be preoccupied, and not paying attention to the dangers of doors, steps and floors. Nothing serious. But, my parents have taken this to be a sign of some kind. A sign of what, I don't know. So, it would not surprise me if daddy asked you to keep an eye on me. He doesn't know about us, so he would assume that asking an upstanding police Lieutenant for a deeply personal favor is the best way to get to the bottom of his suspicions."

"If he is worried about his daughter, he can ask her directly."

"He got to where he is by rarely being direct. His middle name should be circuitous."

"Have you ever spoken to him about Lucky's anxiety about the international expansion of the bank?"

"I may have mentioned it once or twice in passing."

"OK. Here is a wild concept. Suppose your father is cognizant of Lucky's anxiety, as well as his passion for life and success. This creates turmoil. Then he sees the physical manifestation of his daughter's clumsiness, which is created by preoccupation with her husband's turmoil. But, he misinterprets the manifestation to be injuries caused by a bellicose bully, of whom he was not particularly fond."

"You are way off base."

"I told you it was a wild concept. But, maybe not as wild as we both think, given the love between a father and daughter."

Melissa is stone quiet. She stares at her half-empty plate. Then takes the green beer bottle and gulps it empty. When their eyes meet again, there are tears welling in hers. Her shoulders a slumped in the style of submission.

"Sometimes he hits me. Sometimes he shoves me. It's never a lot, nor is it frequent. Only after he has had a particularly bad time for a few days in a row. Then he drinks too much, and becomes pathetic and violent. Once he has hit me, he cries and apologizes profusely. The next day he buys me a very expensive gift. Sometimes we go away for a long weekend. Vale. Paris. Lisbon. He swears he'll never do it again. But he does and the cycle continues. Do you know what I suspect? I suspect that he slaps around his hookers so he won't slap me around. That would explain the long gaps between my accidents. How is that for a wild concept?"

"Very wild. Has he sought help? I mean counseling and not hookers."

"No. If he sought help that would be an admission of vulnerability and the Razdarovich's are not vulnerable. Ask his mother, the iron grand dame. Ask his sister, the freezer. I urged him to seek help, and he punched me in the stomach. So I decided not to bring up the subject again. I let him have his dalliances as a way to blow off steam. Better that than for me to chip more teeth on the floor. I even leave town for some charity so he can play hard. This is my way of controlling the situation."

"That's not control. That's a bad coping skill. As long as you stay in this house, and in his world, you are at risk. If he will not accept counseling as a method of enlightenment and self improvement, then you must extricate yourself from this situation to save your life. Your father suspected as much and now I know."

"A divorce will crush him. It will drive him over the edge."

"Staying married will kill you more likely sooner than later. You have got to move out of this place and in with your parents. Today or tomorrow."

Melissa is trembling, but she steels herself for action. Tony has stepped way over the line. He is not a marriage counselor. He is not a lawyer. He is Melissa's lover. Whatever advice he gives to her is deeply colored by this fact. He has a stake in her actions. He is motivated by feelings toward her and professional responsibility to her father. He is conflicted and compromised.

"Help me clean up. You are right. I almost hate to admit it but you are right. I'll go home to my parents tomorrow."

"And see an attorney. A really good one. Someone, who is so vicious, he or she would take the watches off the dead after a street shoot out."

A small smile appears on her lips.

"You scrape, I'll rinse and the dishwasher will do the rest. I'll tell Rosita to take her things. I'll put her up in a hotel for a few weeks."

Melissa returns the covered large casserole to the refrigerator. She slinks over to Tony and embraces him with all the passion of slave who has been freed. Then she kisses him. It seems to never end. Tony feels the tears on her face and he licks them. She kisses his neck and rubs her body against his, undulating for a different kind of passion.

"Follow me."

They head to the master bedroom, which has been hers alone for too long. Clothes are pulled from two bodies and replaced with long powerful kisses. The two who will become one, tumble into bed. Once horizontal, Melissa slides to Tony's loins and proceeds to devour him. He tries to pull her away and reciprocate, but she is climbs onto him. She will not be denied. He is to lie back and serve. She writhes around and around, and up and down. Suddenly she snaps back, straight up, and her pounding becomes frenetic. The soft sounds give way to loud moans and one final shriek. Her physical and emotional release is experienced thrice before Tony limps into the morning light.

He doesn't read the paper, because getting to the office early allows Tony clear time to plan the day. This is often a futile activity, because some big event or call from the brass disrupts the plan. The telephone ring split the silence. Ballistics reported no match of the Desert Eagles used in the murder and those found in Queens. Damn another rock with just dirt beneath it. He checks his personal computer and sees a note. Attached is a list of telephone numbers, many of which have area codes outside New York City. He spots Atlanta, DC, Virginia. He writes down all forty numbers. As his troops arrive with their pricey latte grandes in hand, the call comes in from the field. Body, found at the Aksum Mission. Female black. The CAT team responds. The four head uptown in a van with all their gear. Two squad cars guard the entrance. More arrive simultaneously with CAT.

"Lieutenant Sattill and the CAT team from the 2-7. What do we have here?"

"Female. Stabbed and slashed. She was butchered. Slaughtered like an animal, cut up for sale. No ID. I have never seen anything like this. There are body parts all over and gallons of blood. I have never seen that much blood from one body. Sir, if you and your team would follow me."

The small group walks rapidly down a series of halls and down two flights of stairs to the tunnels that link the buildings of the Mission. The tunnels are well lit and very clean. Cleaner than the streets outside, and much quieter.

"This is a cross roads of two tunnels. Watch your step it's an incredible mess."

Most of her was there. The crime scene did look like the floor of a butcher shop. There were body parts strewn. A finger here. A foot there. Where were her arms? Her head seemed to be partially removed from her neck and trunk. It was tilted back like a candy dispenser.

"Who found the body?"

"A maintenance man. Bill Smith. He threw up down the hall. You can see his messes in several places. I don't think he contaminated the crime scene. He is sitting against the wall."

"OK. Get him out of here. The riding Detective will want to talk to him as soon as he gets here. My team will gather evidence from the scene. Please secure the entire area at all the tunnel entrances. Do you know who is the riding Detective from the local precinct?"

"Yes, Sir. Detective Hinton will be the riding investigator."

"Shit."

"Sir?"

"Nothing officer, it's just that I haven't seen this much bodily destruction in years. We'll be here when Detective Hinton arrives."

The team is thorough, diligent and fast. Photos are taken and video is shot from every angle. All of the visual evidence will be downloaded into the system ten minutes after the team leaves the scene and returns to the van. Observations are verbally fed into recorders to be down loaded and transformed into text. The system is on the real edge. Blood samples are taken. The National DNA Database will be checked. No weapon is found. There are some minor scuff marks coming from the long hall to the team's right. These are filmed.

"Well, Lieutenant Sattill. I see your team has already catalogued the physical evidence. I'll review it soon, I'm sure. What else has your trained eye seen?"

Catalogued, my ass. The arrogant fuck! There can be no investigation, by a riding Detective without the collection of the physical evidence and the CAT's analysis of possible meanings and implications. Old school still hates new school.

"Detective Hinton, it's good to see you. There are the scuff marks coming down the hall."

"So, you think she was dragged down here and then slaughtered?"

"That may be so. Or she could have walked down here with a known associate and then been killed. Or she could have been carried down here and killed. Or the scuff marks could be simply the residue of an earlier dragging. A dolly with bad wheels. I'll leave the thinking part up to you."

"Thank you. Sattill, I've got to get to Mr. Smith and see if he's strong enough to answer some basic questions. We'll be in touch, I'm sure."

Beneath the thin veneer of cordiality, Tony knows Hinton is seething. Hinton blames Tony for the heat he took for closing the robbery-murder hastily. Did he take a rip for dereliction of duty and failure to maintain the public trust?

"LT, I found something interesting. See, the marks on this arm? I think they are a tattoo. I isolated the area and took some separate shots. Whatever it is, it is not English."

"Be careful gathering up the parts. Make sure we leave nothing behind. The ME will try to put Ms. Humpty Dumpty back together again. I'm going to walk the halls.

Meet you back at the van. Also, better take blood samples from all four corners of the pool. There seems to be too much blood for one person."

Tony heads down the first corridor. He reaches a locked gate after about one hundred feet. The lock is clean. Too clean. No scratch marks. No dust or dirt. Was it cleaned recently? How recently? The hall beyond the gate is well worn up to two doors that look like they belong to storage rooms. There are vents in the doors. People have access to these storages areas, but not beyond. If this is a thoroughfare for the residents of the Mission, why do they not have access beyond this gate? Or is that just for today. Why today? He turns and heads down the hall to the other end. The same scenario. Tony returns to the intersection and turns to his right. He examines the scuff marks. They were not made by a bad-wheeled dolly. They were not made by the vic. The marks appear to have been made by larger feet. Male feet? He takes out his pocket knife, scrapes a little of the scuffs, and places the shavings in a small plastic evidence bag. His dad always told him to carry a pocket knife and a pencil. Even in the computer era, the pencil is a priceless backup. The pocket knife has so many uses it boggles Tony's mind. His team jokes about these two workday essentials to life as a man. The scuff marks seem to start at the gated end of the hall. Another gate. Another clean lock. Storage rooms beyond. The fourth hall is a repeat. All the passageways are clean and well-lighted. It is almost as if they are mopped and wiped daily. Maybe these are part of the therapy of rebuilding so endemic to this place.

"I have something to add to the picture. I took some of the scrapings from the floor for forensics to analyze."

"We already entered our scrapings."

Tony smiles the smile of a father, who is witnessing the growth of his child.

———◦(◦)◦———

At the house, the messages await. Drivel. Drivel. Hospital . . . *Lieutenant Sattill, we regret to inform you that Mr. James Ranck died this morning at 5:35 am. His file indicates that he had no next of kin. You were noted as the one to advise upon his demise. Please contact us as soon as possible to make arrangements for the disposition of the body.*

Tony's body turns cold and stiff. A knot grows in his belly, and tears well in his eyes. A soldier has fallen. Struck down by an unseen internal enemy. The voracious eater has a new meal. Now, the soldier's comrade must be the grave digger.

"I have to go to Mt. Sinai. If you need me, call my cell. Otherwise, let's get today's case processed and off our desks."

This cab ride takes a month. The morgue is in the basement. Tony announces himself, flashes tin and signs the visitor log. He sees people moving toward and around him. He shakes someone's hand. He speaks, but hears nothing. It's like he was on the beach and watching the big waves crash, the noise of the outside world is overwhelmed. This woman leads him to the laboratory with the walls of locker doors. She checks her notes and opens door number 134-M. Jimmy has become a filed thing. The woman pulls the slide out of the wall and there he is. Pale, cold, and very small. Like a sickly child at sleep. But this child of God is dead. There are forms to complete. The attending official suggests a funeral home. Tony agrees and fills in the blanks as to date, time, and place of burial. Next week and next to Pam.

Another funeral. Another moment for Tony to verbally reflect on a friend's life. Unfortunately, he was getting to be good at this. This was a really shitty day.

Who's There?

*T*he explosions shredded the lock and the inverted hinges. This action was followed immediately by a battering ram and three stun grenades. Before the people inside the large room had a chance to look up from their morning coffee, the twelve black masked invaders were poking automatic weapons at them.

"Freeze. You are under arrest. We have a warrant to search these premises and any vehicles in the nearby vicinity for controlled substances and weapons."

There was Lenz barking and growling like a wolf. Everything and everyone else were silent slow moving shadows. I obeyed and shuffled my feet as if I were going to the Dachau showers. All I could hear were the screaming commands to hurry. I offered no resistance.

Another violent dream. It goes with the territory.

———◆———

"Detective LaRue, this is Lieutenant Sattill of CAT in the 2-7."

"Good morning, sir. How can I help you?"

"It's the other way. I want to help you. You caught the murder of Lieutenant Carlita Brown. I have some information that may be of help to your investigation."

"I'm listening."

"Hell, I don't even care if you are recording. On the night Lieutenant Brown was murdered, she and I attended the club called Caliente. At the club, I became aware of the fact that she was snorting blow in the ladies' room and that by then end of the evening she was frightened . . . almost paranoid. She sought my protection from someone or something. I don't know the source, but this fear was apparent after she danced with someone, a club regular perhaps, she knew. As you know the club is the personal property of Diego Seville, with whom Brown had a great deal of contact. I am not sure if all the contact was professional."

"So far you have added nothing to our investigation, except these are the same facts you denied in our meeting. Can you say perjury?"

"Get off your fucking horse and allow me to continue. I say non-professional contact because of the medallion on her necklace. Have you found the necklace that was ripped from her neck by the killer? If not, I will give you a description. Go to the headquarters of Los Hores and speak to Diego. Behind his desk is a painting. The medallion on Brown's necklace is a replica of the art work. My guess is that when you find her necklace, and you'll find the killer. Oh, by the way, have you spoken to Lieutenant's Brown's lover, Kurt Strabel? He is on the job. He may be of assistance in your investigation. He is jealous lover, who could be violent. That's about all I know. If I can be of assistance in the future, call me."

That call will give IAD new places to look for criminals and reasons. One way or another, Lenz will have a perp. Peck's bad boy strikes again.

"LT, we heard from the ME. Beyond the pro forma, Dr. Death notes that the woman was pregnant. About 6-8 weeks. The fetus was also slashed. It was purposefully killed inside the woman. Whoever murdered the woman was damned vicious. I'll bet because she was pregnant. The ME pulled the woman's and the fetus's blood samples and submitted them to the National DNA Database. The samples were sent to Atlanta for identification and cross matching. Dr. Death expects to hear from the Feds in a week, maybe sooner."

Tony calls Detective Hinton and alerts him as to the revisit. Hinton is agitated, and promises to meet Tony there. Old school is really pissed.

"I think I'll pay a visit to the Mission and the crime scene to make sure you all did your jobs properly. Or if you missed something."

"LT, you may want to see this."

We take you live to the Federal Building in downtown Manhattan where the Federal Drug Enforcement Agency is conducting a press conference . . . Today, the coordinated efforts of the Drug Enforcement Agency and local Drug Task Forces in six major Eastern cities confiscated drugs with a street value of nearly 8 million dollars The drugs confiscated at major points of distribution included ecstasy, cocaine and heroin. We are proud to have intercepted this large supply before it reached the dealers on the streets and our children in New York, Philadelphia, Baltimore, New Haven, Providence and Boston. With this single strike we have inflicted a severely damaging blow to the drug trade in these cities, because we were high up in the distribution chain. Now I'll take questions.

"That explains a great deal. That explains the big splash. The X is now in the hands of the Feds. What's next, LT?"

"Brendan, Jesus-fucking-Christ this PR stunt only explains that the DEA and local task forces found drugs . . . what it does not explain is who has the money for the drugs . . . the manufacturer gets paid by a single distributor, who gets paid by the distributors in these six cities . . . nothing is provided on consignment . . . the guys that got busted have paid money for the drugs that they were going to resell . . . now they are out a boat load of cash . . . do you believe the overhyped value of the bust? . . . my guess is that the real street value is closer to 4 million and my guess is that the street vendors collectively paid out a million that they will never see again and the original source received about 250 K . . . you know what an iceberg looks like . . . the reality of the evil destructive bottom bears no resemblance to the visual top, all beautiful and blue white . . . it is all the ugly slime covered bottom nine-tenths . . . and if these jamoaks are stupid enough to rat out the seller, they will be dead before next week . . . the Colombians and the Russians operate that way . . . now the Feds have to find the money . . . we do not have to follow the money, the nearly insignificant 50 large that started us into the whole mess that has gotten so many people killed there are too many unanswered questions to think that this is the end . . . wait forget about the money . . . we have to follow the deaths . . . it's like *Matryoshka* . . . the Russian dolls that fit into each other . . . you see the outer one and you think you have what is meant for you to have . . . then you think there is something inside, because you can hear it rattling around, but you can't open the doll . . . .

then there is a twist and the second doll emerges, but still you think there is something inside . . . each doll lets you believe you have discovered something of value . . . each has a secret way of opening it . . . a twist, a button to push, a point of leverage, something allows you to open the outside layer and discover the what is inside . . . while they all resemble each other they meant to lead you to the core . . . the precious stone or gold coin or key . . . in this case the core is the cause . . . the dolls are the numerous murders we have uncovered, each is connected somehow . . . the real reason, the gold coin, rattles inside the final doll . . . it is all meant to trick, confuse, discourage, and send you off in different direction, unless you can find the lever or button or twist to get inside the enigma, wrapped in a mystery . . . I believe that the fifty large played only a minor part in the purchase . . . or who made the purchase, from whom and how big was the initial purchase . . . it worked this way . . . the gunners were sent to kill Rufus Fulton and rob the store of everything electronic . . . the guys who ordered the hit knew that Rufus knew something that was dangerous knowledge if it became public . . . that's is the only reason the shooters were there . . . once Rufus was killed, and the electronic information turned over, the kingpins decided it was time to eliminate everyone involved in the slaughter . . . cut off all possible leads back to them . . . and that is what they did . . . every time we come to a murder . . . the store, the rave, the *shlub* of a guard, we think or we are supposed to think that we have solved a major crime . . . all we have done is to come face-to-face with the intensity of desire to keep secret what is beginning to leak . . . but we still hear the coin . . . it's not the money it's the man . . . Rufus and

Amanda are the key . . . they are linked . . . the Feds are involved, so the underlying cause must be big . . . now we have to find out who was connected to him whether he knew of the connection or not . . . find out who he was working for . . . who else knew what he was doing . . . we must open all the dolls to find what's inside . . . we need names and connections . . . make good use of your time this morning call these numbers from the secure telephone downstairs and outside on pay phones and record the conversations . . . these are the numbers from the cell phones confiscated from inhabitants of R&B Construction . . . I need to know who they are and how they are connected to this entire mess . . . we need to learn more about the root cause of the killings from Pam, to the guard, to the Euro-trash at the club, to the bodies we found at the Mission . . . we have to dig deeper to the center, because I think all of death and destruction is directly related to something very big . . . why Jimmy's place, who is Rufus Fulton, what did he know and where will that lead us . . . I want to know why a good friend was murdered . . . why, why, why?"

Tony can't breathe. His chest has a Sumo wrestler is sitting on it, sweat is pouring from every pore, and he hears only the rush of his blood in his ears driven by the pounding of his heart. His legs are weak and he has to grasp the desk or fall on his face. Those who have witnessed his rant are silent. Too many facts, too little knowledge, and too many people dead. Tony has imploded. But he can't sit. He staggers off to the stairs and his car. The chief warrior must never allow others to see beyond his armor into his frightened soul. All energies are targeted to stealing his humanity against the intrusion of the light of reality. Is it the fear of letting someone in or letting himself out? This battle causes incredible fatigue. Tony slumps forward onto the steering wheel. He sees a tricycle, a flower dress, dark brown hair in a bun, a mother's smile, the sun is shining, the car widow is open, the girl beside him is laughing, she is wearing a paisley blouse, the squad car roars down the road to the florist, the squawk box is crackling with commands, dad is dead. The shape shifting is disturbed by the ringing of his cell phone.

"Lieutenant Sattill, where are you. I thought we were going to meet at the Aksum Mission to review the crime scene. I have been here forty minutes."

"Sorry, Detective. I ran into some office mess. I'm leaving now. I'll be there in twenty minutes."

Tony turns on news radio to hear more about the big bust. Instead he hears:

Assistant District Attorney Joan Kemp announced today the arrest of twelve members of the street gang, Los Hores in connection with the recently announced massive drug bust. The gang and its leader, Diego Seville, were arrested at the gang headquarters, a bodega located at 235 West 167th Street. The raid and arrests went smoothly. No gun fire and no injuries. ADA Kemp also indicated that Seville is implicated in the murder of Lieutenant Carlita Brown of the Gang Task Force. ADA Kemp is quoted as saying that this is a big step toward putting a big crimp in street-level drug dealing in the gang's neighborhood and closing an investigation into the death of one of NYPD's finest woman.

ADA Kemp is making her bones with a big public face . . . drug bust and a cop killer. The city can sleep better tonight.

⋙◈⋘

Hinton is cold. He is hiding his anger at Tony, but not very well.

"Why are we here, Lieutenant?"

"I am here to be sure that my team did everything they were supposed to, so that you have all the crime scene information at your disposal. I asked you here so you could ask me about any detail we can explore for you. Did you determine the truth about the scuff marks?"

"Some type of shoe. I am awaiting the detailed report from your guys."

"Well, it seems that we did the thorough job we have been trained to do. If we can be of assistance beyond our reports, let me know."

Sometimes it's good to be snotty.

"I have one last question, Lieutenant. Does the AC work in your squad car?"

"Yes, why?"

"Nothing really. It's just that you seem to have sweated through your clothes. And you look sickly pale. Are you OK?"

"Fine, Detective. Call me if you need me."

On the way back to the house, Tony stops by his apartment for a change of clothes. He discards the evidence of his vulnerability. His cell phone jangles.

"Sattill."

"LT, I did some digging about the tattoo on the vic's inner arm. It is Arabic of some kind and it means Flower of God. But the really weird part is the Muslim women are forbidden to be tattooed. Therefore, I deduce that this woman was a Muslim wannabe. I was wondering if she could be the former Amanda Fulton? You know Musin Mahmoud. Or someone like her. Was she part of a cult or movement of women, who want to be perceived as Muslim, but are not true believers? And another thing, the ME reports that both of the woman's thumbs and her tongue are missing. This could be a sign that she would be unable to work or speak in the afterlife. Seriously, LT, this is getting very weird."

"To say the least. I'll be back at the house in twenty. I want to meet with all of you in my office. Make sure that everyone is there, Chris."

"Yes, sir."

———◦(◎)◦———

"LT, we have preliminary results back from the lab and from the Feds on the blood at the Aksum Mission murder scene. You thought there was way too much blood for one person. And you were correct. It seems that there was male Caucasian blood mixed with the female Afro-American blood. Can't tell for certain which came first, but I am willing to assume that the male blood was on the floor and the female was killed to cover up the first crime. But, why kill Amanda Fulton. Why at the Mission and where is the male body? Who is the male?"

"Good work, Brendan. When will we have final results on the DNA?"

"Because of the weirdness, Dr. Death ask the Fed lab rats to make this THE top priority. Maybe tomorrow, but two days of sure."

"In the meantime do your best to confirm the female's particulars. And check the usual places . . . dumpsters, burial grounds on Staten Island and New Jersey for dumps jobs for the male's body. Also ask the Coast Guard if they have any new floaters."

"I'm on it."

"Anything else."

"My calls came up empty."

"I got answers on all but one of mine. It rang twelve times. No pick up. No answering machine. So I called back in the evening. Still no answer. No machine. I think this one warrants a face-to-face."

"Do you know the address?"

"Yes, Sir."

"Good. Go now. Pay a visit to the address. Talk to the person at the other end of the line. Be prepared to enter the quarters. Take backup."

"Folks. Time is of the essence and we have very little of it before One PP closes us down and we all go on two-week vacations. Chop. Chop."

"What about you, LT?"

"Jamie and I are going to pay an oh-so friendly visit to the Aksum Mission. There seems to be more involvement than simply a crime scene up there."

Approaching the entrance to the Mission seems very different without Hinton being there to intercept Tony. Jamie and Tony are met by security at the arched entrance to the fortress. Security is not visibly armed, but the two very tall, very black, thin men are stern. Almost menacing. Their heads are shaved and they are so clean they glisten. Dressed in white shirts, buttoned at the collar, black pants, and combat boots. The shirts and pants are starched enough that the creases could cut bread. Their pants are tucked into black combat boots very well shined. Their belts are wider than would be required for the pants and shirts. The belts resemble garrison belts constructed to carry a pistol, baton, pepper spray and handcuffs. These are belts worn by prison guards. While one guard stands at ease army style in front of the car, the other approaches Tony's side of the car and motions to lower the window.

"Good afternoon. I am Lieutenant Anthony Sattill and this is Detective Jamie . . ."

"What is the purpose of your visit?

"We would like to see Makeda."

"Do you have an appointment?"

"We do not. This is more like a social call than an official police intrusion."

"She is always very busy."

"Please let her know we are here."

"I doubt that she has the time for a social visit. She is always very busy."

"We will only take fifteen minutes from her busy schedule."

"I doubt . . ."

"I would hate to have to drive back downtown and get a warrant, just for a social visit."

"Stay here while I call her office."

"Warrant, LT? Really? You should be ashamed of yourself."

"Jamie, he showed me his and I showed him mine. Mine is bigger, or so he thinks. I won."

"Sir, you may park your car in one of the visitor spaces. Someone will meet you there."

"Thank you."

His English bears an African lilt. At the snap of the security guard's fingers and a nod of his head, the iron gates open. Obviously someone in the guardhouse was watching the entire passion play. Was the other guard armed? The courtyard was nearly a city block in size. Trees, bushes, and a well-manicured lawn were embraced by a circular drive way. There were four visitor spaces; all unoccupied. Tony pulls into the first. His instinct tells him to back into the spot for an expeditious exit. But, he does not want to signal his feelings. Before he turns off the engine, the car acquires two more security guards. From out of nowhere these two simply have appeared. Their attire and demeanor are the same as the guards at the gate. Their hands are on the door handles before Tony and Jamie can reach the handles on their sides. Tony's valet speaks softly.

"Follow us, please"

The four proceed to the entrance. One guard is in front of Tony and Jamie and one behind. The walk is in silence and takes about a minute. At the entrance, the lead guard presses an intercom then steps back to be recognized by someone at the other end of the video feed. The ultra strong, very secure iron gate reverberates and pops open about eight inches. The lead guard grasps the handle and opens the gate, which must weigh a half a ton. What real purpose is served by an interior gate that strong and that secure?

All four enter. The rear guard closes the gate, presses another buzzer and looks up at the camera. His recognition is our cue to continue. The hall is wide, brightly lit, very high, and clean of any items normally associated with large living quarters. No chairs. No couches. No tables. The echoes of four sets of heels on the hardwood floor are disconcerting. No humanity just the noise of shoes clicking. They come to the end of the giant hall. A left turn on to a slightly narrower hall. What was to the right? Tony cannot turn around and gawk. That would be impolite.

"Excuse me, gentlemen. My shoe has become untied."

As he bends to re-lace his shoe, he peers back into the path not traveled. It is dimly lit, but empty. Still no humanity

"Thanks. Carry on."

At the end of the hall there is an elevator. The guard in front stops abruptly and searches for something. He turns to the guard in the rear.

"I have forgotten my key. Do you have yours?"

"Yes. You are a fool for forgetting. Forgetting is not forgiven. I will open the door."

"I implore you to tell no one of my error. It will never happen again. I swear."

"Reporting any dereliction of duty is my duty."

The shoulders of the front guard slump as if he has committed a sin and will be punished. The other guard keys the elevator to our position. In a few seconds the car arrives. But the seconds seem like minutes in the face of the apparent misdeed. The elevator door slides open and the four travelers enter silently. One black in front and one black in back of the two whites. A large human Oreo cookie. The one with the key inserts it into slot with no designation. Is it up or down? The trip is upward. The slow ride is in silence. Tony and Jamie have witnessed an epic of phenomenal proportions during the micro-cosmic of opening an elevator.

The car arrives at the designated landing. The key is re-inserted and the doors open slowly into a well lit ante-chamber decorated with all manner of Ethiopian art and artifacts. A little piece of Africa in Manhattan.

Tony and Jamie are greeted by a young female in a traditional African body wrap with matching head dress. She has a bright smile and eyes. She dismissively motions to the two guards, who disappear back into the elevator followed by closed doors.

"Welcome to the Mission, Lieutenant. Makeda will see you now."

Tony thinks how dismissive this female sentry is of Jamie and the two security guards. Arrogance is a perversion of power. The real power is in serving not abusing. As the three of them walk silently down to the end of the ante-chamber, Tony is awestruck by the paintings of the land, the colorful animal skins, and horns of other trophies. There are no pictures or paintings of the "Lion of Judah", the brave Ethiopian who warned the world about World War II. Strange that such a revered ruler would be absent. There are several large photos of churches hewn from the rocks. Not the face of cliffs, but the top of mountains. Buildings dug into the rocks with steps leading down to the entrance two-three stories from the surface. Tony can easily identify these as churches from Christian crosses engraved on the top. He spots numerous smaller photos of ancient religious artifacts made from wood, stone and leather. Is one of these the true Ark of the Covenant? Perhaps, the chalice from which Christ drank? Tony's imagination is beginning to run wild. His Catholic upbringing does that on occasion. The rug leading up to the double hand-carved black walnut doors is magnificent. Who slept on this rug 2,500 years ago? Tony recognizes the sweet aroma of incense, but not the domestic kind in head shops. This is subtly powerful stuff. As he follow his native guide, her sway and the clicking of the ivory bracelets, are hypnotic. He turns to Jamie. He sees that she sees what he sees. He senses that she senses what he senses. At the double doors, the party of three pauses, while the guide taps gently on a panel to the right of the doors. Are they magical and cannot be touched?

The right hand door opens outward. Strange. Interior doors normally open inward. This opening is one for escape. This is the sanctum sanctorum. The holy of holy places. There in the dark surroundings, beneath two pin spotlights and seated in a large wicker chair strategically placed on a platform is Makeda. On a black walnut slab about four inches thick serving as a desk before her are several stacks of papers, but no lap top or telephone. The rustling of the dashiki indicates that the guide has left. The closing of the door confirms it. The short trip from elevator to wooden door has been a trip. His senses have been played with. But, because he knows it, the alteration has not taken hold.

Cat and Mouse

"**W**elcome. How may we help you? Lieutenant Sattill, it is so nice to see you. I want you to know how much the Mission appreciates your continued support."

"Thank you Makeda. This is detective Jamie . . ."

"Yes, thank you for coming young lady."

Makeda arises from her wicker throne. Her Dashiki is like her flag; blood red, black and brilliant white. Her head wrap does not conceal all her hair. The sparkle of her smile and the twinkle of her eyes speak of a game or drugs. She wears gold and a lot of it. Ten plus bracelets on each for arm, and a large one on each bicep. The etching on the upper arm pieces are repeated on her three-inch gold choker. Is this her crown, her display of ultimate authority and power? From her station of superiority, she rules the roost because she controls the room. The decorations in the room speak of an ancient Christianity. Again, photos of the churches in the rocks, and more artifacts and icons. These icons are in sealed glass display cases. Obviously more valuable than those outside. Probably tied to an alarm system. Then Tony hears the unmistakable breathing of large dogs. Beneath the wood slab, he notices two large muzzles which turn into two large heads of Doberman Pincers. They could be out from beneath the slab and on an intruder or someone who displeases Makeda in about three seconds. After that the miscreant is just so much Alpo.

"Thank you for taking time out of your busy day to accept this unscheduled visit of a friend of the Mission. I wanted make this personal visit to be sure that everything related to the ugly mess in the Mission's basement was handled properly and to your satisfaction. As you may know . . ."

"Yes, I know about the incident. Remember I live here, too."

Abrupt, peeved, and dismissive. Very imperial.

"We at the Mission are pleased with the discretion and professionalism of Detective Hinton and have sent a letter to the Chief of Police stating this. I am not sure what you have to do with the incident."

"We just collect the crime scene facts and report them to the Detective in charge. I wanted to be sure that my squad had not done anything to upset the Mission or offend you."

"No. Nothing was done to add insult to injury. Thank you for asking. Someday, when I am not so busy, I invite you to pay an unofficial official visit. Tour the grounds. See firsthand the good we are blessed to accomplish. I would hope a visit such as that would help you become a greater, stronger supporter."

"I would like that."

"Fine, then it is settled. Call my assistant and set a convenient time for your visit. She will show you out now. I am sorry that I cannot spend more time with you today, but the Mission is my life every minute of every day."

The black walnut doors open and our guide reappears. She smiles faintly and bows her head to Makeda. The back tracing takes ten minutes. Into the car and through the gates.

"Well that was interesting. Like meeting an arrogant chimera. They at the Mission have no love for you, Jamie. Sorry about that. If I had known how rude they would be, I would have done this alone."

"No sweat LT. Did you notice how rich she wants the world to believe she is? I'll bet she wears 15K of gold. And the artwork, furniture and icons? If this is a Mission dedicated to helping the poor and downtrodden, if this is a Mission dedicated to Christian ideals, she has perverted the concepts. She is living the high life on their backs and hiding behind a cross. She acts like the Queen of fucking Sheba. Something just isn't kosher. Really wrong. And her dismissive behavior toward really me pisses me off. I am going to open up the finances of the Mission and Makeda. If I lift enough rocks, I'll probably find snakes and scorpions."

"Be careful. She and the Mission have many friends in high places. The Mayor, and the City Council, as well as the Catholic and Episcopalian dioceses."

"Are you telling me to back off?"

"No, I am asking you to be careful. And before you tell the squad, if you find anything, tell me so we can discuss it."

"Fair enough."

Tony barely sits in his chair when the phone rings.

"Sattill, stay where you are. We need to talk. Now and I mean now!"

The commanding voice of Captain Lenz is harsher than his normal level of threat. Tony pushes away from his desk and puts his head into the squad room.

"Guys, Lenz is making an encore visit. Be on your toes and hide whatever you are working on. Get the shit off your desks."

Tony returns to his emails. Fifteen minutes later Lenz comes barging into the squad room and Tony's office. He did not close the door.

"Sattill, I thought I made myself abundantly clear to stay away from Hinton's case and the Aksum Mission. You are looking at a letter in your file and maybe even a five-day rip. Stay the fuck away. One case is closed and the other is in very capable hands. Capice?"

"Captain, I went to the Mission to be sure that my team had been thorough and had not done anything to upset the residents or Makeda. That's all. And she was told the reason for my visit. She seemed satisfied with the reason. She even suggested that I call her assistant and make an appointment for a formal visit in the near future."

"Don't call. Don't go. Drop your thinly veiled investigation. Now, damn it, now!"

"Yes, sir."

"And that goes for the rest of your squad. Hands off."

"Yes, sir."

"If I have to return on this subject, you will accompany me to IAD headquarters . . . all of you."

"Yes, sir."

Lenz struts out of the office and squad room as if he has just vanquished a foe. Hail to the victor.

"The hell with him."

"I agree, Brendan. Jamie and I obviously struck a very sensitive nerve. Makeda must have dialed One PP before we left the Mission. Any idea what caused such an immediate and virulent reaction."

"Who is IAD investigating? Is Hinton dirty? Is Makeda dirty? Is Hinton in Makeda's pocket? That would get One PP to step on Lenz's toes. Is One PP dirty? A little diversion is always good. Since One PP is hand in glove with the City Commissioners, is a Commissioner dirty?"

"Jamie, that's a lot to ponder. And way above my pay grade. First, we have to get back to the start. Rufus and Amanda Fulton. The robbery. The false leads. Diversions. It all starts there. Does anybody have more information about the real Amanda Fulton?"

Silence.

"I called the Coast Guard, and they informed me that they had pulled a body from some fisherman's nets. The fisherman had acquired the body between Manhattan and Long Island. And since we were the first to call, we won the door prize. They shipped the body to our ME for an autopsy. But they did tell me that it was a male, who had his fingers chopped off, and his teeth removed via a crushed jaw. Obviously, who ever dumped the body wanted it to remain anonymous. Oh, yeah the Coast Guard also said the face, hands and other visible extremities had suffered degrading as a result of hungry sea creatures. So they told me to be cautious with my local seafood orders. They laughed at their little insider joke."

"Chris, call the ME, ask her if she has received the body. If so, we are on our way. If not, ask her to call us when it arrives."

"Already done, sir. She is expecting us. We can just appear."

"Nice work. Let's go."

⸻⸺◉⸺⸻

Morgues are the logical extensions of hospitals; sterile, cold, and foretelling death. There she is Martha, doc, the Chief ME, or Doctor Death. An attractive face often hidden by a mask and plastic shield. An indiscernible body covered by loose fitting scrubs dotted with blood and small body shards. She is eating lunch at her desk. Gawd is she callous.

"What have you found, doc?"

"Well, I know that this male did not go quietly into the night. His fingers were cut off, his jaw was broken and his teeth removed. All ante mortem. He was meant to suffer a great deal. There was water in his lungs, so he drowned. Quite stressful. Another curious item. I found precious little blood in his system. I believe he nearly bled out before he went for a swim. If I were a detective or a Lieutenant of the CAT squad, I would hazard a guess that this murder was payback for some very terrible sin. And, I'd look for a crime scene with a lot of blood."

"I see your point."

"There is something else. Who ever attempted to destroy the recognition factors missed the four teeth that he swallowed during the faux dentistry visit. These four teeth indicate that the vic was not a pauper. He enjoyed the benefits of expensive dental hygiene. Two of the teeth have gold inlays, and two were part of a permanent bridge. So, we have a wealthy male. Now, for the piece de resistance."

The ME pulls back the sheet and Tony gets an eyeful of the chewed, water bloated remains of Latchazar Razdarovich.

"That's Lucky."

"No very unlucky."

"I mean, I believe the body on the table is that of Latchazar Razdarovich, V, President, CEO and majority stock holder in Manhattan Private Bank. The remains of the face are too familiar. How quickly can you get DNA results on the blood you were able to find?"

"Well, I asked the feds to put the two blood types found at the Mission at top of the list. As a bank President, he would have to have his DNA in the system. New anti-terrorist laws after 9-11. So, tomorrow morning by ten. Was he married?"

"Yes."

"Then we'll need his wife or next of kin to make an ID."

"I'll arrange it, at a later date."

"I don't keep bodies in my morgue for longer than a week unless there are extenuating circumstances. Once the DNA results are back, I release the body to the next of kin."

"I said, I'll arrange it. Get me the damned DNA results. I don't want to alarm the wife, unless we are sure."

"Your call."

"Chris, let's go."

"What a mess. Another thing. My brother, Alex, called me this morning. He thinks he is on to something in the gibberish Mr. Fulton left for us to find. He thinks Mr. Fulton was trying to explain some sort of illegal enterprise involving the transfer of funds from one entity to another via a bank. I scheduled an appointment with him in one hour at his place. I thought it wiser to meet him away from prying eyes. We can tell the others if we believe what my brother has to say."

"Why do you say if?"

"Well, Alex has been known to do massive amounts of drugs so he can go on long cyber trips. So, I am not sure what the two grand bought . . . that we can use."

"Let's hope."

One Window

The building was once a brownstone home of some socially acceptable family. Now it is a cluster of run down small apartments that house those new to New York and those existing on the thin line between failure and mediocre success. Chris rings the buzzer for apartment 4-B. No name. Hiding from something or someone. The buzzer responds and the door clicks. The sound of acceptance. The entrance hall that once welcomed home father after a long day's work, once contained a settee, a chair or two and a large brass umbrella stand, is now home to only a trash container. At the top of the wide staircase appears an unshaven head.

"Come on up. You'll have to walk. The elevator has not worked for weeks. Hey Chris, who's your friend? Is he friend or foe?"

"We'll talk when we get to the top of the mountain."

The stairs were once carpeted. Now they are covered with linoleum. The banister on the outer side has been supplemented with a metal rail on the inner. A concession to the building code. The final landing is reached. Chris and Tony head for the open door. Suddenly an unkempt small weasely looking body appears. Hair a mess, dirty stubble of beard, and wrinkled clothes. A far cry from the always freshly shorn cheerful face with clothes cleaned and pressed, Chris. Drugs will produce the former, while a powerful reaction to the drug life will produce the latter.

"Who is the old interloper? I thought we were meeting alone. No outsiders."

"Alex, this is my Lieutenant, Anthony Sattill. He authorized the money I gave to you."

"Ah, my benefactor. Here to extract your pound of knowledge for the pittance you paid."

"Alex, I mean you no harm. I'm here to learn what you have uncovered from the cryptic mess that Chris has been working on. If your information turns out to be useful, I think we might be able to find more work for you . . . off the books."

"The carrot. Where is the stick?"

"There is no stick. We need your help to get to resolve some tricky issues. It's as simple as that."

"Chris, is this guy legit?'

"Yes, he's straight shooter."

"OK, then. Let's begin. Please enter my humble abode."

Tony sees a sty that would be rejected by a pig. A mattress. No sheets. Food containers all over. Some partially covered with dirty clothes. One chair in from of a table that held large and undoubtedly expensive computer with three towers and multiple lines seeming indiscriminately hooked to the unknown. One window covered with brown wrapping paper and a door leading to the bathroom. The kitchen as it is consists of a sink, a half fridge, a small stove. That area of the space contains more food, or what remains of meals. Occasionally, there is movement; the scurrying of cockroaches from one food source to another. And the smell is overpowering. Decaying food and body odor mingle to create the stench of the nearly dead. There is no ventilation in the room. No air movement. Tony goes to the window. It is nailed shut. This guy is a psycho hermit. He could not testify to anything. We have to take his findings and convert into knowledge, we will call our own.

"I'd ask you to sit, but I only have one chair, and it is mine. Stand beside me as I guide you through the mysterious writings of an obviously deranged individual. Do not stand behind me. I really don't like people behind me. OK?"

"OK."

"OK"

"Behold, see and learn. All of this information is connected. The digits represent money or banking codes like accounts and routing numbers or both. The longer sets, the repeated ones, are most likely related to the banking. The shorter sets of digits represent money due to the zeros. Most likely deposited into an account, but removed from another. That, as we all know, is illegal. Or at the least magical, like putting money in one pocket and taking the money from another pocket. Now what is interesting is that the amounts of deposit and withdrawal are different. But the withdrawal is always either larger or smaller by similar amounts. Let me explain. See this set of digits. Let's assume this is a deposit. Then look at this set. Let's assume it is a withdrawal. See the difference in the sets. Don't strain your brains, I did the math. The difference is 66600. The 66600 and 6660 and 666 or are repeated throughout the document as difference between the deposits and the withdrawals. Sometimes more sometimes less, but always by the 66600, 6660 or 666 factors. It is like someone was manipulating the banking process and was too stupid to change his own process of covering up the evil deeds. Or the difference really meant something."

"How can we be sure that these numbers represent deposits and withdrawals?"

"I'm glad you asked little brother."

"Allow me to walk you through the longer sets. You will see nine-digit and ten-digit sets. The nine digit sets represent a bank routing number and the ten-digit sets are a bank account. Now what is interesting is that there are three different sets of each set. That is, the money went into one bank, was mysteriously transferred to another bank, withdrawn and mysteriously sent to a third bank and only to be withdrawn and kept out of circulation."

"How is that possible?"

"Lieutenant, it is only impossible unless there are people at the three banks working together. I believe the law calls that collusion. And that is where it gets really dicey. There is an eerie similarity in the bank number sets. But, there is dissimilarity. This apparent dichotomy could be the result of serendipity, or not, which in as of itself is dichotomous."

"Alex, what does that mean?"

"I'll explain. The last six digits on all the routing numbers are the same. And the last six digits on all the both bank account number are the same. If I am accurate, and I'm rarely inaccurate when dealing with facts, the banks and the accounts are located within banks that are related but not within the same system. Not two different branches of a Bank of America. But, and here it comes folks. Wait for it. The banks and the accounts could be related internationally. That would explain the difference in the first three digits. I don't know routing numbers, but I am sure the police can determine them. Let's say for sake of argument, bank #1 is here in the good old US of A and bank #2 is in Mexico. That would easily explain the deposits here in the states and the withdrawals south of the border. Or, vice versa. Cash in. Cash out. Drugs purchased. Drugs shipped. Drugs sold. Profits deposited. Profits shared. Nice scenario, don't you think Lieutenant?"

"But what about Bank #3? Where is that and why does the money trail end there?"

"My guess is that the profits from the transactions are sent to bank #3, for some yet undisclosed nefarious purpose. Buying influence in a foreign country. Funding a revolution somewhere or revolutions everywhere."

"An hypothesis. Interesting, but an hypothesis none the less. The concept of an international drug cartel using the banking system is at the core of conspiracy theories. Hoped for beliefs of the paranoid. The law tends to discount this ranting."

Alex pushes his chair away from the table and abruptly rises, eyes squinted in anger and fists clenched.

"Ranting my ass. If I were a cop, I would want to pursue this. But then, I don't owe my paycheck to a bureaucracy."

"Alex, relax. Lieutenant Sattill meant no offense. Tell us what else you found."

"Yes, I did not mean to offend you. My years on the force and my training have conditioned me to be skeptical. Forgive me."

It was not easy to seek forgiveness from this asshole fabricator . . . someone who was justifying the two grand he got and used for drugs.

"OK, then. The text I reviewed was equally interesting. And it supports the theory of the banks. There are several references to Satan and holy war. There is also a thinly disguised narrative dealing with enslavement and weaponry. There are numerous hints about the Middle East and illegal land acquisition. It's almost as if the message writer was trying to tell someone about a jihad. I am not sure which side of the jihad the writer is on and to whom he or she is writing. But the number 666 and jihad are close friends."

"Can you show me the support for this?"

"Sure, here are references to land, and home land. See? Here are references to "arms" which I think mean weaponry. Here are references to displaced people lost until they can reclaim their home land. What I don't understand is how this ties into the drug trade. There are two vastly different narratives in this complex message."

"Thanks for your help."

"There's more. By encoding the symbols that appear throughout the document, you can see some kind of ancient language. It's not anything I could find in reference books, but it is a language comprised of symbols not letters. Like ancient Egyptian not modern Egyptian. I just can't find the symbols anywhere. But the groupings appear to be subtext to the written message. Perhaps supporting it. Perhaps they are the real message so well hidden that only one or two people could read it. And one more thing. This message was not created by the person who passed it to you. The message you gave me was sent from an unknown to the person who gave you the message. Someone wrote the message and sent it. So, you might try finding out how the message was received and by whom. I have written all my observations on these pages."

"Many thanks for your help. We will take it from here."

Tony takes the six sheets of lined paper with notes scrawled in pencil and places the paper in his jacket pocket. The use of pencil and paper is odd for a paranoid cyber freak.

"Alex, bro, great job. This is a big help."

They hug and kiss cheeks.

"Yes, thanks for your help."

Tony and Chris exit to the fresh air and car. The ride back to the precinct is quiet. Chris is embarrassed that he revealed a part of his life better left unknown his, and Tony dreads having to tell Melissa and escort her to the morgue.

"Chris, I was serious. Your brother did us a huge favor. Let's keep him on the short list of outsiders we hire for this type of task."

"Thanks."

———◉———

Melissa's heels click down the corridor to the viewing chamber. Tony is off in his own world of reflection. He is deeply saddened. As an adult he has witnessed too much death and now too many friends dead. Too many lives crashed into disarray. Too damned many visits to morgues and their launching pad hospitals. When death deals with others, it is business. When death deals with friends, it's personal. Does death now stalk him for his past sins? Is death his cross to carry up the hill? The door to the chamber is opened from within.

"Good morning. If you stand by the window, I'll raise the curtain. Are you ready?" The attendant is perfunctory.

Is anybody ready to see a mate, friend or loved one in a post autopsy state? No! The curtain rises, Melissa gasps and slumps against Tony.

"Yes, that is my husband, Latchazar Razdarovich. He is grotesque. Tony, how could this have happened?"

"He was in the water for some time and suffered the ravages of the currents and sea creatures."

"I'll make arrangements for his funeral. Can you take me home Tony?"

"Yes, sure."

Another silent car ride. The doorman is at the ready.

"We'll have the service at Heavenly Rest. I'll let you know the date and time. Apparently there is no urgency."

Gallows humor is not funny.

———◆———

The Church of The Heavenly Rest is the bastion of Upper East Side Episcopalian social and political power. The clergy is headed by an heir to a large manufacturing fortune. Serving with him are a former senior member of NOW, the owner of a under garment line, a former black community leader, and a young priest who was or is a disgraced hedge fund manager. The church resides in a one-block estate donated by Andrew Carnegie. The membership is comprised of every level of local society.

It is the great equalizer where the very rich embrace the never-will-be-rich.

The church is resplendent with white flowers and black crepe. Limousines arrive in a steady stream. The local gentry walks. Tony is in full dress blues. Sitting in the rear of the church, he recognizes many as they take their places. He sees the Aylirs alone in the first pew. Three people in a space that fits six comfortably. A spotlight of sorts. On the opposite side of the aisle are Lucky's family. The two families never share a glance. Odd visible tension for the occasion. The attendees reflect their wealth and power. This is the land of the mink wrap and Chesterfield overcoat. The very real pearls and gold crest pinky rings. The service is as stately as one could expect for a member of the royal family, for that is what Lucky was. Tony is sure that the Razdarovich's believed that their son, the heir, married a commoner. A servant. As the church begins to empty, many pay their respect to both sides of the aisle. Tony does not go to the front of the church. That might be conspicuous. Then Tony sees a familiar face and demeanor, Makeda. She is escorted by two tall, lean, and very black men. Black suits, white Euro-trash shirts, and gray shoes. Suede jackets seem to hang on their torsos. Too big. They are hiding something. Guns! Why here? Why now? All three seem out of place. Something to file away for another day. He exits and gets into the unmarked squad car.

———— ◦◉◦ ————

Monday morning briefing of the weekend's events and knowledge gained

"Sir, we got a hit from the Federal DNA data base. One vic was Amada Fulton and the other was Latchazar Razdarovich, your friend, Lucky. Sorry, sir. Mr. Razdarovich was in the data base because of his banking business, both domestic and foreign. Amanda Fulton was in the data base, because she was an employee of the Federal government. Not had been, but was as in up to her death. No known branch. Maybe one of those branches that has no name, no initials, and no members, at least none that the public knows."

"That's two more triggers or button to the next doll. Why was Lucky killed at the Mission? Hell, why was he even there? And, what was Ms. Fulton doing at the Mission? Wait, I saw Makeda and two body guards at Lucky's funeral. So there has to be some connection. He was a big fund raiser for the Mission. Is that it? Chris, good work."

"Brendan, why so quiet? So deep in thought."

"I am sorry if I stepped on toes, but I think that Ms. Fulton worked for one of the very deep cover ops. Else why does her trail end with a name change and re-appear with her DNA in the Federal data base? LT, I think her Mission was to be at the Mission. She had infiltrated the Mission. I just don't know why. And I further believe that she had uncovered something that the Mission wanted kept a secret. Something that could not be explained away or swept under the rug. Now, if we hold that thought process and look at Lucky's death, we can see a connection. Lucky was killed at the Mission, his body was treated viciously, and he was dumped at sea. Obviously, the killers at the Mission were very angry. He had done something very, very wrong. Something that could jeopardize a larger thing. So they vented. Then you see the princess and two body guards at Lucky's funeral. Is that like the criminal returning to the scene of the crime? She goes there to gloat internally, but she takes two heavy hitters. Maybe even the heavy hitters that killed Lucky. So, we have Ms. Fulton uncovering some massive issue and being killed, and Lucky doing something terribly wrong and being killed at the same time. As you have told us many times, there is no such thing as coincidence. The two are connected. We just don't know the connection, except the Mission."

"Jesus, Brendan, that's terrifyingly brilliant. Like Columbus and the round earth theory. We have to determine the connection. Maybe I can turn One PP into an ally. I have a friend or two. While I am doing this, you continue to work the work. How are we coming on the bank routing codes? And, Jamie what have you learned about the Mission's financial statements?"

The Brass

One PP gets an upgrade and a new name every ten years, but for insiders, it is still One PP. The new name reminds everyone who was very important to the life and safety of New York. The upgrade means nicer offices, better communications and more small and arcane departments. Some of these new departments watch other departments. Through it all, the brass rules, thrives, and grows. Growth is required to find jobs for the promoted. They take over the new departments like so many small fiefdoms within the kingdom. The question always asked is how many pieces of the kingdom are there. The department keeps cutting the land until each piece is an incredibly thin slice. Then there is an implosion caused by all the bureaucratic weight. A massive restructuring to "right size the police department for the next decade" occurs. Then the process of bloated expansion is repeated.

Captain Kelly's office, Investigation Coordination Division, is on the eighth floor. Tony is directed in by a matronly Sergeant.

"Well if it isn't my dear friend, Lieutenant Sattill. To what do I owe this unexpected and unannounced pleasure?"

Tony sensed the old man was attempting to distance himself from the visitor and the purpose of the visit. Strange, because Kelly did not know the purpose. Tony sits on the guest side of a large modern work bench-like desk void of the anticipated stacks of paper. Before he could respond, the old man handed Tony a folded piece of note paper. Opened, it revealed . . . *Let's talk outside.*

"I came to give you a personal invitation to my party next month. And I had to take a break from the precinct."

"Party? I wouldn't miss it for the world. To celebrate, let's get a cup of coffee."

As both men are walking down the hall, Tony veers toward the canteen, while Captain Kelly heads for the elevator.

"I prefer the coffee from the street vendor, follow me."

The elevator ride is silent except for the rush of air with each floor. The street vendor is across the avenue on the outside of the park with lots of benches for the noon brown baggers.

"Now what do you really want to talk about."

"First, why the exit from the building?"

"Too many ears. Hell, I can't trust my own space or the cow that runs it."

"That gives me little comfort. I guess the spooks are always spooking everyone. And what better place than the confluence of information and rumors but One PP?"

"Now you know. War horses like us are retired to a laboratory, where we can be monitored and manipulated until our official retirement. Hell, my job is to coordinate investigations so that the big brass can observe how the little mice work together and how they can be controlled. All for the good and safety of the population, of course. Now tell me what's on your mind?"

"Big picture? What do you know about the Aksum Mission?"

"Do you want the party line or the skinny?"

"I know the party line. I want the skinny."

"This is way above your pay grade, and can't be repeated. The Mission and the she-wolf that runs it are very well connected here and at city government. Too well connected. She makes or controls or moves a ton of money through her Mission, and some of it falls off the truck into various pockets. I don't have names, but I do have my suspicions. The Feds. Our own Deputy Commissioners and Commissioners. Councilmen and women. Members of the clergy. Very influential businessmen. Rotten to the core. When a very visible charity does so much good, the visibly proper get paid to look the other way so their skirts are not sullied."

"This is not surprising. The same was said about the mafia during the 90's and early part of this century. Tell me about the money."

"As a charity, the Mission gets tax breaks and some grants from all the governments; federal, state and local. Then the Mission turns around and charges the people they are claiming to help, for all manner of things; rent, food, clothing, education. The place mints cash. It's like an ATM that simply spits money, but only to one person. It comes from everywhere and goes nowhere except into the pocket of the she-wolf and her associates, the wheels that need to be greased."

"Does she deliver bags of cash every month?"

"No, everything is funneled through a bank so it looks legit. The Manhattan Private Trust."

There it is. The magic button on the doll.

"I believe your friend, Lucky, became un-Lucky. My guess is that someone at the cash machine didn't like what Mr. Lucky was doing. Rumor has it that he was funneling some money to that Spanish Street gang to buy drugs. Hoped to quintuple his money in one week. But he got dead instead. Don't you find it strange that his blood was found at the Mission, but his body was found at sea? Don't you find it strange that his blood was mingled with the blood of a black whore? Are you fucking blind?"

"How do you know this?"

"I coordinate. To coordinate, I must know the players and the facts."

"What do you know about, Lenz and Hinton?

"Lenz is keeping an eye on Hinton and his connection to the Mission. Yes, Lenz told you to back off or he would crush your balls. But, the truth, Lenz volunteered to investigate Hinton, Lenz is a tough cop. A little rough around the edges, but a hard driving cop. The brass believes that Hinton is on the payroll of the Mission. And some people even suspect so is Lenz. So they let Lenz investigate Hinton. If Hinton and Lenz are dirty, Hinton thinks he is free to operate as he wishes, because he is protected by the one sent to investigate him. Sometimes the hunter lets the wolf stalk the fox, so both animals can be killed at the same time. In the meantime stay out of Lenz's way. He is vicious. And he may be trying to protect himself. That's all I can tell you.

The rest you'll have to figure out for yourself. I don't want to fuck up my pension."

"Is this enough rope for me to hang myself?"

"No. It is enough information for you to pursue the real reason behind the slaughter at the *Neighborhood Financial & Legal Services*. A word of advice; be very careful, many eyes are on you. Many people don't want any messes uncovered and many people don't want you to uncover the messes alone . . . without their help. Did you ever stop and wonder why you are allowed to operate with freedom? Allowed to investigate a crime or series of crimes into which you should not be poking your nose other than to gather information for the riding Detective? You have gone very far afield from your duties, yet no one has reigned you in. Why? Maybe they want a fresh set of eyes to confirm their suspicions. If you uncover the truth, they will tell the world that you were working for them. If you fuck up and piss off the Feds, they will distance themselves faster than a drunk from a hit and run. Don't get caught in the cross fire. Now, I have to return to my cage to shuffle papers. Don't want my visit with you to raise suspicions."

"Thanks for the information and guidance. I will tread lightly with a glance over each shoulder."

———⋘◉⋙———

During the subway ride back to the precinct. Tony retrieves the one message from his phone. Melissa wants to meet him at Melon's for dinner at 7:30.

Melon's was started by two guys that used to run Allen's, which started by a celestial bartender from somewhere else. They make a business practice out of welcoming and serving important, beautiful people. Tony orders a Balvenie. The young bartender does not know Tony, but the owner Sam Capolla comes from behind his stand to greet Tony.

"Hello Lieutenant. Is this an official visit?"

"Nice to see you again, Sam. How goes the acting?"

"I pick up small parts in movies. Doing some commercials. Working with the theater. Other than that, nothing is going on. Do you want a table or will you be dining at the bar?'

"A table for two thanks. She should be here momentarily. She is now twenty minutes fashionably late."

"Femme fatale?"

"Friend."

Bartenders and saloon keepers on the Upper East Side want to know everything. It's their ace in the hole. Thank gawd, they keep silent . . . for the most part. Enter Melissa. She has a huge grin on her face and a glow about her that seems out of place at the end of the day. A full body hug and a kiss on the cheek tell more. She is putting on a few pounds around the waist. Real comfort food. Eat to assuage pain. Once she realizes her clothes don't fit she will run to the gym.

"Melissa, you look terrific."

"You liar, I look fat."

"Our table awaits. Bartender, send two more of these to our table."

"No, just one for the Lieutenant."

Tony leaves a twenty on the bar. They are seated in the corner with a view of the rest of the patrons.

"Melissa, what would you like to drink?"

"Perrier with lime, please."

The server departs.

"OK, we are here and you are not drinking. *Por que?*"

"For a detective, you're not very observant. Come hither."

Tony lends his ear.

"I'm pregnant."

"Congratulations. It's what you wanted. Something or someone to be your link to Lucky."

"Guess again, LT."

The rush of silence in Tony's ears is generated from the inside as the chatter of the diners and clinking of silverware on plates is drowned out. His heart rate spikes to 85-90. Moisture appears on his upper lip.

"Mine? I mean ours?"

"Yes, and it is something I have wanted for a long time. A child. Our child. This is why no alcohol."

"Does anyone else know? Your parents?"

"You are the only one other than me outside the Doctor's office who knows.'

"I hate to show my police side, but are you sure? I mean me, ours?"

"Yes, I am sure. I counted the days and weeks . . . the missed events. The human inside of me is ours."

"When will you tell your parents? Should I be there?"

"I have a plan. I will tell them that I am pregnant. Let them assume that it is Lucky's. I will not tell the Razdarovich's. They always thought I was kitchen help. So it is none of their concern. Fuck them. I will carry the baby to term, give birth in a nice expensive hospital and retire to the castle with my charge. I deserve the luxury after all I have put up with. The Razdarovich's may be allowed to visit, but only when you are there. I want them to feel the hurt. After an appropriate time of adjustment, you will move in. We will tell my parents and the Razdarovich's. And we will marry."

"It's so nice to have your life planned by someone you deeply care for. All I have to do is sit by and let the events unfold as ordered. But, what if the Razdarovich clan wants to claim their heir? Or when they find out, they claim that all to which you are entitled as Lucky's widow is not yours to have due to infidelity? I assume there was a pre-nup."

"Yes, there was a pre-nup and fidelity was a major clause. That's where you come in. You must find something I can hold over the heads of the Razdarovich clan. Something that would null and void the pre-nup. Something they don't want exposed to the public. You're a detective, you can do that. Can't you?"

"I can't fabricate events or evidence, but I can dig into his laundry, dirty or otherwise. One question. Sex?"

"Yes, I plan on it tonight."

"No, I mean of the child."

"As of now, unknown. I'll know in a few weeks."

"I assume you will tell me so I can start wearing either pink or blue underwear."

"Yes, I'll tell you immediately when I know."

"Enough can we eat now. I need protein. Red meat. Beans. Wheat germ. I read that when the mother eats a heavy dose of protein daily during the first trimester, the child's brain is fed and he or she will be highly intelligent. And, besides that, if I don't eat every three-four hours my hormones go crazy and I could become violent. I have a steak knife right here. If I became violent, you would suffer the consequences, physically and socially. I want a 10-ounce sirloin with a side of black beans and rice. Now."

Tony eats. Melissa devours. If she thought she could get away with licking the platter clean, her face would have gone plate side. Tony orders a third drink. Then a brandy. Pregnancy has a strange impact on the father. A large part of him wants to hide behind alcohol. They leave and hail taxi to her place.

The doorman recognizes Tony, nods and smiles. Once inside the elevator, Melissa pounces upon her quarry. Lips opened, tongue probing, hips grinding, and hand groping at Tony's belt and fly. With the opening of the elevator door at the designated landing, the huntress has to stop, allow the door to close, and locks any escape of her prey. The animal in heat attack starts anew. They both exit their clothes and leave them in the wake as they rush to the bedroom. Covers are torn from the sheets, and the last vestiges of fabric modesty are tossed into the corner. He has never experienced such female ferocity. Kisses become nips. Fingers massaging becomes nails digging. The heat of Melissa's breath is matched by her dampness. Tony is fully aroused. He is ready. The thought of an infant causes him to hesitate.

"Jesus, don't stop now. It has been too long. I need you. I need us. Now and for a long time."

Tony mounts her gradually so as not to harm the infant; his previously planted seed. Too slow and too late. Melissa grabs his hips and pulls him inside with gusto. As he almost delicately thrusts downward, she emphatically pushes upward. Thus is achieved maximum penetration. This horizontal mambo continues until Melissa pushes him from her and rolls on her belly. Her knees are tucked beneath her.

"Be my back door man. I want to feel you deep inside me."

Tony rises to a near standing position and continues his thrusting. Melissa's deep breathing has turned into whimpers. Quickly her whimpers become moans. Deeper and deeper until she begins to utter brief screams of pleasure. He works harder and faster. There is silence. Suddenly, Melissa screams and moans simultaneously. Her muscles inside and outside her vagina spasm. Her legs go tense and she lifts her head as is she is attempting to escape. He sees her mouth agape. She is simply taking in more oxygen. The muscle spasms become trembling. Then the collapse. The only sound now is her deep breaths of exhaustion. Like a runner after a 10K.

He withdraws. She turns to her side. They lay together. She sensually runs her fingers over his chest, belly and loin. He is still erect for he did not finish the race.

"That was marvelous. For me, but obviously not for you."

"I get pleasure from giving you pleasure. My joy is your joy."

"Bullshit. Enter me again. I am ready to give you pleasure."

Slowly Tony does what he wants to do. This time all is on his schedule. Five minutes and he is just about there. In his selfishness he failed to note her moans. She is rushing to be with him at the finish line. The tape is broken by two runners.

Sleep is nearly instantaneous. The combination of alcohol and sex is a powerful soporific. Melissa awakens Tony during the night for an encore. He obliges, because he knows that mindless ambush sex is the best. The alarm comes too damned early. He heads for the shower.

Only to joined by a beautiful black woman with a small baby bump. His baby bump.

The new day brings many new things. Will this be a good day?

New Face

Bank Announces New President

Manhattan Private Trust announced the elevation of Robert Linder from Sr. Vice President of Banking Operations to President of the Worldwide Bank. Alexandra Razdarovich, matriarch of the bank's founding family stated, "Mr. Linder has been a loyal employee of the bank, has risen through the ranks, and was the spearhead of the bank's recent expansion into Europe. We on the board feel there is no one better suited to accelerate our recent growth. Robert has our full support in all he does."

Mr. Linder noted that "The Manhattan Private Trust enjoys a heritage of banking services for those of prominence; those who appreciate the security and personal attention only we can offer. We will continue this loyal customer service here in the United States as we offer it to discriminating individuals worldwide."

Robert Linder, graduate of Yale, with an MBA from Owen School of Management at Vanderbilt, has worked at Manhattan Private Trust for eighteen years. He lives in Manhattan, is married to the former Brenda Middleton of Greenwich CT, and has three children.

Time for a detailed review of matters so far.

"OK everybody, let's put on the boards what we know so we can figure out what to do next. Chris."

"Well, we know that the bank account or bank accounts all belong to the Manhattan Private Trust. I learned that the bank enjoyed special privileges with four countries and thus maintained the same basic routing number. I suspect that made it easier to move money from one country to another. One account is located here in New York, one in the London office of the bank, one in Mexico within the Banco du Popular, and one on the island of the Grand Cayman, the Bank of the Islands. Four banks. Four countries. One account. The signatories on all four are Alexandra Razdarovich, Brenda Middleton, Estella Maria Estefan, Fatima Madri Albar el Sahid, and Regna Blacke. Nobody could move nothing unless all signatories knew. I think the process went like this. Cash was deposited into the account at Banco du Popular. Cash from where we don't know for sure, but I am willing to bet drug harvesting and selling. The cash was gradually shifted over the course of two-three weeks to the account in the Bank of the Islands. Then this cash could be moved quickly, because it was well under the radar, to the Manhattan Private Trust offices, here and in London. By the by, does it seems strange that all the signatories are women? So, I checked. We know Alexandra. Brenda Middelton is now Brenda Linder. Estella is the heffe of a big cartel in Mexico. Fatima is the daughter of a rogue Prince from the House of Saud. The whereabouts of the Prince and his family are unknown. Most likely somewhere in Pakistan or Africa. Regina Blacke is English. She allegedly heads a gun smuggling operation out of Liverpool. This is not your garden variety sorority."

"Gawd, we are on to something. I hope there's more."

"You bet LT. The money transferred here was invested in a private account under the name Melissa Aylir. Large sums purchased significant positions in aggressive companies and some lots of puts and calls. Quick turns. Funds in and out in ninety days. The profits from these investments were returned to the Bank of the Island account, which returned them to the account at the Mexican bank. These profits were siphoned off by parties unknown."

"What about London?"

"It is a little foggy here. The funds deposited in the London branch were wired to a Russian bank designated only as PPKT, Ltd. The wire transfers were in large amounts of fifty to one hundred and fifty thousand Euros. But there were three or four transfers per week for four weeks then nothing. My guess is that the transfers totaled about 2 million Euros. Then nothing. I can't be more accurate than that, because as I was digging on line, my intrusion was discovered and the entire process was killed from within. Somebody did not want outsiders to know anything. But I do know this PPKT, Ltd. is a bank. PPKT, Ltd. is the name of a Russian financial services organization with strong ties to the top three Russian mobs. This so-called financial services company sells insurance, handles IPOs and is a very large weapons distributor in the Motherland, Europe, and the Middle East. They take no side and have been accused of arming both sides in several conflicts."

"Drug money to investments to weapons. But to whom and why? And I find it hard to believe a Mexican cartel is magnanimously purchasing weapons so other nations can kill each other."

"LT, look at it this way. The Mexicans fund the weapons purchases for collateral in the country of the war. Who care who wins? The cartel holds the paper. We just don't know what the paper is. Oil? Land? Mining rights to precious metals? Regardless it is probably worth more than the cost of the weapons. The cartel is expanding beyond this continent. They have so much money they need to something productive with it. Make it grow. Have it be worth much more in two years than today. And the only way to do that is with the help of a bank . . . a shady international bank. My guess is that the bank's profits were kept as cash, removed from the bank's vault, and recycled in the form of real estate here in the US and maybe an island or two in the Caribbean."

"What else did you learn?"

"During the past ten years, the Razdarovich family has purchased hundreds of thousands of acres in Montana, Idaho, the Dakotas, and Wyoming. Plus, the family owns four small islands in the Bahamas. Because it is a foreign chain, there are very few questions asked and even fewer answers."

"Holy shit. That is staggering. Chris, I hope you did not leave much of a trail on the computer. If this gets back to us before we can document the facts, I will be coming to you for a job. But let's press on. We have the dragon by the tail. But we can't prove much for now. We will need the help of the Feds in all initials and demeanors. Plus, we don't know who and why Lucky was killed at the Mission. The logical extension of your discovery already noted is that what he was doing, or about to do, or had already done something that really pissed off his partners."

"Jamie, what have you learned? It's show and tell time."

"LT, I learned that Rufus and Amanda were not married. Their relationship was a cover for their work. They worked for an arcane Federal agency that investigates that, which cannot be investigated. The agency as no name or initials and reports to someone so high up the food chain that simply talking to him will give one a nose bleed. This agency recruited both out of college, undoubtedly with the promise of doing good in the world. This much more we know. Amanda and Rufus were introduced by Mr. Martin, the Fed who died in a mysterious hunting accident out of season. Rufus did work on the West Coast, Seattle. I am not sure doing what, but I am sure he was honing his skills. I found Amanda or Musin Mohammed as she was photographed at a Muslims for Peace and Understanding rally in Charlotte. Then she disappeared. I believe she was united with Rufus here in New York. They both had the same assignment. His was on the outside and hers was on the inside. They were digging into the operations of the Aksum Mission. She went "homeless" in need of shelter and was taken in by the Mission. There she performed housekeeping chores to pay her rent."

"How the hell did you learn all this?"

"I have friends in low places. Before I go on, let me say that the Mission charges a pot full of rent and fees for everything. It is a damned ATM with only one card . . . Makeda's."

"OK, Amanda is living at the Mission and Rufus is living elsewhere. How do they communicate . . . stay in touch?"

"My guess is by way of the internet. She goes to an internet café at a specific time each week. Rufus is at another café. They exchange information. Basically she sends him files of knowledge. Encrypted files. She has a routine. So she is followed. She is questioned. She is killed. The simple ugly truth. My bet is that the men at R&B Construction were guardian angels for Rufus and Amanda. They watched Rufus visit the store front of *Neighborhood Financial & Legal Services*. They suspected a connection with the Rancks, so they put your friends under the microscope. I'll even bet they were nearby when Rufus went to the store front the last time. But they could not intervene without tipping their hands. Maybe they are not so bad after all."

"I will ignore that statement. What about the encrypted files?"

"The ramblings and references to Satan are most likely the utterances of someone under great stress. Stress caused by hiding in plain sight. Stress caused by knowledge that is well beyond her ken. Stress of the job. Also, we learned that she was religiously conflicted. Christian and Muslim make for a bad combination. She saw or thought she saw what was happening and what was coming. Maybe she could see Armageddon, and felt there was no way for her to stop it even though that was her duty."

"Two people manipulated to perform a heroic duty for their country. Killed in the line of duty."

"Brendan, what can you add to the smorgasbord of knowledge."

"I dug into the massive drug bust. And you were right. The real catch was a lot smaller than they announced. A smoke screen to pump their egos. That is no big deal.

But what is the big deal is that the confiscated drugs came from a distribution point here in Manhattan. It seems that some group or guy was trying to muscle into the territory with a flood of drugs. This newbie was connected at the street level with Los Hores. They were his protection. Muscle—nothing else. They were to be paid with the proceeds. But there were no proceeds. They are cranky, but their guy is dead. Found at sea, but killed at the Mission. Lucky. He tried to cut corners and make a big side deal for himself. Makeda is very cranky. She needs Los Hores to find her a steady stream of human refuse for her Mission. She gets $20,000 per soul she takes off the street. She gives Los Hores five. Now, thanks to ADA Kemp, she can pocket it all. She still charges the residents rent and fees. And she collects about one million at the annual fund raiser. The city, state and Federal governments look the other way, because she is cleaning up the neighborhood. I also learned that she has a small standing army at the Mission. About twenty well-trained, well-armed and well-disciplined soldiers ready to die for her cause or just because she wants to be protected and pays them well. The problem is that they only believe they know her cause. They don't know the real reason for the Mission's existence. A front for a huge money machine in Manhattan, the Caymans, Mexico, and England."

"Today, I learned there is an invisible entrance to the next doll. I will share this with you soon."

Tony spends the rest of the day digesting and ruminating about the information on the wall. He re-hears the voices telling the team what the information means. He can't get over the fact that Pam died because she was trying to help some guy, who was using her to get to her husband. A desperate man. Desperate to transfer information about some great evil. A man made desperate by his position. He is caught between his job and the public persona of the evil. He had to transfer information to someone who could help stop the evil. Talk about stress. Rufus and Amanda were being squeezed. Where were their handlers? The couple could not trust their handlers. Were their handlers dirty? That's why Weaver died so suddenly, so mysteriously. This theory works if Rufus knew that Jimmy and Pam knew Tony, the cop. Did Rufus know? How could he know? The picture. The picture Pam kept on her desk. The picture of Jimmy, Pam and Tony in his dress blues at his promotion ceremony. Rufus saw that Pam knew a cop and knew him well. So he knew. He couldn't go directly to the police, Pam and Jimmy had to be the messengers. There had to be distance between Rufus and Amanda and Tony. This means that Rufus and Amanda knew that they were being watched. So he put Pam and Jimmy in harm's way. Rufus and Amanda could only hope that nothing bad would befall Pam and Jimmy. Hope springs eternal. But, in this case, hope falls on its ass. Pam died. And, lots of people died after her. The magnitude of the evil dictates many people had to be sacrificed for the greater good. But, in this case, the greater good is the greater evil.

How does the NYPD in the person of Lieutenant Anthony Sattill, reach out to all the Feds and the various initialed departments with their fiefdoms to protect and tell them what they may or may not know already? How does he tell them what he knows in a quid pro quo arrangement? Who does he contact first? If he tells them, how will the NYPD brass react? Is there a super agency coordinating the investigation? Is there a lead dog? Kelly knows more than he told Tony. The old man is not a player in this game, just an observer. Next stop . . . find a way into the Feds.

The day has been long and enervating. Tony decides to walk to his apartment. Stop and get a pie with extra cheese at "The Original Tony's". Interesting how the early evening brings out a different crowd. Different people on the sidewalks. Different stores lit for commerce. Different traffic patterns. He recognizes many of the differences from previous mind-cleansing walks. Turning the corner on his block, Tony hears the revving of a car engine. The squealing tires is nothing new for his neighborhood. But the bump of a chassis and the scraping sound of metal on metal catch his attention. He turns to check out the source of the vehicular commotion. A black van with the side door open is bouncing and careening in his direction. From the open door, a burst of fire and muffled staccato pulsing. Then the pain, incredible, nearly unbearable pain at his end. The pain starts in his shoulders and runs down his body. He is spun to one side by the impact of the pain giver. He drops the pizza and falls to his knees. Pain engulfs his entire being. The street lights sparkle then dim. There is no more street noise. Before he passes out, he sees more bursts of flame. He rolls over to his side to avoid the pain and watches the van run a red light and turn left. The sidewalk is gooey wet. AJT. The only part of the New York license he sees before blackness overcomes him.

⪫•⪪

"Lieutenant, can you hear me? Squeeze my hand if you can hear me."

One squeeze.

"Good, you've been shot. You're going to be OK. Just stay with me as I talk. OK"

A second squeeze.

"You're in an ambulance heading for Mt Sinai hospital. They'll take good care of you there. A detective named Brendan McLaughlin told me to tell you that they are processing the shooting scene and will come to the hospital when they are done."

A third squeeze.

Tony is aware of the wail of the siren and the lurching of the vehicle as it darts in and out of traffic. He can't feel a thing. He can't see much with only one eye. But, he recognizes the tubes and other paraphernalia inside the ambulance. He tries to move.

"Sir, please lay still. We're just about at the ER."

Tony is lifted out of the ambulance on a gurney and wheeled through a set of large double doors into a brightly lit staging area. There two nurses and a Doctor hover over him and call out some form of medical code. He is shuttled off to a room with a huge X-ray machine that can take pictures from every angle while a patient is standing sitting or lying down. After the pictures, the gurney is aggressively moved into a very quiet room with several more nurses and Doctors. Tony has lost all track of time. From the shooting to here, was it ten minutes or two hours.

"Lieutenant, we're going to lift you from the gurney. OK?

No hand to squeeze. He nods ever-so-slightly and moans.

"On my three. One. Two. Three."

That hurt Tony's shoulders, back, and head.

"Lieutenant, we going to put you to sleep. We need to get the bullets and close the wounds. Sadly, we do this a lot. It's almost routine. You will be fine. Now relax."

"LT, can you hear me?"

Tony recognizes Jamie's voice. It is comforting.

"We're all here now. Hell there are four of us and no cards for bridge."

She takes his hand.

Tony' squeezes it. Human contact. He is alive and with friends.

"Can you talk? Actually can you listen and respond?"

Tony shakes his head slightly.

"Squeeze my hand once for yes and twice for no. OK"

One squeeze.

"Somebody shot you. Sprayed the sidewalk and buildings around you. You took two to the upper torso. Flesh wounds. A third grazed your left temple near your eye. You can't see out of that eye for now. Because it is covered by gauze and a wrap. The doctors said that you'll be fine. Up and about in two to three days. You will be very stiff and sore. They will want you to take it easy for a while. Nothing strenuous."

"Do you want to hear what we know?"

Chris is always working just like Tony. One squeeze.

"We found the casings. There were thirty twenty-two rounds expended. The small caliber is why you have only flesh wounds. Plus, it seems that the car or truck hit a pothole in the street and bounced off a parked car as it was approaching you. This disturbance caused the shooter or shooters to be inaccurate. Is there anything you can remember?"

One squeeze.

"Description of the vehicle?"

One squeeze.

"Car?"

Two squeezes.

"Van?"

One squeeze.

"Color?"

"Black?"

One squeeze.

"Anything else? License plate?"

One squeeze.

"Can you write it on this pad?"

One squeeze.

Tony takes the pen and scrawls AJT.

"Bingo, boss you are the best."

"What is going on here?"

The young Doctor is pissed.

"Jesus, can't you see the Lieutenant is in pain. He needs rest not company. You may come back tomorrow in the afternoon. Do you understand?"

Properly upbraided and with a wealth of information Tony's crew apologizes and leaves he room. Just in time as Tony collapses into sleep.

Hospitals suck! Daytime TV sucks! Lying in bed 24/7 sucks! While pondering his predicament, Tony is left alone except for the regular intrusions into his prison-like solitude by the various nurses and technicians. He understands that the attempt on his life is a clear sign he and his crew are getting too close to a truth that someone or some organization would prefer to remain out of the public eye. The young patrolmen who sit watch at his door are proof positive that the department considers him to remain in clear and present danger.

"Well, look at you. Just lyin' here waitin' for something good to happen rather than out there makin' something good happen."

Captain Kelly's sense of humor is that of a dear friend.

"Yep, I am just lying here hoping they turn on the tanning lights soon. I need to work on my glow. Fuck you, old man."

"That's the spirit. I can't stay long, but I do want to tell you that I heard from a Mister Michaels of the Federal government. Why he called me I don't know. He wouldn't tell me what branch he worked for. But he said he wants to talk to you when you are sprung from the big house. He didn't say what was on his mind, but he gave me his telephone number for you to call. Here."

The number on the scrap of paper has no area code. Local.

"Now I have to git before I am missed at One PP. They clock us in and clock us out. Not with a time punch but with security cameras. Besides, you have another visitor, and she is beautiful. Not that you will be able to do anything with all the wrappings around you. When you are sprung, we'll have dinner. My treat."

His treat! The bastard hasn't picked up a check in the twenty years Tony has known him. Something is off center. Tony painfully reaches to the night stand and stuffs the paper scrap into the issue of Sports Illustrated Brendan left him. He turns back to the patient position and here she is. Melissa is radiant and beautiful. Her entrance is regal. She leans over him and plants a delicate kiss.

"This was the first day you were allowed to have visitors other than your professional colleagues. So your lover and your baby came to say hello."

Melissa opens her coat and bends over to talk to her stomach.

"Listen to mommy, baby Sattill, this is your daddy. He is a cop. He got shot. He is OK. He is a bull-headed bastard. He does dumb things like track down criminals. Criminals who want to kill him. He is fortunate he is not dead. But this is your daddy, for better or worse, in sickness and in health. He is your daddy. I love him madly and you will too."

Tony sees the tears running down her face.

"My father sends his best for a speedy and complete recovery. I can't stay too long. It might look suspicious. Besides hospitals frighten me. When will you be released?"

"Tomorrow."

"Then what?"

"Then rest at home or work light duty. I am opting for the latter."

"I'll come and get you from this place. Have them call me. I'll get you home and lock you inside so you can't go to work. I'll cook for you. I'll bathe you. I'll nurse you back to full strength is the privacy of your home."

"Thanks, sweetheart. I appreciate all the well intended attention. I'll be fine. Soon I'll be able to read with both eyes. The bandages are getting smaller each shift. I am sore, but I'll be fine. I love you and love the fact that you love me. Now scoot! I need my rest."

Sleep overcomes him. Two visitors were too many.

Another Doll

Dressing is forever. The pants are one thing, while the shirt and jacket are nearly impossible to get on. A process that should take ten minutes takes twenty-five. Tony has to rest twice. With the sling and bandage at his left temple, he must avoid public transportation. A cab must be his mode until he looks less like a war vet.

"Welcome back, LT. Do you want to start at your desk or in the conference room?"

"Brendan, nothing on my desk or on my computer will spoil if I don't get to it today. Besides I've only been out five days. There is already too much crap. One more day's worth won't mean a thing. I need to know what you know about my attack."

"First the weapon. The slugs are 223s. They are hollow-points. Meant to cause maximum destruction for a small arm and be untraceable because they split or mush upon impact. The ones in the shrubs and walls at the scene were useless. The ones the docs took from you were fragmented and of no use. That said, this is not a gun of choice for street thugs or your garden-variety mobster. It is a gun of choice for an assault team. A team of professionals."

"Thanks, that helps."

"LT, we tried to trace the license plate and found 4,356 AJTs in the metro area. Of these 196 belong to vans. Of the vans, 12 are black. Of these, all can be accounted for. On the job, at the garage or under repair. My guess is that the plate was stolen for this purpose. So, it had to be stolen very recently. We went back and learned that 3 of the AJTs had been stolen in the week prior to the shooting. One in Queens. One in Brooklyn. One on Long Island. Manhasset. We checked with the owners, all of whom claim their cars were garaged during the plate disappearance. None of the owners appears to have any connection to the netherworld. It seems like the thievery was a crime of opportunity, by someone who need a specific item at a specific time."

"Chris, keep digging."

"Jamie, what have you learned?"

"The reason you were not killed is that the van, as it was coming toward you, hit a pot hole and the driver apparently lost control momentarily. Thus, I believe that the driver and the shooter did not know your neighborhood streets. The van careened into a light blue Toyota which was parked on your side of the street. There was black paint scraped off onto the car. Thus, there was light blue paint scraped onto the van. By checking the paint samples, we learned that the van was a Ford Econoline. 2006-2010. So we know what we are looking for. Another thing, because these guys were waiting for you at your house. They must have known when you would be getting home. I surmise they followed you on your walk from the precinct. If this is true, they may be watching you and us on a regular basis. Scary, eh what? So, I reviewed the video input from the security cameras outside the precinct. From the evening you were shot, we can see a black Ford Econoline parked across the street. There you are leaving the building, and there they are pulling away from the curb. The side windows are tinted so we can't get a peak at a passenger, if there is one. Most likely he is in the rear. But look when I freeze the picture. LT, I'd swear that is one of the security guards from the Mission. He also looks like the Euro-trash that was gunned down at the rave. I maybe jumping to conclusions, but that's what I say."

"Very nice work. Now, if they were waiting, they must have known I was here. How did they know that, Jamie?"

"Did you get any calls after five that day? Did you receive any packages?"

"No packages. I made and received calls all day long. But, none after five. Wait, I called my old friend, Captain Kelly late in the day. Bitched about how tired I was. And that I needed a night to be alone with no thoughts. He called me a wuss. No big deal."

"Maybe our phones are bugged. Maybe Kelly's phone is bugged."

"Jesus, Jamie, you may be right. My guess is that Kelly's phone is monitored. But to be safe, sweep our lines and phones."

"Why Kelly's phone?"

"The PP in One PP really stands for One Paranoid Palace. The commissioners collect all the old dogs in one place, give them small jobs with big pay, and listen for secrets. And I will hazard a guess, as to who is bugging his phone—IAB at the command of the Commissioners.

I suspect they even bug the commissioners' phones for insurance. The entire place is filled with people who think they are above the law. So it's only natural that everyone at One PP would be monitored. Not just phones, but comings and goings. And who is our favorite IAB inspector, none other than Wolf Lenz?"

"Sir, if that's true it means he is in the loop. That is hard to believe. How do we prove it? Hell, how do we investigate it? One other piece of insider news. Kurt Strabel was taken into custody by IAB in connection with the Lieutenant Brown murder. It seems he was her lover and very jealous of her relationship with Diego Seville. A relationship that was way more than professional. So the heffe of Los Hores is off the hook for murder. Not drug trafficking."

"Can that rumor be confirmed? Permit me to posit several queries? Have any of you thought how we have been able to pursue this complex and arcane investigation without the brass coming down on us like a ton of bricks? We have been left alone, because someone wants us to do the heavy lifting. There have been no complaints about our real work. So, if you all get the picture, we have been given an unofficial green light. Let's use that unspoken permission and move full steam ahead. Sorry for all the trite metaphors. Let's let Lenz be our provocateur, while that hand that guides him is on our side or so it seems. Now get to work. Find the SOBs that shot me and link them to whomever."

Tony slumps in his chair. Even this bit of work has tired him out. Maybe he'll just work a half day. First he has to look at the e-mail. *Crap!* Two-hundred and forty-five unread messages. A daunting task he wants to, but cannot, avoid. He must trudge through them. First the normal reports. His team has those. Then the PBA notices. He will file them for late night reading at home when he cannot sleep. Messages from his fearless leaders addressed to the entire PD. Those get deleted. Questions from his peers. They will be read immediately after the screen cleaning. Messages from organizations that want a police man to help them in a charity drive. Deleted. Messages about submitting medical leave and insurance forms . . . fourteen including reminders. What a fucking waste of cyber space. He is finally down to thirty-four messages. Reading them and responding will be his work for the afternoon. Maybe a nap before lunch. First call this Fed Michaels.

"Mr. Michaels, good morning. This is Lieutenant Anthony Sattill of the NYPD. Captain Kelly advised me that you wanted to talk to me."

"Yes, Lieutenant. Thank you for calling so soon after your incident. I would like to talk, but not over the phone. Can we meet somewhere at our convenience? Can we meet today?"

"Sir, how about tomorrow at Soldier's Gate in Central Park."

"That's fine. Say noon."

"That's fine, sir. How will I know you?"

"Not to worry, I will recognize you."

"Excuse me, I need to know . . ."

Click.

This is disconcerting. Being recognized by a stranger. Hopefully, Kelly vetted this guy. The lead weight of paranoia hits Tony's gut. Followed by a huge wave of fatigue. Call a sector car to take him home to rest.

Soldiers' Gate is an opening to the inner road way of Central Park and across from the Church of the Heavenly Rest. Cars can enter and exit the opening only at certain times of the day. The bulk of the time, it is reserved for pedestrians, runners, and bicyclists. The huge white marble wall commemorates the men and women who died in the first quarter of the twentieth century protecting the freedom of the rest of us. Each name and year of death is preserved for all to see. No one does. There is a long white marble bench twelve feet in front of the wall. Tony sits and waits. In about five minutes he is approached by a slender man about 5'10" 165, wearing khaki pants, a dark pullover shirt, black shoes and painfully obvious Ray Bans. This man slides beside Tony.

"Lieutenant Sattill?"

"Yes, and who are you?"

"Mr. Michaels."

"OK, Mr. Michaels, before we go any farther, I need to see two forms of ID; a driver's license and your company card. And take off those silly glasses, unless your team is using them to spot you."

"Here is my New York driver's license and my NSA ID."

Off come the glasses.

"OK, David Michaels. I believe you are legit. Before we talk about the reason for this meeting, let's go for a walk deeper into the park, where no parabolic mics can follow."

"OK, if you wish."

They head over the inner road way onto the large playing field. Tony heads to a bench. Sitting is required as fatigue is becoming a regular factor.

"Now, tell me why are we meeting?"

"I will be direct."

Tony notes the first sign of lies to come.

"We understand that you are investigating a series of murders that seem to be connected. And the connection centers on the Manhattan Private Trust and the Aksum Mission. We would like you to share with us all that you know."

"And I would like to be taller and younger. So there are three things that aren't going to happen soon."

"Lieutenant, don't be foolish. First, we have a good idea of what you know, second, sharing it with us would accelerate your career, and third, you don't want us to be a road block to your investigation and get you in trouble with the brass at One PP."

"I was waiting for the threat. The carrot and the stick won't work. And you can't be both the good cop and the bad cop. But you tried. I'll tell you this; we will cooperate with your agency if, and only if, we can sit down at a neutral site with Captain Kelly and do the old quid pro quo. I'll show you mine, and you show me yours."

"Our involvement in your little escapade is way above your pay grade and that of your beloved Captain. You and the NYPD have only begun to see the enormity of the issue that drives all that you are investigating. It is on a need to know basis and you two don't need to know."

"I am tired. Remember I was shot. So . . ."

"Yes, we know you were shot. 223s I believe. The shooters got away in a black van. They are ruthless. If they can go after a police Lieutenant, they can go after his family. But, you don't have a family, do you?"

Another dead weight of paranoia hits Tony's stomach. This thinly veiled threat has been successful.

"Ouch, you are not playing nice. But, if memory serves me, you called this meeting. Therefore, I know you think I have something you want. To get what you want, you will have to tell me how it fits into your work. It is that simple. So simple even a Fed can understand it. You do understand, don't you?"

"That will never happen."

"Then my lips and files are sealed. Do us both a favor. But you have a chance to redeem yourself. Go back to your higher-ups and tell them of my offer of conditional cooperation. See what they say. Then get back to me. In the mean time, if I feel threatened or in danger in any way, I will come down on you personally. Remember, I work with certain people who don't give a shit about who they hurt. And these people owe me for keeping them out of jail. You will never know the where or when, but hurt will happen. With that I bid you a fond adieu. You can put the glasses on now. I wouldn't want any runner to recognize you."

Tony remains seated while Mr. Michaels, or whatever his real name is turns and walks away. They both got what they wanted. Michaels learned that Tony's squad had information to share. More information than they thought and the Tony was willing to share it. Tony learned that The NSA, if that is the real agency, really wanted Tony's information and would be willing to give him a peak under the tent flap. He walks slowly to Soldiers' Gate to grab a cab. There it is; the painfully obvious unmarked car with two front seat passengers. Michaels crew. Dinner tonight with Melissa. Maybe some tea and sympathy.

The doorman smiles his "I-know-what-is-going-on" smile. A two-legged Cheshire cat. He nods to Tony.

"How's the arm, Lieutenant?"

"It aches a little, but on the mend. I hope to be out of this damned sling in a few days. Thanks for asking."

The doorman announces Tony and keys the elevator up to Melissa's floor.

"Good night, sir."

"Yes, good night."

The uniformed man is getting friendlier as if Tony were a resident.

The elevator opens up to a construction site. Scaffolding, ladders, and tarps.

"We are so glad to see you. Baby Sattill wants to get to know the father. Don't you baby?"

Melissa is dressed in loose fitting clothes. Comfort and disguise simultaneously. Her hair is swept up and tied in the back and her face, a little larger, than he remembers, is damned near shining. She takes his hand.

"Come. Look. See what is going on and what it will be. First, I am cutting a double door between the master bedroom and Lucky's former office/den. That will be the baby's room. Once the book cases are removed and the window enlarged, it will be a beautiful home for the newborn. The double pocket door will provide easy access to the new room, as well as the obvious sign that mother and father are nearby. I am increasing the size of a laundry room and buying all new appliances for it as well as the kitchen. Rosita will come back as a live-in. So I am creating a two-room suite for her. Take a gander at the twin bathrooms. Each is fully equipped, again all new fixtures. Plus, and here is the *piece de resistance*, the room between the bathrooms will hold a two-person tub for special evenings. If you play your cards right."

"Jesus, Melissa these changes are monumental."

"That's not all. When the interior is complete, in about four months, I will have the terrace built out and child proofed. So we can sit outside and play. The three of us. Look at the paint colors and wall paper. Everything to soothe. Grays, blues, yellows. Bright white trim and accents. Plus, plus, I found this incredibly beautiful wall paper called South China Seas. Gender neutral. Intricate design, with an adventuresome feel. Well, what to you think? Before you tell me how much you love it, you should know that baby Sattill and I adore what the finished product will be and look like."

Tony is struck by the enormity of the change that is about to occur in his life. His heart rate increases and he feels flush. He is about to go from single cop with no one to worry about except himself to serious Lieutenant husband and father with all that entails. The new emotions; his, hers and the baby's. New patterns of life, eating sleeping, hours at work. Obligations. Obligations. Obligations. A brave new world.

"I love it. It's just that here is so much going on here, that I will need time to absorb it all. You have been living with it. I have just been introduced to it."

"See, I told you, baby, he would love it. We have to give him time to adjust. You know the lock-step mind-set of a police man. Tony, you look tired. Let's sit in the living room."

"Melissa I have never seen your energy level this high. It's almost as if you were on speed."

"I am on the speed of love. Love for my new life, life without the jailer. Love for my new life with the new life.

Love for my new life with you. I am even learning how to cook. I want to be the complete lover, wife, and mother. I am so happy, I could cry. And every once and a while when I am overcome by the enormity of the new about to be that I do cry. Tonight we will feast on quiche, lamb chops, potatoes au gratin, a three-bean casserole, endive salad, and a dessert of lemon gelato to cleanse the palate. The Food Channel and I are becoming friends, joined at the clicker."

"May I have an adult beverage?"

"Yes, one. I don't want to slow the healing process. You sit, I will pour."

Now it starts. The controlling. The monitoring. The alpha female emerges.

"Oh, in case you were wondering, we will make love tonight. I asked the Doctor and he said we can make love until the ninth month. I must warn you, I am very lust filled. Notice I did not use the colloquialisms. I don't want baby Sattill to hear the harsh vulgar words. I bought some clothes for you. Two pairs of slacks, four button down shirts, three pullovers, two pairs of shoes, six boxers shorts, cute ones with teddy bears on them, a reversible belt, a blazer and three ties. Plus, in your bathroom, you will find a complete set of toiletries. It was so much fun buying clothes for my man. Now, you won't have to skulk out of here before dawn to get ready for work. You might as well get used to it. We are a family."

The first sip of Balvenie goes down so smooth, yet hits Tony like a hammer. It eases him into his new world.

This was a strange day.

The Meet

"Jesus, boyo you really kicked the hornets' nest. Before 8 AM, I was doing my famous back and fill for you with the big guys down here. They are getting their Johnsons squeezed by one of the Federal agencies, the one that sounds like the National Shopping Association. They want the department kept in the knowledge loop, but not in the involvement loop. They want credit, but no risk of blame. That's where you come in. I just got off the phone with your Mr. Michaels. He is pissed at your demands. After ten minutes of him yelling in my ear, I convinced him that you would come around and share your information with him and his agency."

"Did you tell him that he had to come clean with me, or us, the NYPD?"

"I suggested he would be well advised to tell what he knows. And he told me that was well above our combined pay grades. The arrogant prick. So, we agreed that we would all meet at my house on the island, discuss the very complex case and share information. I got the distinct impression that he, too, is looking to take the upside, while you take the downside."

"When is the meet?"

"Seven-thirty tomorrow."

"Who all will be there?"

"Me, you, and him. No team members from either side."

"I'll bet your pension that he will try to bring others and to somehow record the evening."

"I promise you this. If he arrives with more than himself, alone, there will be no meeting. And I will check all cases, yours included. And take all side arms. You have a day to gather the paper work. Now get hopping."

Tony tells his people to gather up all the information so far and to create files with summations. He does not explain why. They don't ask. The rest of the morning is devoured by his own files, reports and paper work. Whatever happened to the promise of less paper in the electronic information age? Lunch time is the best time to take a stroll and see humanity.

Il Supremo is a pasta dive in mid-town on the far west side. An area where the Italian mobs and the Westies fought over turf, until the truce and the ensuing slaughter of the Irish. This checkered table cloth restaurant serves the best homemade pasta dishes. Locals, construction workers and mid-level office drones love the food, the prices and the ambiance. Real Italian. The place is owned by Jerry and Angela Troisi. A few years back, Tony assisted in the arrangements to get Jerry's dad transferred to Rikers from upstate so the family could visit the very sick old man. He also, got Jerry a sweet deal on an extortion charge. Net, net. Jerry owes Tony.

"Tony, great to see you. How long has it been?"

The hug is one of family.

"Too long, my friend. How is Angela?"

"As beautiful and bitchy as ever. She is in the back. I'll call her."

"No need, we'll go to her. We must be away from these ears. Let's go to your office."

No questions. Just a turn and deliberate steps to beyond the kitchen. Tony acknowledges no one in the kitchen. He is not there for social reasons.

"Jerry, I need your help."

"Name it."

"I need to know about a guy who works for the NSA."

"Whoa, that's heavy. Not sure . . ."

"Cut the crap. You have twenty-four hours, by noon tomorrow I need to know the skinny on a guy named David Michaels. I know you can do it. I just don't want to know how. OK?"

"Jesus, Tony, the NSA, that's big time. I'm not sure I have the resources or the time."

"Remember you said anything, any time. This is the thing and now is the time."

"Noon tomorrow. Come back and have lunch. We will talk."

"By the way, how's your dad doing?"

Tony drives the nails of importance and urgency deeper.

Back to an afternoon of office work and review in the file summaries. Incident reports in this complex case that has spanned nearly fifteen months with stop and go moments, multiple deaths, and numerous reveals. His team is diligently gathering the pieces. His job is to make sure everything is in chronological order. Tony will turn over copies of the reports. His team will keep all the back-up information. He must decide what to leave in and what to leave out. Sources, suppositions, false leads are out. So are the details of the international banking involvement. Just domestic items. Hell, Michaels is NSA. Let him supply information to the international cops. One by one the files are placed on his desk. He reviews them and extracts only the summary sheets. His gifts of cooperation. Each one brings back the memory of quirky details. Seeing Rufus' hand move in the video. Jimmy's agonizing death. The messy life of the store guard. The territory poaching at the Nite Lites. Carlita Brown's drug use and her necklace. The weapons of choice signaled by casings at various scenes. Lucky's penchant for black hookers. No need to tell him about Amanda. What about Weaver, one of his own? The visit to the Mission is out. Bank records are out. Jesus the hits keep on coming. Wrap up with a brief meeting tomorrow after lunch when all the files are ready. Tonight, a nice evening with the family. Odd thought. Family. Pleasant, but odd.

———◦◉◦———

The last of the files, 26 of them are ready for a final review. But, lunch at Il Supremo is first.

The walk across town is enjoyable. Seeing all the people scurrying about. Men all dressed to impress. Women dressed to conquer. They are getting better looking as Tony ages.

"Tony, I missed you yesterday. You should have said hello."

"Angela, you were so busy and my visit had to be brief. Today, we eat. If the food is any good."

"You putz."

"Can I trust the chef?"

"Be careful or she may poison you."

A big hug. Angela has the full body of a woman who has lived well and produced three teen children. She smells warm, like a kitchen. A peck on the cheek.

"Let go of my woman, you bastard."

Jerry's whisper is not subtle.

"Come we'll eat in the kitchen. It's more private there. I recommend the veal. It goes on the menu for the dinner special tonight. So thin you could read a paper through it. So sweet, you'll swear it has nectar of the gods in it. Angela, honey, please. Three Veal Troisi. Wine, Tony?"

"Not today. I am still taking meds for the damned wounds and I am on the job. One glas and I would fall asleep. Tough afternoon."

"I meant to ask, did they ever get the bastards that shot you. I'll tell you this. It was no one I know or that we know. I haven't even heard a word on the street about it. Must have been an outsider."

"We have a good lead. None of your people."

"Tony, when are you going to get married and settle down? You need a family. Are you getting serious with anyone?"

"Angela, you sound like my mother. She used to ask these questions ten years ago. Like all good cops, I am married to my work. Actually, I am a slave to my work. Always on call. Always the next promotion. Always the next big case. I can't have two masters or mistresses at once, now can I?"

"A good woman is not a master. She is a partner. She grows with you and helps you grow. She shares burdens to make them lighter. She shares good times to make them better. Just as you do. She lifts up. Just as you do. And your children are the beauty of the relationship."

"Angela, you sound like a Catholic priest during a pre-marriage conference."

"I am happy in my marriage. I want the world to know. Now I cook for my boys."

"Jerry, I don't want to sound rude, but it sounds like her hormones are talking."

Jerry's smile widens.

"They are. A late pregnancy. A blessing. Made possible with your help. Getting me out of a jam. I was here for her and the boys, and she was here for me. Now we work together. Life is good. The baby is proof."

"Congratulations. At your age. At her age. This is really terrific. I am happy for you guys."

"Tony, let's get down to business before the meal arrives. I don't like to talk this kind of stuff in front of Angela. It raises too many questions. Here's what I learned. Your David Michaels works at the NSA, downtown. His job is low level. Records or something like that. Maybe computers. Definitely not a field agent. He lives in Brooklyn. He is married and has two children. We don't have a picture, but his description is 6'2" about 210 to 2235. A big guy behind a desk. What a waste. And he is black."

Tony can barely contain his desire to scream.

"Are you sure this information is accurate?"

"It's dead on. The source works in the building."

In the sea of cacophony and seeming confusion, Tony has to be calm. The din of the kitchen and niceties among friends. The congratulations about the impending birth. The success of the restaurant. Tony has to block these and plan his next moves with deliberation. The voice in Tony's head is the voice of reason. Saved by the meal. A slice of veal with penne. Arugula salad on the side. A glass of Pellegrino. Topped off with a cappuccino A meal fit for a king, but Tony concentrates on what he has just learned.

———◈———

"Chris, get me the drivers' license dupes of all the David Michaels in the state data base. I need them for our review."

There are several small files on his desk that weren't there before. Over the next hour he reviews their content differently now. He tries to see how each file is part of or related to each other. What is the connection? The Mission and the bank. It all comes down to money. The numerous and various murders are cover-ups of something really big. Big money. Really big money. Enough to grease a lot of wheels and still buy land all over the western hemisphere.

"LT, here are the print outs of the state driver's licenses. Three hundred and twenty-six David Michaels. One hundred and ninety-six in the five boroughs. We meet in thirty minutes."

Tony pours over the pictures looking for the man he met in the park. Zip, nada, zilch, zed and zero. Then he looks for the black David Michaels in Brooklyn. Bingo. Height and weight match Jerry's description. The wave of dread is back. Now for the team review of all the files.

"Guys, listen carefully. First you have done yeoman-like work in pulling together all this information. Second, I don't need it."

Quizzical expressions in silence.

"Let me explain. The man who I met in Central Park, ostensibly the man who demanded to Captain Kelly that we share our files, is not the David Michaels who works at the NSA. They are as different as black and white. Something is afoot. Somebody wants to know what we know. And that somebody is not on our team. Now to tonight's meeting. Here is what we are going to do. We are going to trap the trapper. Obviously, this phony Michaels wants our information. And, just as obviously, he is planning to give us nothing we don't already have. In fact I bet he is planning to give us less than we already have. So when he and I exchange files, I will arrest him."

"What about Kelly?"

"Jamie, he must not know. He must be innocent."

"What about guns?"

"Kelly will ask me and Michaels to give up our side arms, but he will be unaware of the little 25 caliber I keep on my ankle."

"What if the faux-Michaels is not alone?"

"That's where we trap the trapper. You will be stationed near and at three points around Kelly's house. If Michaels brings back up, you must be behind the back up. Be on the alert for a black van. That will be the tip. If there, the van will be close enough to listen and protect if need be. So, my guess is that Michaels will be wired. And, I will be wired. So, when you hear me make the arrest, you come aggressively into Kelly's house. The department will pay for the damages. If the black van is near the house, one of you arrest the occupants. If they try to escape shoot the tires. We need live bad guys. Dead bad guys are of no use. If there is no black van, all three of you come into the house. Understood?"

"Now, wire me up. I want you at the scene by 5. Well before the meet at 7:30."

—————••••—————

There have been times when Tony wanted to live outside the city. Long Island or Westchester. But during a mind numbing drive, like the one to Kelly's house at the height of rush hour traffic, the thought of living out here and commuting each way each day made him very glad he lived in the city. How long does rush hour last? Certainly longer than an hour. And just as certainly here was no rushing. Ninety minutes to travel thirty miles from mid-town. When Melissa and he are married, he will finally have the space he has wanted for a long time. What will their home in the clouds be like? A private enclave for escaping the slings and arrows of outrageous fortune. His kingdom by marriage. His family in waiting. What shall they call the baby? Is it a boy? A girl? No Russian name. Something Italian. No ties to the evil empire whatsoever. Life has become more complicated. But it is a pleasant and exciting complication as Tony moves from an existence to a very different life style. Finally the exit to Manhasset. Kelly moved here because his wife, Katherine, demanded it. The city was no place to raise her children. Regardless that her husband was a cop dedicated to make the city a place safe enough to raise children she would not have children and live there. Tony always suspected Katherine wanted to be near her family. White shoe, lace curtain, linen Wall Street Irish types who looked at Kelly as if he were a throwback to the old country. The Kimballs and the Kellys never really fought. They never loved either. Kelly's folks shied away from weekend visits. They could feel the tension and disdain. Because of Katherine, Kelly would come into a boat load of cash when Richard Kimball, the scion, died. Maybe that's what the old cop was waiting for. Payment for services rendered. The GPS in the unmarked squad car is spot on. Tony parks in the driveway to be noticed. He is fifteen minutes early. No van in sight. A knock on the door turns on the porch light.

"Hello boyo. Come in. Sit take a load off. First I will have to take your sidearm. I'll do the same for Mr. Michaels. Before you ask, Katherine and the boys are at dinner and a movie. Helluva an easy bribe to get them out of the house. I'd offer you a drink, but that will have to wait until after the meeting. You'll stay a while. Katherine wants to see you and nag on you for being single."

"One department issued 9 millimeter at your request. You've done something to the first floor since I was last here."

"Added a sun porch. A nice and expensive way to save wear and tear on the living room furniture. Build a sun porch and buy new furniture for it. Women have a strange form of economic thinking. Wait I see head lights behind your car. The game's afoot."

The knock on the door produces the appropriately casual response by Kelly.

"Welcome to my humble abode, Mr. Michaels. Before we get into the negotiated swap, I must ask that you relinquish your side arm. Thanks. I'll just leave it here next to Lieutenant Sattill's."

Michaels has an aluminum case. Standard issue for the Feds. It creates the impression that the contents are very important or valuable. Tony has an extra large manila envelope with the opening flap folded over. The three men walk down the stairs to the man cave. Big screen TV, refrigerator, large couches, two coffee tables, and card table. This is the special place for Kelly, his two sons, and their friends. Saturday and Sunday football games. The holy panoply of manhood.

"Please be seated, gentlemen."

Kelly positions himself between Michaels and Tony. The location of the arbiter.

"Now who shows first?"

"I will, because Mr. Michaels is a guest of the NYPD. Let me show you this. This is the real David Michaels who works at the NSA and lives in Brooklyn. You will note the extreme difference between the real David Michaels and yourself, sir. Kelly, this guy is an imposter. I am not sure who he is or what he wants, but my guess is that he works for someone who wants to stifle our investigation."

The first shot breaks the glass of the basement window and strikes the wall behind Michaels. Tony instinctively pushes Kelly to the floor and follows him down under the table. The next five shots cut into Michaels' chest. The reports are from a small caliber automatic. Like 223s. Then Tony hears two more pronounced reports. Glock 9s. The shooting stops. The surprise is over in a few seconds.

"LT, are you OK?

"Yes."

"Captain Kelly?"

"Yes, bruised but not broken. Someone has a lot of explaining. To me, the Manhasset police, and Katherine."

"LT, there is one dead bad guy out here and we got the driver of the van. Shot out two tires."

"Jamie, call 911 and get the local police here after one of you get the driver of the van into one of our cars and headed for our house. Make sure he is in the special room in the basement. Someone will have to babysit him until the morning. You and I will have to stay here a deal with the locals. Others must disappear. Old man, I'll explain everything as best I can so we have the same story for the outsiders. Then they will have their chief call our chief."

The multiple siren noises increase the urgency of Tony's explanation. He hits only the high points. This will suffice for the locals, but not Katherine. A small smile creases Tony's face as he thinks of how Kelly will have to tap dance around the truth to the grand inquisitor. This was a better day.

Afterglow

Manhasset, New York.

Two Intruders Killed.

Last night two men attempting a home invasion and robbery of New York City Police Captain, William Kelly, were shot and killed by Captain Kelly. Manhasset Police Chief, David Ellis, reported that Captain Kelly "was defending his home". "This marks the third time that a home in the town was invaded. The other two were robbed", said Chief Ellis. "I think we finally got the men who have been on a crime spree in Manhasset." The identities of the two men have yet to be confirmed.

Copenhagen.

Three Mosques Bombed ... Forty Killed.

Copenhagen police reported that three of the city's five mosques were hit by car bombs placed at the front door of each. The explosions destroyed the front and roof of each place of worship. Although the bombs were set off at 4 am local time when no one was at *prayer, forty Sunni Muslims were killed in the explosions. "The death toll would have been much higher had the bombs been set off during prayer", said Police Chief, Tom Diek Held. "This appears to be the act of terrorists. But no one has claimed responsibility for the attacks". The nation's anti-terrorism force is working with corresponding groups throughout Europe in an effort to track down those responsible.*

New York.

Banker Hangs Self.

Robert Linder, newly appointed CEO of Manhattan Private Trust was found hanged at Broadway Arms, a small exclusive hotel in mid-town Manhattan. "I went to his room when he did not answer my calls. He was just hanging there," reported Julius Brown, night Manager of the hotel. "He checked in yesterday and paid in cash for two weeks in advance. I needed to speak to him about the delivery his mail. This has not happened before." The New York Police Department noted that the body was at the city morgue awaiting confirmation of the body by Mr. Bender's wife, who is on a two-week cruise.

$$\Longrightarrow \!\!\!\bullet\!\!\! \Longleftarrow$$

"Well, Brendan, who do we have here?"

"Sir, the perp had no ID. No license. Nada."

"Does anyone else know he is here? Has he talked? Did you read him his rights?"

"I kept the door locked especially when I went to the head. I read him his rights and he gave me this telephone number. LO5-4545. I called last night and got an answering machine of a law firm, Davis Reed Oswald

Driver and Livingston. Googled them. Huge firm with 450 partners worldwide specializing in international trade, commerce, and banking. Then I dug through the newspaper archives. Seems two of their big local clients are the Aksum Mission and Manhattan Private Bank. So, they are way out of this guy's league. Given his coal black complexion, tall boney features, and his Euro-trash attire, my guess is he works for the Mission. He may even be related somehow to the shootings we have been chasing; the Nite Lites and you. Yes, I printed him and sent the prints to national and international data bases. I await their responses. Now that it's daylight, shall I call Davis Reed again? By the way, how did the Manhasset mess turn out?"

"Good work, Brendan. Two wannabe intruders were killed by Kelly as he protected his home. You know the old story about a man's castle. The van is in the Nassau County impound lot. Today, one of you will have to go out there and examine the vehicle for any reference to my shooting. Let us permit our guest to make his one call to his lawyer. I can't wait to see who shows up and what excuse he or she gives for the actions of this asshole. Now take him outside through the side door and in through the front door to the holding tank. We'll meet at one today to learn what we know."

———◆———

"LT, there is a Mister Elliot Livingston II to see the prisoner from last night. Here is his card. I checked out his credentials. He is legit."

"Mr. Livingston, how can I help you?"

"You have detained my client. He has invoked his right to legal counsel. I am his legal counsel and demand to see him immediately."

"Well, first of all we have detained numerous people during the last twenty-four hours. Which one do you represent?

"Bodrum Bogatta."

"And where did we acquire Mr. Bogatta?"

"On long island which is way out of your jurisdiction. So you are holding him illegally."

"Well, yes and no. Yes, we apprehended Mr. Bogatta in Manhasset. And, no since he is directly linked to a murder of a skel unknown and attempted murder of two New York City Police Officers, his apprehension falls within the fugitive laws. The Manhasset Police Department will confirm this. We have set up a room in which you two can converse, before Mr. Bogatta is sent to the tombs prior to arraignment. But, before you enter the room, you must be searched. Wouldn't want someone to get hurt, now would we? Please follow me."

Mr. Livingston and Mr. Bogatta sit next to each other and whisper. Tony heads upstairs to the locker room to shower and shave. He must (that's a strange word) . . . he wants to call Melissa and have breakfast before the review meeting.

"Melissa, sorry I didn't make it home last night. I was involved in something on Long Island."

"Baby Sattill and I missed you. When will you be home today?"

"Around 6. Until then, I send kisses and hugs."

Has he become mushy? How domestic will he be? Living the big life on a Lieutenant's salary and someone else's money. Will he become a kept man? Ultimately a eunuch? No. Damn it, no. But this new world that awaits him is disconcerting. A domesticated Tony will not become an emasculated Tony.

Kelly calls. All is fine with the locals and at One PP. The Manhasset Police and the Nassau County Sherriff have relinquished the investigation to the NYPD, but, and here is the expected but, they want to share in the credit; pictures and press releases. Quid pro quo. Ah, the politics of police work.

Breakfast consists of an egg, ham, and cheese sandwich from the local deli. Really greasy, really salty, and really bad for the body . . . really good for the soul. A bottle of apple juice. And a large coffee. Black. No double espresso, mocha, latte with extra foam crap from Syd's. Hell, Syd's coffee can be used by the DOT to tar the streets.

The conference room is filled. The boys and girl are ready.

"OK. Let's stop farting around with the myriad details of this case. Let's look at the many facets and incidents from 10,000 feet. What the hell is really going on? Why? Who? Please think outside the box. I'll start, because I can. I am the LT. I think we have seen the outer face of the first three or four dolls of the Matryoshka. What we are looking for is the last doll that contains the coin, jewel or key. All the killings that appear to be random and unrelated are, in fact, related to a massive cover up. The thing being covered has to be huge to require so much violence. Big money. Big international money. So many dead bodies. The Fultons were on to something. They were both killed to silence them. Unfortunately, we can't get to their handler or handlers to learn what the happy couple had learned. But, because Amanda was killed at the Mission and Rufus was killed trying to hand over the disc, it is safe to say the Mission is neck deep in shit. The princess is one of four queen bees who run the huge scheme. But, why was Lucky killed there? Why the wholesale slaughters at the store and the rave? Let's table those issues. Brendan, please write them on the wall panel. The guys that shot me and that killed the faux Mr. Michaels appear to be on the same team. A team that was involved in the rave shooting and acts as security at the Mission. Back to the Mission. I was shot, because I made the Mission, in the person of Makeda, uncomfortable. I was nosey and getting in her food bowl. Makeda surfaces as member of a financial cabal that moves tons of money internationally. Money that ultimately winds up in the hands of the Russian gun dealers. Why? The banking beauties don't take possession of the weapons. They go to rebel or terrorist forces throughout the world. These forces have promised the girls land, mineral rights, or some such as collateral for the loan of cash to buy the weapons. What we are seeing is a huge international conspiracy to establish greater wealth than we could possible image. All financed by drugs in Mexico and fed by a banking game controlled by women. The weaker sex, my ass. Let me hear it. Jamie?"

"I think Lucky was killed because he had become a liability. Let me explain. We know he had a weakness for young black hookers, and that he was not afraid to snort Andes candy. He was tangentially connected to Los Hores, and that he was involved in the drug deal that the Feds busted before it started. He may have even financed it to some degree. To him it was easy money and no more illegal than what the bank was doing. When momma and the girls realized that his actions might bring scrutiny to their grand plan, they had him killed, thus, eliminating the liability. This also allowed them to puppeteer Robert Linder to head the bank. The fact that a mother could kill her child tells me how deeply evil the sorority is. So they asked him to come to the Mission. Like taking a child to the woodshed for a spanking. In this case they spanked extra hard. And because Amanda' efforts had been discovered, they decided to cover up one murder with another. Fiendish, but stupid. I think that Los Hores and Lieutenant Carlita Brown were involved with Lucky. She was killed, because Los Hores feared a leak to the NYPD about their big drug deal. One loose end tied off. Or maybe the rumor is truth, and she was murdered by Strabel. The jealous lover. Regardless, the gang remained a street force until ADA Kemp busted them. She walked back on the trail of the drugs and find Los Hores holding the bag. Another loose end will be tied off. If they try to blame Lucky or LT Brown or whomever, they are screwed. It's too late. The drugs and the buck stop with them. Chris?"

"The shoot out at the Rave was to eliminate the guys who had committed the store robbery. And the tire fire was simply an old fashioned neck tie party to silence voices. It seems that we have been chasing our tails. It's as if someone on our side who knows how we operate and prioritize is driving us all over the ranch in search of one-offs, rather than the real force behind the numerous crimes. Assuming that all that has been said is true, what the hell do we do now? We just can't go into the Mission and the bank and arrest the two moms. There is no ADA or judge who will give us the warrants needed. Somehow, we need the Feds, multi-jurisdictional Feds. Brendan?"

"How about RICO? Couldn't we use the RICO statute as support to rip apart the Mission and the bank? I understand that some of our information is sketchy and may require a quantum leap of faith, but it is worth a try. Our case would be stronger if we could get the support of the Feds. But, how do we do that? They have been amazingly absent or stonewalling us at critical junctions. I think they are already involved and are letting us do the heavy lifting."

"You are on to something. You have already pulled our case together in detail, connecting as many dots as we can. I'll find someone in the agency mélange that wants to make his or her bones. Jimmy Ranck gave me a few names. I'll dial and smile. Review the report I was to use with Mr. Michaels. Go over all details, but link all of them to something or leave a question to be answered. We will use what we have to get subpoenas and warrants."

Back to his notes about conversations with Jimmy. Jimmy's voice rings loud and clear in Tony's mind; "Kill 'em. Kill 'em all." The all is now a very large complex group. He cannot kill them, but they will suffer very long ugly prison time. After trying Jimmy's fed connections, Tony must once again lean on Kelly for his connections.

First stop, Bill Wilson retired from Treasury. He gives Tony the name of someone he trusts, Paul Ziegler. Paul remembers Bill fondly and listens intently. Tony bets the call is recorded, because Paul says little and nothing incriminating. He will get back to Tony. Once again the Federal camp is alerted. This time they know that the NYPD knows a whole lot more than before. Kelly gives Tony two names, Ellis at NSA and Leonard at CIA. Same call as to Wilson to both of these new contacts. Same guarded reaction. Same "I'll get back to you." Tony has kicked three hornets' nests. Nature and the ardent desire to protect sacred turf will run their courses. Tony estimates that calls to the Manhattan District Attorney's office will start in fewer than two hours.

Next stop, lunch tomorrow with an aggressive ADA, Joan Kemp. Tony is banking on her taking the facts and connecting with the Federal Prosecutor who will have been contacted by Treasury, the CIA and the NSA. Two more hornets' nests.

"Lieutenant Sattill, what can I do for you?"

"Well it's what I can do for you. You caught a small tuna the other day and it made the news. How would you like to land a whale and make international headline? If you would like, you can help facilitate a huge investigation and garner a ton of favorable press for you and your office."

"How is that all going to happen?"

"In a short period of time . . . say two hours, you will be hearing from the Federal Prosecutor's office and maybe even three federal agencies. They will be dancing around the facts and implications of a case involving the Manhattan Private Trust and the Aksum Mission. Dancing as if their pants are on fire. And they will hint that I am withholding vital evidence about their undisclosed secret investigations. Unknown evidence, but vital to their case and National security."

"Do tell. You can read tea leaves or Tarot cards or some such?"

"No I can investigate, collect, and provide you sufficient evidence that supports the fact that multiple detailed warrants can be issue by your office. And here is the best part; I'll even pay for lunch tomorrow. A picnic lunch where no one can hear us. Waddaya say? Take a lunch and gain big headlines."

"OK. Where? When?"

"Wagner Park at noon. Do you like pastrami or roast beef?"

"Pastrami. Light on the mustard. Two pickles. Lots of slaw. A bag of chips and a Celray Tonic."

"See you then. I'll be waiting by the main entrance. We can sit by the river."

"Sir, Mrs. Razdarovich is on line two."

"Hello, Melissa. What can I do for you?"

"I have told my parents. Not about you and me, but about the baby. They simply popped into see me. Unannounced. I could not hide my baby bump or the work in the apartment. They are convinced that baby Sattill is baby Razdarovich. By-the-by baby Sattill is a boy."

"When were you planning on telling me about my son?"

"I just did. I learned yesterday, while you were out on Long Island saving the world."

"Now all four interested parties know. And don't go all pissy on me. I am beginning to feel very hormonal, and I have access to steak knives."

"I love you, too. Do your parents suspect that I am living with you?"

"No. They were so blown away by their impending grandson, they didn't notice your shoes under the couch or your necktie and jacket in the closet that you leave open or the active second bathroom."

"I think they have a right to know."

"Not yet. One trauma at a time. Are we still on for dinner?"

"Yes, six."

"Good, because as I told you I am beginning to get very hormonal, and I want dessert before dinner. Love ya."

Melissa never ceases to amaze Tony; forthright, assertive yet seductive. And, she has steak knives.

Time to dive into forms and responding to blanket e-mails.

"LT, wanna hear something illegal, but interesting."

"It better not be porno, Chris."

"Way better, so I have been told. When Livingston and Bogatta were conversing in the room before Bogatta was transferred to the Tombs, we must have left the mic and the recorder on. Such a silly mistake. Not the first time, but very silly. Take a listen. It is whispered, but the sound can be amplified for clarity sake, if we need to."

"Bogatta, listen to me. Do not worry. You will be taken care of. You have many friends in high places who will protect you and your secrets. You may have to do a little time. They do have a strong circumstantial case against you. But, you didn't know what the two men were up to. You simply gave them a ride. Do you understand?"

"Yes, I understand. But, what about my family? Will they be protected?"

"Yes, they will be taken care of also. Now, go willingly to the Tombs. When you are arraigned, I will be there with whatever bail money is required. Others have seen to it."

"OK. Thank you. And please thank Makeda and the Mission."

"Chris, this is dynamite. Make sure it accompanies the written report. But you cannot indicate how we got the information. So paraphrase it as if you overheard it in the hall. By the way, how are you guys coming on the report? I have lunch date with ADA Kemp tomorrow. I want to hand over the report then. Every step along the way must be spelled out. All conclusions drawn must be obvious and verifiable. I want to hand the legal eagles cases so simple even they can't screw them up."

"Sir, one more item. The ME said she found a needle mark in Bender's neck. It was disguised by the rope's ligature mark. Disguised, but not hidden. In a very preliminary tox screen she found a huge dose of Thorazine. She claims, there was probably enough of the drug in his system to put a bull to sleep. Her final report will be available in a few days. But, based on this, it is unlikely Bender hanged himself. He had a lot of help. Maybe Mrs. Bender is just cleaning up a mess before it occurs. Obviously not her, but her surrogates. Guys from the Mission must have paid Mr. Bender a visit and helped him to his end. One last item cleaned up. Now, once the final report is created deconstruct it into as many small pieces as you can possible imagine. So if we are asked for the details, we can provide them. Just not the final reports. And shred any loose pages."

"Make sure the ME report and the conversation between lawyer and client get in the report I will be taking to the ADA. I want to pick up the report tomorrow morning. Tonight I dine with a beautiful woman and small child."

<hr />

Lovemaking before dining dramatically increases Tony's appetite. Lovemaking between courses makes the evening meal last twice as long as usual. Lovemaking on the floor beneath the table holding the dirty dishes completely enervates the male of the species, but fails to slake the sexual desire. Tony calls for a time out. Thank gawd there were no steak knives.

The Beginning

The day is sunny and warm. Nearly perfect for lunch in the park. Except for the wind and purpose of the lunch. This will be no idyllic basket on a blanket meal. Two lovers laughing and whispering. This lunch is all business. Big business. Big bad business. As Tony enters the precinct he is acutely aware of the silence. The uniforms are just sitting at their desks. The sergeant is not barking out orders. Then he hears the noise from upstairs. The squad room is a cacophony of shouts and commands. Purposefully he heads upstairs.

"Nice of you to join us Lieutenant."

"And you are?"

"I am William T. Davis, Special Agent, Treasury. And I am here to acquire all of your files that are pertinent to an on-going investigation of my office."

"On-going investigation? And, just what might be the subject of this on-going investigation?"

"Illegal wire transfer of money, both domestically and internationally, by the Manhattan Private Trust."

"Well, ya know, I read something about that somewhere in a departmental memo a while back. Maybe I can find that memo for you."

"Cut the crap Sattill, we have a federal warrant and the understanding of your superiors that you will cooperate. But, we have received no cooperation from this precinct or your squad. Now where is the file?"

"Chris, please make a copy of our Manhattan Private Trust file for Special Agent Davis."

"Yes sir."

"See how easy that was. Here ya go one file requested, one file delivered. Just like Syd's Deli. Is there anything else you would like today? A ham sandwich? A cup of coffee? If not, get the fuck out of my squad room."

The boys from Treasury depart.

"Now, Chris, get me the complete file on a thumb drive. We need just two copies, one for the ADA and one for us. The deconstructed crap is for everybody else."

"Yes."

"Very soon we will be visited by the other alphabet teams all wanting our files. We will willingly give them paper versions of the components that apply to their area of authority. So, because of their historical Chinese Wall operating procedure they will not share what they know with the other Feds. It will take them a while to figure out that we have scammed them. By then we will have taken the initiative and closed the case."

"What about One PP?"

"Well, they will be pleased that we cooperated, but displeased that we have did not cooperate completely. They will love that initiative, but we will be yelled at. Maybe even given rips. But, after the news media and the adoring public understand what we have done, we will get our back pay and maybe even accommodations."

"Genius."

"Nope, just not my first rodeo, partner. Now give me the complete file and break down the components. The smaller the pieces, the longer we have to operate. You may even want to omit a few pages."

Tony puts the thumb drive in his pants pocket next to his money clip and places the printed version in a manila envelope. Gifts for Ms. Kemp.

The grease smell of Syd's is like a valium after the mild confrontation. Food in hand Tony heads for the park. During the eight-block walk, he suspects he is followed. He ducks into a hardware store for no reason and waits five minutes. Upon exiting he sees the guy in the black windbreaker across the street. The same guy he saw as he left the precinct. On this side of the street he recognizes the middle-aged woman in slacks and a bulky sweater. The famous federal parallel tail. Tony waves at both of them. Neither acknowledges. They know that he knows and that's all that matter.

As he enters the park, he spots Ms. Kemp sitting at a table. Near the river the wind is more aggressive. Her skirt occasionally shifts to reveal a pair of dynamite pins. Is the rumor true? Did she climb to the top on her back? Given her conviction rate of high profile cases, how she got there doesn't matter. She is the Executive Assistant District Attorney for Manhattan. And a damned good one.

"Good afternoon Ms. Kemp."

"Good afternoon Lieutenant Sattill, and call me Joan."

"OK. Call me Tony."

"I don't know what you want to discuss, but I will say my phone has been on fire all morning. Apparently you knocked over a few lemonade stands yesterday. My source at federal court tells me there have been several search and seizure warrants issued for files in your possession at your precinct. I am sure the warrants have been or are being executed as we speak."

"Yes, indeed. So we have to act quickly. We may have only a one-day window."

"Explain. And, why are we meeting here in the open?"

"Many walls have federal ears."

"Yes they do."

"It would take too long to explain in detail. That's why I brought the complete file of our information and activities. Both paper and plastic. You read. By the time you get to page four of the summary, you will know how big the issue is. I'll set the table."

As he empties the bags of food, he rips the bags into place mats. He looks up and here are his two pals from the street. He wonders how many other people in the park are watching them. He spots a man picking up trash. But he has no mandatory Sanitation worker badge on his upper arm. There is couple sharing a newspaper, soaking up the sun. Tony discounts the mothers with children. There are two guys tossing a disc. The park is alive with interested parties.

"Holy shit. This is nearly unbelievable. If half of what you allege in this document is accurate, we have a huge international crime syndicate in our backyard."

"It's all true. The murders, the attempted cover-ups, the money laundering, the weapon buying. It's all true. We need you to get us warrants so we can seize the files within the bank and the Mission and arrest the leaders of the cabal. Can you do that?"

"You bet your whatever. Under the RICO statute, I can close these places down in a mille-second. But, and here is the big but. Because the Feds have been alerted, they will want all the glory. Their processes individually, could take days. I want to move on this tomorrow morning."

"Fear not. They will be pouring over the bits and bytes. Only you and I have the complete file. All dots connected. All players named. All links confirmed."

"How did you deliver partial information?"

"They will each have a portion of what you have in front of you. Only the portion that pertains to their sector of influence. And since they don't talk to each other, we will have time to act."

"OK. But, I want to invite them to our party. When we serve the warrants, I want them as backup. They can stand with me in front of the cameras, and share in the glory of the NYPD."

The woman is a political *playah*.

"How soon can you get the warrants?"

"How soon will your posse be ready to ride?"

"The horses are saddled and canteens filled, ma'am."

"I want to review all this in detail then run it by my boss. I'll have the requisite paperwork signed by five. I'll return the numerous calls of this morning after five. We ride at dawn."

On his way back to the precinct, Tony notices that his two traveling companions are not with him. More than likely they are debriefing their superiors about the little they learned. By now all the alphabet leaders know that ADA Kemp has a file of unknown origin. A file each thinks that his or her agency has. But, they are not sure. Maybe she knows more than they do. Tony trusts Kemp to let them all know what she wants in due time. Her rise to the top cannot be fettered by some arcane unrealistic protocol. She will do as Tony hopes. Arriving at the precinct, he is greeted by Captain Sanchez and his Commander Jocko Lane. A meeting is called for the conference room. Tony lays out all the details. His superiors are satisfied that the proper channels have been kept in the loop. His team is excited to finally get a chance to close this case.

"If ADA Kemp is successful with the process, and she will be, Chris, Brendan, Jamie and I will take the lead. We will serve the warrants and make the arrests. Kemp will carry the necessary back-up paperwork. I request that we have SWAT at the Mission, but not when we arrest Hinton and Lenz. We'll take care of those two. I am sure the Feds will be at the Mission and the bank as a show of force for the media. We will not get between them and the cameras. And, let's make damned sure they don't get between the bad guys and us. One PP will alert the media ten minutes before the warrants are served. I don't know the time yet, but I'll bet it will be very early in the morning. I stress early. Five or six AM at the Mission. Then we move to the bank just as it opens. More Feds. Between the Mission and the bank, we will arrest Mrs. Razdarovich and Mrs. Linder, the grieving widow. I know the media will be at the Mission, the bank and our precinct when the two ladies are brought in because they will be told to be there. Any questions?"

The ring master is in control of the circus . . . he hopes.

"Since we can expect resistance at the Mission, and since there are more than several well-armed guards, what fire power will we have beyond our service pieces?"

"Jamie, we will requisition department issue MP5's. Each of you is authorized and range-trained on these. Now you get to carry them. They are for show. Only for use if circumstances requires it. Like returning fire. SWAT will have heavier pieces. Who knows what the Feds will bring to the party? Maybe an RPG or two. Maybe a tank. But, please carry the weapons in full safety mode over your shoulder. I repeat, use them only and I mean ONLY if fired upon. Go that? Did I miss anything Captain? Commander?"

"No."

"No, Lieutenant. I will add, be very careful. In making these arrests, you will be taking something very valuable from people who are used to getting their own way. I am concerned that they will not go quietly into the night. Wear you vests and helmets."

"Thank you Commander. Now we wait for ADA Kemp to call with our marching orders."

A call comes at 4:12 PM.

"Lieutenant Sattill, I have the warrants. When would you like to serve them?"

"Which warrants do you have?"

"One for the Mission, one for Makeda, one for the bank, one for Mrs. Razdarovich, and one for Mrs. Linder."

"What about Hinton and Lenz?"

"Shit. I can get those in a few minutes."

"I think it advisable to hit the Mission between 6:35 and 6:45 AM. While they are still wiping the sleep from their collective eyes. Then we will hit the bank at 8:30.

Tell the Feds and media to be at the Mission at 6:45. After the Mission, we will get Hinton and Lenz. Then we will go to the bank. The Feds and media can meet us at the bank. Keep them away from Hinton and Lenz and the two women. So don't call any of our collateral support until 6:30. The Feds must know by now that something is going to happen. They just don't know when or the scope. OK?"

"You're the foreman on this ranch. I am just the rancher's daughter."

Coy, seductive, and devious. A great combination for an ADA. Tony lays out more details his Captain and Commander. One PP will make the appropriate calls and the appropriate time. Now to wait. It's like having a baby. Boy, that's ironic. His team is getting rest up in the crib. No sleep. Just rest. Bathroom visits are more frequent than normal. All too soon the bewitching hour arrives. Tony calls Kemp. He will pick her up on the way to the Mission. She is already dressed and on her way to the precinct. Coy, seductive, devious, and aggressive.

Joan Kemp is given a vest and helmet. On the outside of her white blouse, make up, pressed slacks and white sneakers, she looks like a member of the team armed for battle. The van is loaded with bodies and equipment. Police EMS is alerted to stand by. Radio silence is required to keep the media and groupie scanners in the dark. The van is quiet. Tony's heart rate at 76 is way above his normal 52. No traffic to speak of. No sirens. A long ride before the destination is reached.

"Warrants?"

"Got 'em."

"Make sure your badges are clearly evident. Extra zip ties."

"I have six strips."

"I have four."

"I have eight."

"Jamie, you are so prepared."

"LT, may I cuff the princess."

"Yes, indeed. I'm sure she will be glad to see you again, young lady. I'll take a few extra strips. Not sure how many bad guys we will encounter at the Mission."

"Intel told me there are fifteen to twenty security guards. We'll need all we have. Maybe some from the SWAT team."

"Time, Chris?"

"6:28 AM"

"OK, boys and girls, let's make a movie. I'll lead. Jamie, you go the Makeda's quarters. Brendan, you and I will secure the first guards then have them lead us to the barracks. ADA Kemp will stay in the rear. Your job is to have the paperwork ready when we exit the building and to be the face of the operation. So you will be close to the cameras and out of harm's way."

"Do I have a choice?"

"No. Keep one eye on me and one eye looking for SWAT backup. When they arrive, send them in. That would be a big help."

"Remember, radio silence until we have achieved our objectives. Unless, of course, you encounter trouble you can't handle."

No one on Tony's team will admit they need help unless they are in dire straits. They are too well trained. Too tough. Too proud. The van side panel slides open at the first gate of the Mission. The sentry on post is taken by surprise and cuffed before he can announce the arrival of his new BFFs. The guard walking the circular drive reaches for his phone.

"Drop the phone and drop to your knees, NOW!"

Brendan's loud whisper echoes off the walls. The guard does what he is told, is cuffed and told to lie on his face and to be quiet. The SWAT team arrives and rushes into the courtyard to scoop up the first two bad guys. Brendan and Tony lead four of the team to the barracks in the basement. They ram open the door, toss in two stun grenades. Three seconds after the explosions and clouds of smoke, the SWAT team enters the large room. The denizens are escorted or dragged out of the barracks demanding to know why they are being abused and harassed. The team leader is curt and forceful. Tony's phone squawks.

"Hey, LT, guess who I have in custody? Without all her makeup, gold and jewelry, she looks like an abused street walker. So much for royalty."

Tony hears cursing in the background.

"Jamie, great job. Was the secretary there?"

"LT, interesting back story. The princess, the secretary, and one of the security guards share a bed. I'm bringing all three to the front gate in their PJs. A big dose of humility will help us get answers at the initial line up."

All interested parties are lined up at the gate. Warrants are served. Tony notices blood running down Makeda's left cheek. And her eye is red. She must have fallen against a piece of furniture. At least that will be the story. Jamie would never strike a suspect, regardless of any history between the two. Makeda, the secretary and the security guard, in their nightclothes are connected by zip ties. Pictures and videos display the entourage to the public, while ADA Kemp, Tony's Commander, and the federal alphabet boys preen and talk to the media. Joint task force. Investigation lasting two years. Great interagency cooperation and coordination. Money laundering. International terrorism. Multiple murders here in New York. Blah, blah, blah. Counterbalanced by screams of harassment, lawyers, and law suits. They are bleating like sheep before being sheared. Tony's team now moves on to Hinton, Lenz, and the two remaining female US members of the conspiracy.

High fives in the van.

"Not so fast guys. Lenz and Hinton may aggressively resist. Be on your guard."

Tony's personal cell phone vibrates. A text message: *"Baby Sattill has decided to arrive. Headed for Lennox Hill. Meet me there."*

"LT, anything wrong?"

"Nope all is right with the world. I am about to be a father."

"That is fucking great. Who is the mother?"

"Chris, that information will have to wait for a few days. Everybody clear?"

"Yes. Yes. Yes."

"Now let's get on with the job at hand. We are closer to Hinton, so he is first. Then, my pal, Wolf Lenz. We will knock. Listen for a response. Knock again. Listen for a response. If none is forthcoming, we use the ram. Chris, got the ram?"

"Sir."

Here we go."

Hinton was easy. No ram needed. He pissed and whined about a brother in blue. This quickly became a cry for his union rep and attorney. Into a sector car.

"You can make your call from downtown, asshole. You are a disgrace to the uniform."

Jamie is proving herself to be the more intense of the species. Not unlike a tigress or lioness.

Lenz was passed out on the couch. Reruns of mediocre sit-coms were dancing in his head. A second sector car is used. He was still in a fog when he arrived at One PP. Taking them downtown hides them from the media until the department can get its story straight. He and Hinton make the requisite calls.

Off to the homes of Mrs. Razdarovich and Mrs. Linder.

"Here is where the fun will really begin. Threats will be made. Threats upon threats upon threats. We must not use force. If they are in nightclothes, that's the way they go to the precinct. A big splash of humility will go a long way to making our point that their days of wealth and power are over."

Mrs. Linder is stunned, confused, and tearful. She still is trying to play the role of the grieving widow. The warrant is read slowly so she understands that she is done. She wants time to get dressed and call her lawyer. No fucking way. Jamie finds a long coat for modesty sake. Her sneakers don't match. Mrs. Linder is placed in the back of a squad car partially coveed. Who knows who or what was on that back seat last?

Mrs. Razdarovich is defiant, arrogant, and angry. Her hair is not yet washed, nor has she had the time to apply makeup.

"I want to call my lawyer, now."

"If you give me his number, I'll call him for you."

"There, Eliot Livingston."

"Oooops, my phone battery is dead. You can call from the precinct. I'll make sure he meets you there. You will be in the same holding cell that held Mr. Bogatta before he was transferred to Rikers and murdered. Did you know this low-level errand boy was murdered? I'll bet you did. Mr. Livingston will know where to find you."

"Loosen these straps. They are hurting me."

"You're a whiney bitch. The zip ties are for your protection. Without them you might try to escape. Then we would have to shoot you and we don't want to do that."

"I promise, I won't try to escape. Just take the straps off and get me my clothes."

"Sorry, department regulations require that all scum bags must be cuffed when arrested. You are a scum bag. This is an arrest. Ergo, the cuffs. Now let me find you a big ugly rag to cover you. Let's look in the maid's closet for her uniform that should do nicely."

"I will not wear that."

"It's either that or your dressing gown. You're call sweetheart."

The uniform is chosen. Jamie is enjoying this a little too much, but no harm no foul. Tony tells the third sector car to take a circuitous route to the precinct so the media have time to assemble. He will make sure they are there. Park the car in the lot across the street and walk the two ladies in through the front door. He wants a big-time perp walk.

The bank is the last stop. The Feds are there first, but only ADA Kemp has the warrants. She arrives in the Commander's car. Entry is easy. No resistance and no arrests, because the employees have had no part in the scheme. Boxes of paper files and boxes of discs and

thumb drives are walked out through the front door.
Techies connect the system to the downtown system and
download everything. The media are again treated to an
interview. The dots are beginning to become obvious
and they are beginning to connect the dots. A monster is
emerging. An international, hydra-headed monster. The
media is handed a kit with some pertinent information
about the on-going collaborative investigation. Local,
federal and international law enforcement agencies
working together to stop crime and put a serious dent
in the funding of terrorism. Kemp is in her element. She
will be crowned queen. The Commander is so proud of
the work of the NYPD. The alphabet boys each have a
moment in the spot light. Each praises the other members
of the team. No one was injured. The entire morning
went off without a hitch. Surgical precision, clockwork
timing and well-trained team work. All spearheaded by
Lieutenant Anthony Sattill and his CAT squad. The
internet will be bombarded as the news researchers and
junkies learn more about the organization. Film at noon.
The book in a year.

"Where is Lieutenant Sattill?"

"He will be made available to the press after a
complete debriefing."

"Hey, guys, I want to duck out to see my child. I'll
meet you back at the house in about an hour. Cover for
me. Tell anybody who asks that I went back to the house
early or some such. I am taking the van. Find your own
way home."

"Congrats old man."

"Now be nice Brendan."

The ride to Lennox Hill Hospital is shortened by
the siren. He takes off his vest and tosses the vest and

helmet in the back. Badge on the outside of his jacket. He has sweated through the damned thing in several places that mark the location of the vest. Parking is easy. No one wants to question a cop who is sweating profusely. Looking back on the morning, Tony is pleased. Everything went flawlessly. Planning and controlled execution meant that no shots were fired and no one was injured. He thinks, *"Nobody moob . . . nobody dah."*

Baby Sattill

Entering the hospital is different this time. No friend or fellow policeman is sick or dying. Tony remembers Jimmy and says out loud, *we didn't kill them all, but we got them all and they all will pay for their sins. Rest easy soldier. You fought a good fight and won.*

The maternity wing, the Kenvin Wing, is on the fourth floor. Off the elevator straight ahead, the nurse's station is decorated with bunnies, birds and flowers.

"Excuse me. I'm looking for Razdarovich."

"Sorry, sir, we have no on by that name on this floor. Are you sure you have the correct floor. This is maternity."

"Yes, ma'am. How about Aylir?"

"Yes sir room 4276. Down the hall to my right and turn left at the T."

Tony assumes that running and giggling is not appropriate. His paces are long and purposeful and they quicken. Turning the corner he hears laughter and happy talk coming from every door way.

There it is #4276. He sheepishly enters. The elder Aylirs are standing beside their daughter and new grandson.

"Lieutenant it's nice to see you. What a pleasant surprise."

"Mrs. Aylir, it's nice to see you again. Mr. Aylir, it's nice to see you."

"Since you have come to see our grandchild, Lieutenant, we can use your help with two issues. First, who does the baby more resemble, Melissa or Lucky? Second, what shall the boy be named?"

"Ma'am, I think that despite the wrinkles, the boy looks more like Melissa than Lucky. As for a name, I am out of the arena entirely. What do you think, sir?"

"Definitely more like my daughter than the baby's father. As for a name, I vote for anything that is not Slavic or Russian."

"Hey, does the mother get a say in this? The baby boy looks a lot like his father. So, I am naming him after his father . . . Antonio."

The silence in the room was ear shattering. Two elders do not even breathe. Two sets of grandparental eyes bounce from daughter to Tony and back again like ping pong balls. First mouths open wide the smiles emerge.

This is a really good day.